Grace Humiston and the Vanishing

A novel

by

Charles Kelly

For my sister Mary, who has done so much to nurture our family.

This work of fiction is based on a true story. The Crime Lawyer, Mary Grace Winterton Humiston, was a legend in her day.

Grace Humiston and the Vanishing

CHAPTER ONE

THE DISAPPEARANCE OF RUTH CRUGER, wrongly known as the White Slave Case, came our way on a blustery day in March 1917. Later, this case would cause *The New York Times* to call my employer Grace Humiston a "sleuth extraordinary," which she was. *Literary Digest* would also label her "A Feminine Sherlock Holmes," which she was not, her methods differing sharply from those of that cocaine-addled Englishman. The reporters would also dwell on her detecting, forgetting that she was, in fact, a working lawyer who spent her usual day tunneling in law books, composing arguments, and pummeling officials on behalf of immigrants caught in the web of so-called justice.

Still, none of that sort of thing was occurring on this particular afternoon. No, indeed. At 2:15 p.m., with the wind trembling the windows in their casements and the clip-clop of hooves and the strangled-goose honk of auto horns clamoring below on crowded 42nd Street, Grace was lifting a revolver, centering it on the forehead of the death mask twelve feet away on her Greek Revival mantel. It was a fine revolver, the type I often had used myself in my past career as an operative of the Federal Department of Justice—a .32-caliber Colt Pocket Positive with a 2 1/2-inch barrel and a feather-light single-action pull, requiring a finger pressure of only three pounds.

It was not the type of weapon I associated with Grace Humiston, not that she was too delicate for it. She was a fine-bodied, athletic

1

woman, and her spirited nature belied her wealthy, quiet upbringing as the daughter of the late Adoniram Judson Winterton, the old-time New York merchant, real estate magnate and lay worker in Baptist affairs. But Grace was not one for pistols. Normally, her weapons were her granite determination and her quicksilver mind, plus her knack for stirring things up. I never saw anyone, man nor woman, more eager to set flame to a brouhaha, nor one more likely to warm the world with the ensuing fire.

Today, though, with no furor to raise, she had taken up the Pocket Positive. Watching from the doorway, I thought that perhaps she meant to try its single-action pull, cocking the hammer, pressing the trigger. But she did not fire it single action. Indeed, at first she did not fire it at all. She lowered her arm gracefully toward the desk where she sat, then let the arm flow upward again to firing position, a gesture—given her natural sinuousness—as smooth and mysterious as smoke gusting in the wind.

Her finger pressed firmly on the trigger, forcing it back in a nine-pound double-action pull, a smooth, rolling stroke that ended when the hammer fell on an empty chamber with a metallic snap.

"Target practice?" I asked.

Grace looked up, showing me her usual demeanor: dark hair folded gently and precisely above a face that was full and true—compelling eyes, clean-cut cheeks, straight nose, sensitive mouth, a jaw as direct as a boxer's jab.

"No," she said. "The reconstruction of a crime."

She laid the revolver on her desk. A window rattled in its frame, shivering in the intrusive wind. "That revolver belonged to the murderer King," she said. "You have heard of the case?"

Who had not? The newspaper and magazine writers had given the story full rein. It is not every day that an innocent man is snatched from official death with the clock running down, saved by simple idealism and hardheaded investigation. I inclined my head, trying to make the movement smooth. But nothing is smooth about a body-battered, beer-fed Transylvanian detective who has fought his way up from Hell's Kitchen.

"Everyone has heard of the case," I said. "Everyone knows of the midnight ride, of the saving of Charles Stielow." I shrugged, wet my lips in anticipation. "But no-one knows the details."

Grace rose from her desk, and I could see her full rig now, though I tried not to focus on it too much. She was, after all, a married woman, and I a bachelor of low tastes. It wasn't wise, therefore, for me to spend my eyes on Grace's body, full in the right places, encased stylishly in black-kid high-lace shoes and a dark gray dress that swept cleanly from ankle to neck.

"That is true," she said, "and no-one is going to hear the details just now, because we have a client, or more than one, in the outer office. Or so I assume, based on your sudden appearance."

I smiled, put a hand to my mouth to keep her from seeing the disfigurement of my oft-knuckled teeth. I coughed and, once more, I nodded.

Henry Cruger's expensive shoes creaked on the polished-wood floor, shifting nervously, as his wife sat hunched into herself, fixing her eyes on Grace Humiston with raw, fearful hope. Cruger was drawing himself up, squaring his shoulders as I supposed he often had when preparing to mouth some flatulence to the odd fraternal society or businessman's group. "As I'm sure you know, our daughter Ruth has disappeared," he said. It was the type of pointless preamble I would have expected, and it only made him seem more absurd—a public accountant with an elephant nose and sparse hair, clothed in expensive wool, fingering his wristwatch, an effeminate bauble.

"We have followed the case in the newspapers," said Grace, her hands opening slightly as if she wished to reach out with a comforting touch. "Is there no progress?"

"Worse than none," said Mrs. Cruger, looking down at her hands, smoothing away imaginary wrinkles in her tailored cape-coat suit—a Bonwit Teller special, I knew, for I've an eye for clothes, both women's and men's. "Now they are making up wild stories, they are saying she is a bad girl."

Her voice broke, and her husband moved clumsily to lay a hand on her shoulder, saying, "The police believe she went off on her own."

Grace rose from her desk, her face fixed with concentration, and moved to the nearest window. I shifted with her, though I took care to keep my distance, and found another window. On 42nd Street, a horse-drawn carriage struck an outmoded note amid the morass of clumsy Chevrolet and Model T Ford automobiles jousting stiffly for street space with Hudson, Chandler and Westcott machines. Only the horse looked graceful. At her window, Grace laid her hand on the rattling glass, seeking to calm its agitation.

"It has been three months now since the disappearance," she said, turning. "Do you seek my services as a lawyer?"

Mrs. Cruger half-glanced at her husband and he cleared his throat. "Oh, no, Mrs. Humiston. As a detective."

Grace hesitated, looked at me. "I have recently employed Mr. Julius Kron as an investigator," she said. "My husband and I are increasingly busy, involved as we are in our work at the People's Law Firm on behalf of the poor."

Henry Cruger composed himself. "We were hoping for your personal involvement, Mrs. Humiston."

Still, Grace hesitated, and I knew why, though nothing had come to me directly. Though I haven't the brains of a Grace Humiston, still I am no mean investigator. I see personal signals and I read them, I finish half-sentences, I note how people react to telephone calls. Grace Humiston had told her husband that she would undertake no more investigations, giving in to his arguments that the danger was too great, that the general good served was too small. Her husband was a fine, well-educated man, given to great thoughts. Well, God bless him. I don't pretend to that myself. I'm a saloon hound, a man more interested in beefsteak than the Bible, a frequenter of gambling hells and race courses. But I have my own thoughts, too, and one thing I believe is that you should let a thoroughbred run.

Grace Humiston sat. Her desk was of bulky, dark mahogany, well-polished, decorated only by a small bust of Julius Caesar. She pressed her hands to her mouth as if in prayer. The Crugers' plight had moved her, I knew, but acting on that emotion would not be easy for her.

Still, she was her own woman. After a long time, she released a sigh.

"Of course," she said. "I will investigate. Kron will assist. Now, you must tell us the details yourselves. The newspapers sometimes take liberties."

I relaxed and let my heart swing free, though I didn't dare smile. I found a place to brace myself against the mantel. Cruger, too, felt the release of tension. He settled into a chair next to his wife, spread his precise, paw-like little hands, and I was sure we were in for a humdrum recitation. "First of all, you must know the type of girl Ruth is," he said earnestly. "She is 18, a good girl, a good student. She is in the senior class at Wadleigh High School. . ."

We knew all that, of course—the newspapers don't get everything wrong. Fortunately, he broke off and told us something we needed to know, watching his wife's face as he did so. "Mrs. Humiston," he said. "She loves us—you must know that. She has never gone off, she would not go off. We feel she is being forcibly detained."

Mrs. Cruger's wife began to weep silently. I could see her shoulders shaking under his hand. With an effort, Henry Cruger looked away, licked his lips, began his tale. "On December 13, in the early afternoon, Ruth went out," he said. "She told her sister that she was going to retrieve her ice skates, which she had left to be sharpened at a shop." He pursed his lips, raised a finger. "The address of that shop is 542 W. 127th St."

Grace nodded. "We have read of the place."

"Yes," said Cruger. "Then you know it is a repair shop owned by an Italian. His name is Alfredo Cocchi—a tradesman who does motorcycle and bicycle repair and odd jobs." Cruger paused. "He has not been very helpful, but I suppose he has done what he can. He said Ruth came for the skates and went away with them."

Grace leaned forward slightly. "And the police, what have their investigations turned up?"

"Very little, I'm afraid. They say they spoke to people in the neighborhood, businessmen and passers-by, who saw a girl fitting Ruth's description going off in a taxi with a young man."

Mrs. Cruger's chin rose defiantly. "We do not believe that. Not at all."

I stirred, tapping a knuckle on the mantel. "Has the taxi driver been located?"

"No," said Henry Cruger.

"So the police could not find him." Grace looked thoughtful. "How was your daughter dressed when she went out?"

It was Mrs. Cruger who spoke. "She wore a blue serge suit, a white waist, a blue velvet sailor hat, brown shoes and a long blue velour coat. And kid gloves." She dropped her head. "It was very cold."

"And did she take her purse?"

"Of course," said Henry Cruger. "She had to pay for the sharpening of the skates."

"Other personal possessions—beauty aids, clothing, photographs?"

"No. A watch she treasured is still on her dresser."

"Is she given to migraines or spells?"

"No."

Grace looked at me, rose, and began to pace deliberately. The office was small enough that I had to shrink back against the wall each time her pacing brought her within my orbit, so as to give her room to range. She marched with a fist compressed under her chin, thinking, asking questions without turning to look at the Crugers. "Was Ruth carrying a great deal of money?"

I kept an eye on the Crugers as they prepared this answer, for it was a crucial one. "We never could be sure," Henry Cruger said.

Mrs. Cruger picked up the reply. "She had a small trust fund—an old friend of the family had doted on her and left her something when he died. She received regular checks, and sometimes she cashed them and saved the money." Mrs. Cruger breathed in deeply, began to pick at her clothing. "Ruth did that so she could surprise us with gifts. She loved to be mysterious about her secret fund."

Grace paused in her pacing, nodded. "Did she have a particular male friend?"

Mrs. Cruger's shoulders stiffened. "We never allowed that."

Grace now gave me a measured look. "Was there a particular reason?"

I saw Henry Cruger dabbing at his mustache, nervous but determined. "Ruth never fixed her affections on any boy. Then she met a foreign young man while ice-skating one day and. . .she hinted that she might see him again." His lips pinched in with obvious distaste.

Grace surveyed the Crugers. "Was that so terrible?"

Henry Cruger looked resolute. "Mrs. Cruger believes that foreigners are bad business."

Silence fell, briefly. "I see," said Grace Humiston. "And what do we know about this particular foreigner? His description, his antecedents?"

Cruger clicked his tongue. "No description. Only that he is Argentinean, so he said. And that he has some expertise with jewels."

Grace stood pondering for a moment. If she had something in mind, it wasn't clear to me what it might be, and the information was very sparse. "Well, at least that is something," she said at last, "but we will go about this methodically, beginning with Cocchi."

She picked up the revolver. It had lain unnoticed on a corner of the desk until now, but now lamplight winked off its polished metal as she drew out a drawer, began to place it inside. Shocked looks from the Crugers stopped her.

"Excuse me, Mrs. Humiston," said Henry Cruger. "Do you expect violence?"

Grace's mouth was set. "In this world, one does well always to expect violence," she said. "However, this is not a defense weapon. Erwin King was carrying it last March when he used another pistol to kill the farmer Charles Phelps and his housekeeper, Margaret Wolcott, in Orleans County."

Cruger said: "Of course we know of the case." He paused, touched his mustache, then went on hesitantly, as if he feared committing an indiscretion. "Could you tell us how you induced King to confess?"

Grace laid the pistol down, made a dismissive gesture.

Cruger coughed. "Please?"

She caught the eagerness in his voice, looked ruefully at me, still hesitated. Grace Humiston hated show, but she ruminated constantly on the meaning of everyone's actions, including her own. Why did people act as they did, what power did some hold over others? I had heard her expound on some particular instance of peculiar human behavior before, and now she seemed to be seized by the same sort of mood. When she took in a breath, I knew I was right.

"As you know," she said, "I was retained by friends of Charles Stielow, Phelps' hired hand." She paused, recalling. "Time was short. Stielow sat on death row at Sing Sing, and the state had determined that he would not sit there much longer."

She began to move around the office. "King, who lodged near Phelps' farm, had been overheard discussing specific details of the crime. He quickly became my chief suspect. But King was a hardened criminal. Detectives had tried to break him, and he had not broken."

Grace stepped to the mantel and unconsciously touched the death mask. "I arranged for him to be arrested in Buffalo for a minor crime committed in Cattaraugus County. And I arranged to ride with him and two detectives in an automobile traveling at night to the county seat."

Grace once again moved to the window and looked out, absorbed in her narrative. "King lived roughly, and cared nothing for fine clothes. He was wearing an old Army coat and, in the coat, just above the left pocket, there were two pin-marks." She turned, illustrating with forked fingers. "In just that location, a soldier wears decorations. I could see that King, though evil, was a proud man. I asked him, 'Have you braved death for your country only to let an innocent man die in your place?'"

As Grace said these words, the Crugers leaned forward and I leaned forward with them, seeing the scene unfolding—the dark interior of the automobile rocking on the uneven road, the lights of farm houses far off over the fields, the night pressing in outside, two faces close together—one burning with purpose, the other hard and ruined.

"'You have saved lives on the battlefield, have you not?' I said. 'Will you not do a manly thing, and save another?'"

Grace paused as the Crugers sat there barely drawing breath, and I could feel my own heart beating in the silence, feel the pulse tattooing in my temples, feel a yearning in my chest. Grace's eyes were wide and bright, their depths as elusive as a bird song in a dark wood, a melody that draws you on and on down trackless ways. At that moment, I knew how King might have been glad of his chance to confess murder to Grace Humiston.

For a few moments more, the silence continued. I listened to my own breathing, the Crugers sat as if carven. Grace Humiston pondered, drawing a finger to her lips, the electricity in the air drawing the dark hair away from her pale temples. Then her expression changed. Traffic creaked and rattled in the street. The window shook in the wind. The spell was broken.

"So," said Grace, turning a hand. "King told his story. And that was enough to turn the case. The governor, Mr. Whitman, commuted Stielow's sentence."

She shifted her gaze as a young man appeared in the office doorway, a blond young man, blue-suited, with translucent skin, a patrician nose and, as usual, a smug expression. "This," said Grace, smiling, "is James Whistle, who always seems to come when wanted."

Whistle bowed deeply, an over-elaborate business that never failed to annoy me, though for some reason Grace found it charming. I suppose we all see things differently but, to my mind, there is such a thing as too much charm.

"Whistle is an embryo lawyer who is learning the business," Grace was saying to the Crugers. "As our investigations continue, you may consider him your faithful liaison."

When the Crugers had gone, fully examined as to detail, with Whistle acting as the stenographer, I patted my pockets for my pipe and came up empty. Tobacco is my great relaxer, and I was being denied it. And Whistle, of course, had put me off my feed.

Pettishly, I cocked my head to one side and looked narrowly at Grace. "The magazine hounds would call that speculation about the Army coat a great deduction," I said, with more edge than I meant to use. "A nimble leap—jumping from pin-marks to the conclusion that King was a war hero."

Grace puffed out her lips coolly, and the way she tossed her head put me in mind of a yearling named Broadway Bess on which I'd once tripled my stake at Saratoga.

"As you well know, I do not proceed through deduction," she said. "When I questioned King, I had his mustering-out papers from the Mexican conflict in my pocket, as well as a full account of the action that led to his citation for bravery." She fixed me with a look. "Do you know that he went out three times through machine-gun fire to save comrades, and sustained seven wounds? And that a week later, in a drunken fit, he got angry at one of the men he had saved, and removed his eye with a bayonet?"

"A remarkable man," I said. "And a remarkable story. Why did you tell it?"

Grace laid a hand on the bust of Julius Caesar. "To comfort the Crugers. To convince them that I will find their daughter."

"And will you find their daughter?"

Grace Humiston removed her hand from the bust, picked up the revolver, considered it. She held it for some few seconds, until I half expected her to raise it again, to test the faith of its action. But she merely gripped it tightly, looking up at me.

"Yes," she said. "But, I fear, not alive."

Chapter Two

THE PICKLED-PIG'S-FOOT-AND-sawdust crowd I tipped steins with sometimes ribbed me for working for a woman, and sometimes the ribbing turned to knuckling. It didn't happen all that often, of course, for I was known as a man with workable fists and one who appreciated a fight. I'd been that way since the age of 16, when an extortion racketeer shot my father to death in his second-hand clothing shop. I'd had to solve his murder myself, helped by one of the few honest detectives on the force—now long dead. That murder hunt, and his tutelage, had turned me into an investigator. And a fighter. So, as a connoisseur of conflict, by 1917 I was well fixed to judge the fighting qualities of women—Grace, of course, but others, too.

There were plenty of wars that year. In the workhouse on Blackwell's Island in the East River, a hunger-striking woman was rolled in a blanket and fed milk, eggs and a stimulant through a rubber hose thrust down her throat; she was fighting for the right to counsel the poor about birth control. Suffragettes picketed the White House, and were arrested; they were fighting for the right of women to vote. Across the sea, Frenchmen, Englishmen and Germans in thick wool uniforms slipped about in the sucking mud, absorbing the spitting lead of Maxim guns; they were fighting for their lives. Miss Jeannette Rankin of Montana, the only woman at that time ever elected to Congress, fought against giving young American men the privilege of dying in that war. She lost.

But for all the fighting, the world was entering a new age of technology and morality that would bring heaven to earth—that's what the newspapers said, at any rate. Like most people, I wanted to believe it. Unlike them, I didn't.

But New York City, being my own universe, showed plenty of evidence that what the newspapers said was true. Subway trains had been whooshing through the ground under our feet for more than a dozen years, and more were being added all the time, though you could still take a horse-drawn cab if you wished to go leisurely. Automobile production had passed the one million mark the year before, and *The New York Times* was reporting that 60 vehicles per minute were passing the intersection of Fifth Avenue and 42nd Street, less than three percent of them horse-drawn. Movies had transformed entertainment: Norma Talmadge was starring in "Panthea" at the Rialto on 42nd Street, "The Temple of the Motion Picture." We hadn't yet benefited from the healthful effects of total Prohibition—only 19 states were dry, and New York wasn't one of them—but I drowned my sorrows over this with the occasional pail of beer enlivened by a whiskey shot.

And women were making remarkable progress. Why, a *Times* advertisement for Shanley's Restaurant on Broadway went so far as to venture the opinion, in headline type, that "Women Are People." It went on to proclaim: "Here they can dine or lunch in perfect security and with as much freedom from constraint as if they were in their own homes; and this is as it should be."

This admission of women to the human race might have been a boon for Grace Humiston, but I doubt that she needed any formal acknowledgement, since she always made her own space. By the time the Cruger case fell to her, she had carved out a striking career, some of which I learned about only following her unusual solution to that mystery and its accompanying adventures, which nearly put us both in the grave.

After graduating from Hunter College in 1888, Grace had determined to support herself. That in itself, if not a scandal for a young lady, was a departure, especially for one whose father was so well situated, owning properties all over the Upper West Side. She taught for a while at the Collegiate School on West End Avenue and 77th Street, but that didn't fulfill her, so she went to law school, and when the 1904 class of the New York Evening Law School went forth, Grace ranked seventh. The fact that she was in the class at all was shocking, since in those days, only one percent of all lawyers were women. More shocks were in order. A clerkship with the Legal Aid Society immersed her in the sorrows of the poor, and showed her she could use the law to ease them. After she was admitted to the bar in 1905, she set up the People's Law Firm, a sort of five-and-ten-cent affair to which the clients paid only what they could. Shortly, she opened two branch offices of the firm, and engaged assistants to run them.

She was not only capable, but sympathetic. Perhaps that is why her work among the poor led to a curious development: Her clients and their friends would drop by to tell her about relatives or acquaintances who had disappeared. She began to see a pattern: A surprisingly large number of the missing people were reported to be in the South. At that point, she was retained (by whom, I don't know) to travel to that region and to find out what was going on.

What was going on was this: The turpentine camps of the South needed laborers, and the camp owners employed agents in big cities to recruit help to fill the sap buckets. Once a worker got down there, he generally stayed there. If he got other ideas, he was chained up and his attitude was rearranged with a whip.

It was an intriguing story. Supposedly the South's slaves had been freed forty years before, and many of the freed men and women had moved north to the big cities. Now the slave trade had begun again, supplied by a reverse flow of people shanghaied from among the ragged classes of those Northern cities. S.S. McClure, owner of *McClure's Magazine*, was eager to get that story. He offered to finance Grace on a trip through the camps. She accepted, leaving the work of the People's Law Firm in other capable hands. She disguised herself— sometimes as an old woman selling scissors—to penetrate many of the camps, wandering from plantation to plantation for a full year. Then she supplied the details to *McClure's*, which resulted in a round of lively muck-raking.

Our law-enforcement officials in Washington, D.C., who hadn't noticed peonage of Biblical proportions going on under their noses, now awoke from slumber. Rather than work up a sweat themselves, they drafted Grace to serve on the staff of the U.S. Attorney General, to continue her work and turn over the credit to them. She was more than happy to do so, for it meant she could put the oppressors out of business.

That was where I came in: She hired me as a federal investigator. She knew I had the background for what she wanted, for she'd encountered me while dealing with the many nationalities that crossed the portals of the People's Law Firm. While many of the turpentine workers were shanghaied from among the Italian immigrants of New York, many others were of Balkan extraction—my own specialty.

I had been working the precincts of Hell's Kitchen in the employ of a drunken Irish investigator who valued his own hide too highly to sally forth among the head-breaking Hungarians and Rumanians, and who wouldn't have been able to understand them if he had. I speak the languages, you see, being a Transylvanian brought here at the age of eight by my father, who owned a fine clothing shop in the old country. My language ability helped him, and it helped Grace with her shanghaied Hungarians, but she was even more attracted by my general knack for dealing with immigrants and for using my elbows in a tight spot.

One other item also caught her eye, she told me later. I had recovered a diamond necklace that had been stolen from the daughter of a U.S. Congressman by the agents of a Hungarian gangster. In the course of the investigation, I had turned down the gangster's $500 bribe to leave him alone and the Congressman's $100 bonus for quick work.

It made sense to me. I hadn't contracted for the bribe, nor for the bonus, so why should I take them? Grace said that showed I was honest. Well, so be it. If it put me closer to her, so be it. But all it meant was that I keep things simple. There are enough things that complicate a detective's life; he must be steadfast. And I am steadfast, my people are steadfast. Note well: I am a Transylvanian—calculating, slow-going, proud. We Transylvanians, formerly subject to Hungary, suffered greatly under Hungary's rule, but stayed faithful to our nationality for a thousand years. Do not cross us. We will grind you down.

Of course I was not privy to the scene that ensued at Grace's home the night after the Crugers visited our office, though I was able to reconstruct it later through some throwaway descriptions from Grace and my careful knowledge of her and of her husband, who also was a lawyer. Things did not go easily.

"I have taken another case," she told him. With that, I'm sure she folded her hands in that particular way she has of signaling she has made up her mind. Of course, she had taken some precautions, not relying solely on determination to see the thing through. She had gotten Howard Humiston settled down in the front parlor of their brownstone flat with an after-dinner pot of steaming Oriental tea near him and chamber music selection playing on the Victrola. I have since seen the room, and it is comfortable enough to make any man feel secure—sturdy and American, exhibiting hardy Mission furniture in the Gustav Stickley style.

Howard Humiston filled a cup and shielded it with a massive, freckled hand. I know that gesture, too, and his customary expression when performing it—his forehead wrinkling quizzically above his broad, straightforward face, fair hair spilling in poorly-combed rivulets down all sides of his dome. He looked a fool, but was not.

"I could tell you had," he said, peering into his tea. "You came home happy." They had been married for some time—a second marriage for Grace, the first for him. The union had taken place in Lima, Peru, on a world tour they had taken after Grace had left the

U.S. Attorney's office. As a woman of property, she could afford it, and as one who had been under great strain for some time—vilified by plantation owners, shot at, undercut by politicians—she needed it. She and Humiston had known each other for years previously, had shared the legal work at the People's Law Firm. I viewed the marriage from a distance, fatalistically. Grace and I had worked together for the U.S. Attorney, but nothing of personal import had passed between us, though we had had a few fast-breathing moments together, particularly on one occasion when a lumberyard manager got his shotgun on us and his double hammers cracked back before I could bull into him, thrusting the gun up, sending the twin blast skyward instead of into our bodies.

I had said nothing to her when she quit her job with the U.S. Attorney, though that night I did repair to the Old Ebbitt Grill, stayed late and had, perhaps, one more stein than necessary. Over the years, I had written the whole thing off. Still, when she had summoned me two months before from my secure government position, I had packed my bags within the hour. Now, though we were merely employer and employee again, I had spent some time considering what had drawn Grace to her husband, and what had pushed them, curiously, apart.

"Actually, your separate practice has worked out well," he said now, dolefully. "It appears to be lucrative."

At the sideboard, she had been rearranging the tea service. "What a thing to say! The money goes to you to support the People's Law Firm." She checked herself, spoke more calmly, marshaling a rational argument. "That was the plan, to give our charitable enterprise more substance. Even so, my practice is not that lucrative."

Howard Humiston plucked at his lower lip. "Still, you can afford to pay those young men."

She sighed with exasperation. "I took on Whistle and Kron expressly so I could turn the detecting over to them."

He sipped at his tea, tapped the side of his cup. "Yet you have taken on another case."

She wheeled. It was still windy that evening, and the curtains from the open window billowed and flapped. Outside, the darkness of New York was cut by the yellow eyes of a thousand windows, framing slivers of otherwise-hidden lives. "This is a special case. The police have failed, or worse. For the Crugers, there is no other recourse."

"A special case! They are all special."

She lifted a finger to make a point, then clenched her fist and shook her head. Sorrow lined her forehead, anger pressed her lips into a line. "I still take cases from the People's Law Firm. Don't you accuse me of not doing so!"

"I would never accuse you of that."

They stayed poised for a few moments in unhappy silence. From the Victrola, a violin overrode its fellow instruments, sawing at the charged air. Howard Humiston looked away from her and sipped his tea, then looked back.

She ran her eyes over him, and I know what she was thinking. In a weak moment, she had once confessed it to me. Whenever he was depressed, he seemed to shrink inside his clothes. When she had met him, he had always bulked up so large, roaring at the capitalists who forced young immigrant women to grind out a living in freezing shirtwaist factories, battling the laws that forced those same women to bear flocks of unwanted children, smiting the brassbound merchants of war. Now, when gloom descended upon him, his clothes bagged away from him. Only his broad head, buttressed by old-fashioned mutton-chop whiskers, maintained its size, floating like a large moon above the dark landscape of his raiment. "I only want us to be together," he said, trying not to make it sound like an accusation.

She turned back to the window, still framed by the curtains beating in the wind. In the dark sky, icy cirrus clouds scraped the heavens, and unknown cosmic disturbances stirred. It would be a violent night.

"We are together," she murmured.

But on this issue, they were not together. Both knew that the decision had been made. And both knew it would drive them further apart.

CHAPTER THREE

A DIRTY STREAK, LIKE THE trail of a tainted teardrop, made its way down the center of the shop window at 542 W. 127th St., eddying past a painted motorcycle. The building showed wear, but retained a certain solidity and crafty style. Above the ground floor, deep-set windows were arched with decorative brick, and the plaster edging the roof three stories up was entwined with motifs of leaves and vines, pocked with the gaping mouths of gargoyles. Pre-Civil War, I judged. In recent years, we had required less cleverness of our buildings, more efficiency and function.

The loose-swinging doorbell jingled and Grace pushed through as I followed close behind. The shop was a jumbled mess: Crusted mechanical parts clustered around a Harley-Davidson Racer motorcycle, a deflated tire tube straggled away from a bicycle with one wheel off, boxes holding for-sale monkey wrenches cluttered one end of the counter that cut the shop in half. Permeating all was a heady, dangerous chemical odor concocted of spilled gasoline, cleaning solvent, and lubricating oil. A firetrap, I thought to myself. What would have brought a well-bred young woman to a shop such as this—a low, smelly place?

The jingle of the doorbell hadn't roused the small man in streaked coveralls. He crouched over a workbench at the back of the shop, next to a door that appeared to open on a staircase. His rapt attention was fixed on a miniature Ferris wheel, and his fingers moved slowly,

19

deliberately, as he manipulated its driving mechanism, producing a monotonous squeaking.

"Alfredo Cocchi?" Grace asked abruptly.

The man looked up, startled. "That's my name," he said. He looked from Grace to me disconsolately, his misshapen nose twitching as if to hold back an imminent mucus-drip, his hands sweeping to the red bandanna that draped his neck. He polished off the most recent layer of grease and asked, "You have job for me?"

Grace smiled. "We would not take you away from your Ferris wheel." She swept forward eagerly, her morning dress rustling lightly above the filthy floor, and ran her eyes over the toy. "It is a beautiful creation."

Cocchi's back straightened, his spreading mustache quivering beneath his lumpy nose as he bowed slightly. "It is a plaything for the new world—modern," he explained. "For every child. Every child will want one."

"Yes," said Grace. "The modern age. What *Life* magazine called, if I remember correctly, a 'get-things-done-quick age.'" He nodded, but Grace's eyes moved away from him, inspecting the shop's decor—an odd combination of color and low sentimentality. The walls displayed a crucifix that appeared to be of real gold, a painting of Jesus with glowing heart and pale skin, and unremarkable murals depicting scenes of Italy—olive trees, country lanes, mountains and valleys.

Cocchi took the opportunity to run his eyes openly over Grace's body and grin widely at me, inviting shared appreciation. The gaping separation between his front teeth seemed to expand with the grin. I scorched him with a look, and he collapsed into confusion and dismay, rotating his head and shoulders toward Grace, seeking refuge.

"This one," the little man said, looking at me obliquely, "he does not like the Ferris wheel, he is a rock-face. Why does he frown?"

Grace's eyebrows lifted in amusement. "Kron comes from the solemn sector of Rumania. He is quite fierce and hard-hearted." Her voice dropped, acquiring a touch of mystery. "His work makes him so. He is a detective."

I screwed my face into my best people-eating expression, drawing my eyebrows downward, crunching my teeth together, and pivoting my nose over to one side. Cocchi crossed himself, his chin vibrating as he cowered closer to Grace. "And you, lovely lady," he whispered. "You are detective, too?"

Grace laid a hand on the counter as if laying it reassuringly on his arm. It came to rest near a box, that—to judge from its inscription—held a monkey wrench. "No, a lawyer for the parents of Ruth Cruger. My name is Grace Humiston."

Something moved in Cocchi's eyes. "A lawyer? No. The newspapers say you are detective. The greatest detective."

"The newspapers say many things."

Cocchi was still for a moment, his work-beaten palms scraping at the coarse overalls covering his thighs—an unsettling movement, as if he were itching to get his hands on someone who had wronged him. "Yes," he rasped. "They say many things, write many things. Many things that are not true." He shook a finger at her. "They accuse me."

He began to gesticulate, to stamp around the shop, raising dust from the floorboards. My throat closed and I coughed, but Grace showed no reaction, except for a widening of her eyes. "They try to say I kill this girl, I hide this girl!" Cocchi exclaimed with injured fury, stabbing a finger at the floor. "The detectives go through my cellar, move everything, look for holes in the ground." He struck himself on the side of the head. "They slap me, grab my clothing. Beat me."

"That is outrageous." said Grace. "But they are upset. You say they believe the girl was murdered. I believe so myself."

He went quiet, and his eyes were wet. "Why?"

"It is obvious. She loved her family and made no preparations to leave, she has no mental defect, there has been no ransom demand."

"Still, perhaps she is held."

"She has been gone for months. The odds of surviving are vanishingly small."

"Sad...," he said. His face flushed, the anger returning. "But I didn't murder her! Don't slap me. The damn police...outrageous! Slap those other people! Grab those other people's clothes!"

The shop was dim, and Grace moved closer to Cocchi, coming within inches of his face to read his expression more closely. "What other people?"

"Those Spanish," Cocchi spat out, spraying mouth-mist into the slanting, weak illumination filtering from the front window. "Those high-hat Spanish in their shop next door, with their fancy clothes, and their jewels and their pretty girls that come and go. . ." Heavy footfalls rumbled on the enclosed staircase.

"Alfredo!"

The exclamation cracked through the shop and all three of us snapped around toward it. A behemoth of a woman stood at the bottom of the staircase. Her dress was rough and grease-stained, her broad forehead crusted with eczema above porcine eyes, her left cheek glowing dully with a birthmark that stained the skin like the mark of a devil's claw. She balanced her cargo of skin, bone and muscle on a cane, but the cane seemed to be a convenience rather than a necessity, for in the next second she lifted it and swept forward on the attack.

"Time-waster!" she said. "Trash-builder!" She slashed her cane at the Ferris wheel as the little man rushed forward, too late. Little passenger-baskets, gears and pieces of the wheel exploded outward as the toy collapsed. Cocchi stumbled to a halt, tears sluicing down his cheeks, his hands fluttering as the woman turned abruptly and disappeared. All that remained was the sound of her retreat—the cane clattering on the staircase, her harsh, fading breathing, her stumping footsteps mounting upward.

Grace moved to the broken wheel and began to pick up and arrange the shattered parts on the counter delicately, carefully, giving Cocchi time to recover. At last, he gathered himself, sniffing. "Thank you, lovely lady," he breathed. From his pocket he pulled a mucus-splotched cotton handkerchief, flipped it wide and honked into it.

He straightened his back. "My wife," he said, flinging his hands about apologetically. "She is not well, I upset her with my foolish things. She is right, I should spend more time on the police motorcycles."

He flung a hand vaguely at the staircase. "I go and talk to her, make her feel better."

"I understand," said Grace. "Perhaps we will talk again."

Cocchi pressed a finger to his lips. "Okay," he said softly. "Only don't come when my wife she's around. Pretty ladies make her more ill." He rolled his eyes and wobbled his head from side to side, so that Grace swept a hand to her mouth to stifle a smile. In spite of my supposed fierceness, so did I.

"He was right about one thing," I said. "The pretty girls, they do come and go."

Grace and I were finishing a third cup of coffee in a cafe with a view of the jewelry shop next to Cocchi's. I was examining the jewelry shop's latest customer—a woman of about 20 in a fanciful hat and a Scottish Mole coat. She was hesitating, reading the window legend. In curving, antique script, it announced "De Souza Jewelers." Oddly enough, the inscription was enclosed by the tail loop of a stylized monkey.

"That's strange," I said, but I was thinking about the customer, not the inscription. "Why do they spend so much time chewing their fingernails before they go in? It's not because they can't afford the goods, for any one of them could probably buy the place out." Well, the preliminaries were over. The young lady, after first checking the street, stepped resolutely into the shop. I lifted my chin at Grace. "How do you read that?"

"Very simply," she said, sipping coffee. "It is not the jewelry case each intends to look over. It is a man. A very good-looking man of a somewhat lower-class disposition, I would say, or, in the alternative, one with a racy reputation."

I smiled. For all that she was brilliant at this sort of thing, she was not reserved about it. Her intensity glowed in her eyes. "And how do you read that?"

"You will have noticed that these young ladies primp their hair before they go in, and they primp it furiously when they come out."

I shook my head. "All right, that accounts for the idea that they are going in to see a fine-looking specimen, but how do you come up with the idea that he's either lower-class or racy?"

Grace nodded. "It is the hesitation that tells me. These are well-to-do young women, sure of themselves." She placed her pointer finger on the table. "Take our last customer, for instance. Her Scottish Mole coat cost her at least $260, even if she got it on sale, and it was the cheapest coat we've seen this morning. Such women are straightforward. A few years ago, they would have been expected to blush and hide their faces at the thought of a man. Not any more. Now, they are bold. If they felt—I emphasize felt, for it is exactly a feeling, not a rational conclusion that inspires this behavior—if they felt the man they are going to see was suitable, they would roar on in there, guns blazing."

I sighed. I prided myself on interpreting behavior, but there was always something to be learned from Grace. "So have they met this young man before?" I asked, "Or have they heard about him from someone else?"

"They have information from others, I would say, and most likely from their women friends. They go in singly, rather than in pairs or threesomes—that in itself is unusual, suggesting that they are deliberately slipping away from their friends to enjoy this little adventure." She paused. "And the adventure they are seeking out, the man they are interested in, is a strange sort of businessman."

Perplexed, I said, "He sells jewels."

Grace cocked her head. "I wonder. Four young ladies have gone into his shop in an hour and a half, and not one has come out with a package. Not one has seen fit to buy a trinket from this very good-looking man as an excuse to linger a few moments longer."

I lifted my shoulders. "Interesting. But whether his business is strange or not, it's not likely he made off with Ruth Cruger. He's still here, after all."

"Or perhaps he's back from where ever he went," Grace said. "That's a riddle, though. Ruth was not equipped for a long trip, and she certainly was not dressed stylishly enough for a honeymoon."

I mulled that. "She might have equipped herself, and she might have dressed herself in style after she left. There is the matter of her secret fund, after all."

"True." Grace was biting her lower lip. Her thoughtful expression convinced me I'd scored a point, and that emboldened me.

"Even so, we might be focusing too strongly on this man," I said. "All we have on him is a scrap of suspicion, and that was thrown our way by Cocchi, who may be trying to divert our attention."

"Why do you say that?"

"Just a thought."

Grace touched her chin with a long, delicate finger, and her eyebrows went up, forming two dark, regular arches. "A very insightful thought. You are doing well, Kron. That thought is based on things you have unconsciously observed."

"Such as?"

She waggled the finger. "Such as the fact that this motorcycle repairman, who wastes all his time building toys, still has enough money to buy a cross of real gold for his wall." She paused. "And such as the fact that he makes a great show of saying the police beat him. My experience is that the police excel in that area and are remarkably thorough. But Cocchi shows no marks of a beating on his face or hands, or at least none I could see when I drew close to him. No bruises, no lumps, no lacerations."

I made a face. "You are wasting money paying me as an investigator."

"Not in the least," she said with a smile. "It's useful to have an ally who can make frightful faces."

As she said that, she put a hand on my arm and I stayed perfectly still so as not to disturb the feel of her fingers. They were warm and firm, and I imagined I could feel the blood pulsing in them, a rapid beating that meant she was excited, on the chase.

"So," I said, trying to keep my voice steady. "Will we concentrate on Cocchi, or on our jeweler friend?"

She removed her hand, reached for her handbag. "We will concentrate on neither, until we find out which man has drawn the interest of the police."

I snorted. "The police! Why the police? They've cocked up this investigation. Why talk to them?"

Grace nodded significantly. "In this city," she said, "anyone interested in crime should always begin with the police."

CHAPTER FOUR

POLICE CAPT. MICK "STOKER" MCCULLAGH was a meat-eater, one of those neatly-pressed predators in blue who had been prowling the streets of New York for decades, gobbling up payments for the big boys downtown, leaving toothmarks on gamblers and saloon-owners who didn't pay tribute, bullying drunks and lamp-post-hangers into voting correctly in municipal elections, ignoring—and sometimes performing—murder.

It's true that in that year just before the war—or rather, just before the United States involvement in the war, there being no real war, in our estimation, before we were in—the city was relatively quiet from the standpoint of graft and violence. We were experiencing a spasm of reform. John Purroy Mitchel, a humorless, youthful man with self-righteous blue eyes and the energy of a Midwestern dry-goods dealer, was ensconced at the Mayor's mansion, doing the Lord's work. The bribe-takers were lying low, the gangs were on the run, and the murder rate was plummeting—alarmingly, from my standpoint, since I derived a large part of my income from probing the ultimate departure of my fellow human beings. Homicides, which had numbered a comfortable 265 in 1913, had dropped to 244 in 1914, slid to 222 in 1915, sunk to 186 in 1916. There was a real danger that our citizens would quit slaughtering each other altogether, and turn all human carnage over to the automobile-makers, who were producing machines that—pressed to their utmost—could whiz along upwards of 100 miles an hour, destroying all men, women, forests, factories and outbuildings that got in their way.

McCullagh, though, remained faithful to his vision of ultimate human corruption. In fact, he seemed to exhibit that corruption in his person. Physically, he exuded a strong odor of rare meat and alcohol, like a bloody-fanged hyena that had fallen into a whiskey vat. He had a tight face, a thin, bony jaw, eyes black as rotting peach pits and poorly-clipped hair bunched in clumps like squirrels jostling for position on a dead branch. His blue uniform, in contrast, was fresh as morning air, the wool nap tightly pressed, and his message was reassuring.

"You don't want to be working yourselves up over nothing," he said, inclining his head as if it were being driven downward by the weight of his considerable experience. "These young girls are always going off. It's a pity, indeed, but it's the times, there's no help for it."

I smiled wryly as Grace got up and began to pace. McCullagh's office in the Fourth Branch Bureau at 342 W. 123rd St. was a dowdy room dominated by a monstrous oak desk aflow with reports, hard-spined ledgers and trails of gray-and-black-speckled cigar ashes skirmishing around his green-shaded banker's lamp. The floor was a tangle of wicker trash baskets, bulky electrical cords, leather gear and nightsticks, the wall a photo gallery of stiffly uniformed cops. Grace took some time examining the portraits, then did the same to McCullagh, who sat leaning back in his chair.

"Ruth Cruger has been missing now for three months," Grace said quietly. "All that time you, supposedly, have been looking high and low for her. What are the results of your search?"

McCullagh emitted a smile, though the teeth that made it shine seemed very plentiful and sharp. "I'd love to tell you, now. We always co-operate with the lawyers," he said. "They're soldiers fighting right beside us in the constant battle we're waging for justice. And we're especially co-operative with charming lady lawyers like yourself, we being but men, and subject to the weakness of our breed. But Mr. Kron can tell you that our cooperation can go only so far, and not so far as to release information concerning our open investigations."

Grace leveled a finger at him, meaning to provoke. "I am well aware of what you release and what you don't release when it serves your turn," she said. "Don't play with me."

It is hard to imagine true fury until you see it exhibited by a man who rises each morning, sips his coffee, eats his roll and jam and puts on his uniform in the sure and certain knowledge that at some point that day someone will cower before him in abject terror—some thieving newsboy, some barkeep short on his tribute money, some streetwalker who has let slip an impudent word, who has gone too far, who has seen your hickory stick rise to batter her wrists and elbows blue, to stain them red-and-purple with broken blood vessels. Such was the fury of McCullagh. He coiled, his face scowled as if it would never smile again, his right hand made a fist, his boot kicked the side of his desk like a sledgehammer booming into a coffin.

"You are howling in the wrong graveyard this time," he ground out, finally, pounding his fist thump-thump-thump. "This girl went off with some fancy fella she met skating at Van Cortlandt Park, and no doubt they were up to some fancy business. She was seen getting into a taxi."

I shifted my weight, teetering my chair so that two of its legs struck the floor with a crack, warning McCullagh not to carry this too far.

Grace hardly seemed to notice. Calmly, she said, "Did this man go by the name of De Souza?"

McCullagh wet his lips. I could hear the harshness of his breathing, ragged up by lungs that had spent too much time squeezing pipe-smoke. "And what the hell makes you think we know his name? Wouldn't we have hauled him in for questioning if we knew that?"

A bit of redirection was called for. Before Grace could reply, I interjected, low and insinuating, "You tell us, Stoker."

He had been furious before, now he was beyond that. I could tell because everything about him—his voice, his movements, his facial expression—went deadly quiet. He rose slowly, and he was tall and he was hard and he was a speciman you didn't want to trifle with. His reply was a whisper. "Only my friends call me that."

This is the sort of game that, being in, you cannot slip out of, whether you feel like it or not. You must fold or press your bets, and my nature is to press my bets. I said, "Then I guess you never hear it."

He paled. His voice, which could not get softer, did get softer, and now it was a hoarse, hissing sound. "You don't value your health much, do you, boy-o?"

I rose. I would have had to in a moment, anyway, for he would have come around the desk and clouted my skull while I was tilting awkwardly between sitting and standing. I got my fists out to the side, snapped hard together so that I stood less chance of breaking a hand on his knotty brain-box, got my weight braced. But Grace took two steps, cutting off the path he would have taken to get to me.

"When this investigation is finished, I'll arrange for you two to face each other in an earthen pit," she said. "You'll be armed with Bowie knives and your free hands tied. That'll please you, I'm sure, but until then—"

McCullagh, his eyes on me, coughed like a cougar. "This investigation *is* finished, so far as you're concerned. This girl went off with something in long pants that got her nether parts wet, they do it all the time." He broke the stare-down with me, looked at Grace. "This is the sixth one in the last three years, tender high-class females. How do you like that?" He laughed coarsely. "And I suppose her parents told you she was the Virgin Mary?" He laughed again. "Well, they all do. They all do."

He continued to breathe harshly for a few seconds, then choked on a rough, half-heard curse, shook himself, resumed his seat. He felt he'd scored a point, I could tell that, and that made his recovery much easier. It took some time, but at last the redness of his face began to fade and he took a long, long breath. "Well now," he said. "Well now."

He allowed himself to lean back in his chair and put his hands behind his head, inside himself again. The transformation was complete. His control had returned, he was in the mood to play. He cleared his throat. "You know, you two are quite too good to waste time on some little business like this." He smiled broadly, and his Irish brogue had bite. "Look at you, now. Mrs. Humiston, you'd ought to be modeling face powder or Albrecht Furs. And you, Kron, if you were too good for the Department of Justice—or vice versa—you'd ought to go in the ring and pound fellas into paste. You've the attitude, and the money's good."

I sat down again, waited to see where all this would lead.

Grace returned McCullagh's smile. "We appreciate the career advice," she said. "You think this case is too murky, even for talented amateurs?"

McCullagh's expression was an odd combination of smugness and wariness. He lifted his right hand and began to examine his nails. "Oh, I wouldn't say murky. Oh no, not for you two." He looked down at his desk. "But it's getting so you don't know who your friends are out on the street."

He got up, slid to the wall on his left, and stopped near a framed photo of a policeman with full lips, a broad nose and troubled eyes. On the policeman's high collar, which dipped to a "V" in front, there were lieutenant's bars. McCullagh touched the frame with a long hook of a finger, squaring it up. "Lieutenant Charles Becker. God rest him, no matter what they say." He turned. "They say Becker was crooked as a dog's hind leg, that he would break your bones, make you bleed. But he wasn't a thoughtless type of man, indeed he wasn't. I knew him. He had a theory about controlling the gamblers, the muscle boys and the gang fellas."

I looked to Grace. Her expression seemed to show nothing, but I knew that face. The light blush of color about her cheekbones, the tilt of her jaw—they betokened that well-controlled excitement that meant her mind was feeding on whatever she was seeing and hearing. Somehow, she was getting what she had come for.

McCullagh half-slanted an open palm at us. "He figured you had to be out among 'em, else how would you know what they were doing?"

The palm swept at the air. "The honest folk don't care about these mugs, 'long as they keep their diseased selves out of the public eye. The public don't even care to know. But Becker knew who they were and where they were. And if they got out of line (here, McCullagh's palm chopped at the air like a hatchet) smash 'em! Bust up their joints!"

"Kill them," Grace said flatly. "That's an excellent technique, too, isn't it? Fill them full of bullet holes, as Becker, or someone, did to the gambler Rosenthal."

McCullagh's mood seemed almost cheerful now. He strolled back to his seat and sat down. "Yes, well, now. Some said Becker, or somebody, went too far on that one." He almost giggled. "But, really, there couldn't have been much doubt that Becker was the one did Rosenthal, seeing how they broiled him up at Sing Sing."

Grace put a finger to her lips, appeared to be considering all this as if McCullagh had been making a difficult philosophical point. "Let me see now," she said. "Becker is dead, but his spirit isn't. His style, his techniques, live on. Is that it?"

McCullagh hugged the arms of his chair and began to rock back and forth. "Well, now," he said, "that's what some might think."

Grace and I sat next to each other on the downtown subway. The car rocked roughly, and the wheels shrieked on the turns, the curved walls flying by the windows.

"A dangerous man," said Grace.

I pulled my woolen trousers back from my knees so that the stretching would not destroy the crease, shrugged my shoulders inside my tightly-tailored suit coat. "That's certain."

"I've never heard him called 'Stoker' before."

I watched the speeding walls, or tried to. I was mesmerized by the darkness outside, the speed, the clicking and swaying of the car. "Many call him that, but few to his face. They hung that tag on him ten years ago, when he was making his way up through the ranks. It goes to when he found the body of Sid Pearlstein, the gambler, in the furnace of that office building in mid-town."

"That was a major triumph for McCullagh, or so the newspapers said."

The speed of this trip was making my stomach queasy. Not that I preferred horse-drawn conveyances, but there was something about too much speed—

"It turned out that way, but it could easily have gone bad. The D.A.'s men walked in on Stoker and found him with the furnace door open and a coal shovel in his hand. He claimed he was trying to pull Pearlstein's skull out of the flames to preserve it for evidence." I hooded my eyes and dropped them away from the windows. My stomach settled, slightly. "The papers bought it, and the D.A. finally decided to go along with the game."

"And the truth was?"

I shook myself and smiled bleakly, trying not to show too many of my teeth. "Street talk says Stoker shoved Pearlstein in there himself, and was just putting on the finishing touches."

"And why would he do that?"

"The usual reason. Pearlstein was getting ready to rat out some cops."

The train slowed, coming into the 42nd Street station. My equilibrium reasserted itself. I began to feel better. A mechanical voice croaked above our heads. When it fell silent, Grace spoke: "We've been warned off, but we don't know whether we've been warned off Cocchi or De Souza or some scheme that involves neither. We need the police reports on the six disappearances."

"McCullagh brought those up. Why would he do that if the reports meant something?"

"I don't know, and I won't know until we get them."

"How will we get them?"

"We'll buy them," Grace said. "Everything in this city is for sale."

Chapter Five

IT WAS GRACE'S IDEA TO brace De Souza alone, to survey his shop and see what she could see. I had nothing against it, but I suppose that her husband put up some argument, and that she was forced to satisfy him on the point. She and Howard Humiston had made up their recent quarrel, so it would have been necessary to walk softly so as to continue the negotiated peace.

That's the way of it with married people, I'd always been told—much shaking of newspapers and clinking of coffee cups in the wake of fights, many half-started sentences in attempts to make up. I'd done the small version myself, of course—I'd been sweet on a few women and they on me, and we'd had our fallings-out and tried to get back to where we'd been, but in the end one of us always chose to walk away. It was easy to do. With marriage you can't do that, or at least you shouldn't, that's my bottom feeling. And that's why I'd stayed as I was, a bachelor. Marriage is a tougher swim, so I'd never gone the route.

Still, I could imagine what the scene with Grace and Howard Humiston must have been like. Typically, he would have joked awkwardly with her about her plans for the day, telling her he was glad she was shopping for jewelry and not shoes, since the scarcity of leather had sent the price of ladies' shoes, formerly $6 a pair, shooting up to $14. He'd have asked—trying not to kick up a fuss, but desperate to know—if she was in danger. She'd have kept her temper in check, would have been cool, would have dismissed the idea.

35

He, of course, would not have believed her. I wouldn't have believed her myself.

We could have taken on De Souza Jewelers together, Grace and I, pretending to be sweethearts shopping for an engagement ring, but Grace called that poor strategy. If some man in the shop was romancing women, why, then, it was best to give him a chance to strut his business, to exhibit his style. Strategically, I agreed with her. And, of course, strategy was the only real consideration. All else had to remain unspoken.

After her encounter, she gave me a report in detail. Even at the moment before she entered the shop, she wasn't sure what her approach would be: to disguise her identity or make it plain, to play a role for the information it would bring, or to tell the truth, to see what effect that would have.

The door opened on a surprisingly well-appointed shop for a neighborhood that was dowdily commercial. Sophisticated electric lighting glowed on the green velvet of the jewelry cases, the floors shimmered with fresh wax, and the furniture was French Provincial. A few chairs in the front were arrayed around a coffee table, so that waiting customers might lounge in elegance.

A young man who had been taking advantage of a Louis XIV chair in just this fashion, chin on palm, apparently alone, sprang to his feet. He moved toward Grace with a sharp smile and the sinewy movement of a whipping hemp-rope.

"May I offer you some assistance?" he said, a slightly breathy quality to his tone.

The words were correct, just fitting an upscale shopkeeper, but the usual air of obsequiousness was absent both from his dress and manner. His high silk ascot was rich and haughty, and aggressive confidence glowed in his dark, lustrous eyes. They highlighted the muscular sensitivity of his Hispanic features—high cheekbones, lips full and slightly misaligned.

"I wish to examine your wares," said Grace, and, though she did not make a point of it later, I'm sure that she, too, dropped her voice intimately, lowered her eyes. She is fine at many roles, but this is her best.

"A natural enough desire," he said, his eyes lingering on her face. "Though it will be difficult for our little sparklers to compete with your natural beauty."

His body had a rich, strong fragrance—a crushed-almond scent composed of cologne and his own body oil. He had stepped in close to her—closer than an American clerk would have—and she was trying to decide whether he had done so tactically. Concentrating on the question helped her control her breathing, I suppose, and her breathing would have grown faster—the young man had that effect on women.

"Beauty is shown off best by competition, is it not?" she said.

"Always."

"Then let the competition begin."

He nodded graciously, led her toward the jewelry case.

"You are Mr. De Souza, then?"

He stopped and turned. "I am Ricardo Alvarez, the Count de Clements." His lips drooped, eyes clouded. "Surely you are not fixed on dealing with my uncle?"

"Oh, by no means."

He paused. "Still," he said, "if you wish to deal with him, he is here."

He gestured toward a shadowed doorway at the rear. Grace saw the silhouette of a corpulent, suited figure standing bolt straight, holding a slim cigar at a distinct angle, smoke curling around the man's head, some strange creature clinging to his shoulder. The man took a step forward into the light, and she saw a bearded face laced with red veins cutting outward from haunted eyes. On the man's shoulder, a lascar monkey minced and chittered.

Ricardo bowed. "My uncle, Carlos De Souza."

Uncle Carlos swept forward, discarding the cigar in a convenient ashtray. He, too, bowed elegantly in the Continental style, the monkey hanging on for dear life. Uncle Carlos' trousers were sleek, coat collar high, whiskers razor-trimmed. A diamond stick-pin set off his apricot vest, angled so the stone would catch and throw back the light. "Welcome," he said. "Your beauty honors our place of business."

Grace nodded. "It is a privilege to meet men with such dedication to beauty. My name is Grace Humiston."

She thought she saw a flicker in Uncle Carlos' eyes, but Ricardo continued to regard her with the same ironic courtliness. "Mrs. Humiston," said Uncle Carlos, recovering. "Excellent. May we show you something?"

She moved a step forward to emphasize her words. "Indeed," she said, "I hope you will show me everything."

Uncle Carlos emitted a little laugh, a not-entirely-comfortable little laugh, and spread his hand invitingly at the jewelry case. "I should warn you before we begin," he paused for a beat, "our business is somewhat unusual."

Grace's eyes were on the monkey. "I had gathered as much."

"You had?"

"Yes," said Grace, smiling innocently as she strolled toward the jewelry display. "I've been told by a young friend, Ruth Cruger, that you have an unusually lovely array of gems."

This had the intended effect. Grace saw Uncle Carlos' glance lock for an instant with that of Ricardo and, instinctively, Uncle Carlos began to caress the quivering monkey's back. What would his response be: outright denial, pretended ignorance? He smiled ingratiatingly, swayed his head slightly, and moved his right hand to the side, palm upward. "A recommendation, however it comes, is always welcome." The monkey squeaked, its tittering catching the man's exact tone.

Sly, sly. He had slipped away neatly, neither confirming that he knew Ruth Cruger, which could have led to more questioning, or denying it, which would have proved embarrassing if Grace had contrary evidence. He turned abruptly, back in command. "I was speaking not of the unusual beauty of our line, but of our out-of-the-ordinary merchandising process. You see," he indicated the display, "these jewels are only samples. We take orders, then return to our native Argentina to select the gems personally from among an array provided by trusted wholesalers there."

Grace moved to the case and looked down into the winking lights of dozens of emeralds, rubies, diamonds and pearls. The dimness of the shop and the unworldly brightness of the case—inscribed with the monkey logo—made the gems seem curious, abandoned and forlorn—like the leavings of ancient shipwrecks, flung across the bottom of the sea. "Strange," she said, turning her gaze on Uncle Carlos. "I have traveled in Argentina and I don't recall that the country produces gems."

The ropiness of Uncle Carlos' facial veins became a degree more distinct, the skin tightened across his cheekbones, his jaw jutted—but he controlled himself and passed a hand over his face, a gesture of embarrassment. "You have caught us out, I am afraid."

"How so?"

Ricardo shambled forward. "We are very poor merchants," he said. The backlighting of the jewelry case burnished his features and the vulnerability of his expression lent him a touching charm. "That is to say, we are wealthy people, but no good in the line of trade."

Grace looked from one to the other. "It sounds like a fascinating situation."

Uncle Carlos held up a hand to Ricardo, claiming the tale for himself. "These jewels are all that remain of one of the great fortunes of Spain—a branch of our family that has suffered certain reverses," Uncle Carlos said. He smiled with self-deprecation. "Ricardo and I have been lucky. God has blessed our cattle-ranching operations in our native country. We travel, we enjoy ourselves." He grew doleful again. "But our relatives—they are proud, but sinking. Rather than spend all our time in America wastefully, we market their lovely gems."

Grace nodded with understanding. "And rather than risk traveling with a large store of treasure, you bring them over a few at a time."

Uncle Carlos chuckled, thrusting a finger at the monkey, who seized it and began to suckle it like a grotesque baby. "You are as clever as you are lovely."

Grace smiled gently. "Cleverness has its own beauty," she said. "And once attained, it is preserved with fewer cosmetics."

Both men laughed. "We obviously will not take advantage of you in commerce," said Uncle Carlos. "Shall we do business?"

Grace gave him a direct look. "Almost certainly, we will."

CHAPTER SIX

HAPPY JACK MULLRANEY HAD A stale, disused smell, like a room shut off in winter. I noticed it as soon as I put my foot up on the brass rail next to him in Murphy's, a saloon on the edge of Hell's Kitchen. The place was run by a Tammany pol who still remembered when the Irish gangs could deliver the vote and was sentimental enough to offer a free drink once a year to the ex-faithful.

Jack looked up at me with a smile. Of course, whenever Jack looked up, he looked up with a smile, whether he felt like it or not. Happy Jack had gotten his nickname because the left side of his face was paralyzed, pulling the facial muscles up into a grotesque mask of happiness.

"Jack," said I, in simple greeting. We didn't shake hands, it wasn't a hand-shaking kind of place. If you put out a hand at a man it had better be fisted up, because he'd come back at you as if it was. I showed a thumb to the bartender, a muddy-faced man with knobby eyebrows, and he trundled over, roused by the unusual sight of a customer in a laundered shirt.

Happy Jack examined his beer as if trying to read his future in the swimming foam. "Today's my lucky day," he said, with neither humor nor bitterness. "Seein' you, today's my lucky day."

I considered this, flipped a few coins on the scarred surface of the bar, told the bartender, "Two beers, quick, before Prohibition gets here." My attention returned to Jack. "Why is that?"

41

"Because I'm goin' to get my second free beer of the morning."
He tipped a cigarette at his pale lips, and the smoke made a trip up his
face, wandered off into the brew-smelling air. "As well as a chance to
get myself in some bust-face trouble."

Jack was 25, looked 40. He was undernourished and runty and his
gray eyes were furtive. His collarless striped shirt and patched trousers
hung on him like a bathrobe on a closet hook, and the opposite ends
of him were covered by a woolen flat cap and someone else's brogans.
Scraps of newspaper—makeshift innersoles—showed through the
holes in his shoes. Hunger had increased the natural translucency of
his Irish skin, lending an odd delicacy to his wasted face.

"Can't I look up an old pal without having something in mind?"

I checked out the back bar, dominated by a huge mirror edged
with gilt fretwork interspersed with cherubs and shining women
comfortable in their flesh. In a painting above the mirror, another
nude with heavy thighs lounged and simpered. Jack half-turned,
showing his smile that meant nothing. "Not you."

I laughed, making it come from my belly, letting it rumble and
soar and boom, though to tell the truth, I didn't feel happy about what
I was doing, putting the arm on this little donkey with his starved lips
and dry-straw eyebrows and his disease grinning on his face. "Well, are
you up for the game?"

The bartender arrived with the beers, settling mine carefully,
cracking Jack's down, letting a bit slop over the rim. He wiped his
hands deliberately on his apron and looked at Jack without contrition,
taunting him, waiting for a reaction. What his problem was, I don't
know, except that perhaps he didn't agree with his boss' sentimental
policy toward freeloaders. Jack looked up at him slowly, cocking his
cigarette to the side, letting the ashes fall wherever they chose, saying
off-handedly, "I once gave a bartender a third eye for acting
disrespectful."

The bartender puffed like a steam engine, his shoulders straining
the striped sleeves of his shirt, an ancient scar over his right eye
glowing as the blood came up behind it. His eyes moved savagely

beneath his knobby eyebrows: He was a bruiser, and glad of a chance to show it. On the other hand. . . I put a hand on Jack's arm.

"I remember that business," I said. "It was Paddy the Priest, wasn't it? And afterwards, they couldn't figure out if you'd done him with a revolver or jammed him with a crowbar. They're still picking pieces of his skull out of the mirror in that dive on Tenth Avenue."

The bartender choked, his big hands working, his eyes going away but his arm-muscles still twitching, cranking up, pleading for action. At last his brain got the upper hand, his muscle-flutters eased, he turned and edged away from the bar.

Jack laughed softly, a rippling, lost sound. "Old times, right Kron? Old times. The oldest trick in the book." He blew some smoke, released a gust of air. "The way I remember it, we both watched that scene over the top of a whiskey bottle, but didn't participate. I was so pie-eyed I couldn't tell who did the deed, and when I hit the floor after the pistol went off, you'd slid down there before me and was in the midst of a little nap." He laughed again, shook his head. "Well," he said, "this changes my plans. Tomorrow, I was goin' to start working on Wall Street, wearin' a clean collar and a top hat and gettin' rich." He coughed. "But that can wait. I guess I can do your little job, if there's a meal in it, and maybe a nice casket."

I spoke quickly, before he could change his mind, and I kept it short, telling him about Ruth Cruger, saying I needed police reports on the missing women, describing Stoker McCullagh's warning. When I finished, Jack nodded. As usual, it was impossible to tell how he really felt—resigned, frightened, resolute? He scratched his chin, figuring the angles. "The Stoker has put out the word not to do business with you, so you need a stand-in?"

"That's it."

Jack stubbed the rag-end of his cigarette on the bar, shagged a soiled butt out of one pants pocket, found a match in another, lit up and blew smoke at the big-thighed nude in the painting. He flipped the match at a sign on the wall that read, "Gentlemen will not, others must not, spit on the floor." The sign was doing some good. Spit that otherwise would have hit the floor had ended up on the sign, dried in splotches. Jack drew another huge lungful of smoke and expelled it.

"The Stoker is the big man these days," he said. "He runs the dirty-handed cops, and he don't mind making business for the coffin-maker. He don't see eye to eye with the mayor, so he has to run hard and low, and he does. None of the cops wants to cross him."

"It's a closed shop, then?"

Jack's mouth moved wryly. "Not to me. I had cops visitin' me in prison, beggin' me to keep my mouth shut about things, hauling goods in to make me comfortable, not that I got any of it. One of them brought me a turkey." This time his laugh was an asthmatic wheeze. "I hope the warden enjoyed it."

"Then you can get in?"

"With money, I can get in."

Jack's butt-end erupted in a final explosion of smoke.

"Gettin' out, now that would be the beauty part."

I was back in the office by noon, none too happy when I saw that Grace had had sandwiches brought in. I liked a hearty lunch myself, something with plenty of sausage, cabbage and potatoes in it, perhaps with a moist chunk of bread pudding for dessert, with vanilla sauce. That wasn't Grace's style, though. When she was on a case, she had no regard for food or sleep, and those around her had to get used to that.

James Whistle was laying out the sandwiches on Grace's desk, precisely of course—he was a neat little bastard—arranging the cut halves symmetrically on squares of butcher paper, placing them in parallel with the pickles and the apples. When he ate peas, he probably weighed and counted all those little green globes, then racked them like billiard balls.

"I think that last pickle is about three degrees out of plumb," I said, tossing my hat toward a chair. Whistle watched the hat go flying, and a quaver of disapproval crossed his sensitive young face. Christ, he should have been a valet, the world of crime was too untidy for him.

"Hard day at the saloon, Mr. Kron?" His blue eyes were forty feet deep and innocent all the way down. They would have looked better with bruise rings around them, but he was too small for that kind of treatment, it would have been murder in the first degree. I could never figure why Grace had picked him up, she never seemed one to be impressed with a nose-in-the-air Harvard attitude like his. Why hire this choir boy? There were other lawyers who had scrambled, who knew the streets.

"Hard enough," I said. "And you? I hope your tweezers didn't slip while you were plucking your eyebrows."

Grace looked over from the file cabinet she was involved with. "That's enough. We have business, and if you don't want to get down to it, you two can always be replaced with a dog and a cat."

I kept my eyes on Whistle, said, "But then who would walk the... pussy-cat?" That triggered a hot glow on the feline bastard's cheeks, and his ears twitched with anger, which put me in a reasonable mood for the first time that morning.

Grace was paying no attention. She scooped a file from the filing cabinet, closed the drawer and began to read as she walked toward the desk, while I pulled up a chair and downed half a sandwich—one bite.

Whistle waited with Grace's chair, helped settle her into it, then primly took his own chair and waited politely for her to begin eating. He didn't even bother to look at me, but I got the message. I shrugged, put what was left of my sandwich back on my slab of butcher paper.

Grace, engrossed in the file, at last looked up and saw Whistle with his hands folded in his lap. "Oh, begin, gentlemen," she said. She looked at my plate, noted the half-eaten sandwich, smiled just enough. "You too, Kron."

My face got hot, and Whistle's leer put me in a mood to destroy furniture, but there wasn't a thing I could do except work out my frustration on the rest of the sandwich. I got my teeth into it, wishing to God it was Whistle's jugular, and tore it apart, taking care to swallow quietly.

Grace let her own meal lie uneaten in front of her as she

consulted the file folder, made a few notes, then looked up again. "Well, what do we have?"

I was halfway through my apple and I couldn't get any words out around the crunching, so Whistle won this round, too, blotting his mouth with a corner of napkin, drawing himself up for his reply. "Very little so far," he said. "From what you've told me, you have your suspicions about Mr. De Souza and Mr. Alvarez, but little else."

I wasn't going to let this pass. I tossed the apple core down, started to lick my fingers, then reached for my napkin instead and wiped my mouth as neatly as a wet nurse clearing the damp from a baby's bottom. I snorted. "Little else except the fact that Stoker McCullagh falls out of his trousers when we barely mention De Souza and spends the next 30 minutes telling us to point our noses in another direction."

Grace tapped the folder on her desk. "Whistle is right, we are merely going on speculation at this point. Still, I would like to know what's got McCullagh upset."

"We'll find that out before you can say Jack Sprat," I said. "Happy Jack Mullraney will be bribing it out of some copper before tomorrow dawns."

"Do I know Mullraney?" asked Grace.

"You wouldn't forget," I said. "I'll bring him in for a show after he gets the goods."

"We won't waste time between now and then. Though we only suspect De Souza and Alvarez, we'll take a short run at them, nevertheless."

I liked the sound of this. "I could batter them around a bit, just by way of softening them up."

Grace smiled. "Let's stay with finesse for now. Tonight, you and I are going to see José del Campo, the ex-Chilean Consul. He knows Latin America well. Perhaps he even knows its jewel retailers."

Happy Jack Mullraney's efforts for us are described in our files. Going over them, as I've done many times, I find nothing we could have done to save him, nothing that I could have changed, though Christ knows I would have changed things if I could. He moved swiftly, and, before any of us knew what exactly we were doing, the die was cast. The very night I hired him, he set a meeting, and 10 p.m. found him shivering under a street lamp gouging a hole in the darkness near an alley off West 28th Street. The alley was a foul place—once, it had been the rear approach to a slaughterhouse, and long-dried animal blood lent the air the pungency of decay. There were ghosts there, but Jack was not an imaginative fellow. He coughed stoically and wished desperately for a cigarette as he fidgeted, glancing at the alley, glancing away. Mist dampened his forehead, chilled his face, set his torso shuddering.

A plainclothes cop came bustling up the street, ducking away from the streetlights. Jack, with a swivel of the head, slipped softly into the alley. Seconds later, the cop slid in, too, his thick soles slipping and catching on the unseen cobblestones. "Where the hell are you?" the cop whispered, his big head bucking.

Jack hissed lightly and clicked his tongue. "Can't you see my teeth?"

"No jokes, for Christ's sake," the cop panted. "Let's get the job done. Where's the money?"

Jack put his head close to the cop's, smelling the beer he'd had an hour ago, the damp-wool sourness of his armpits. "Where's the goods?"

"It's just a list. Of names."

Jack's head popped up and back. "What in hell? We bargained for reports."

The cop made an angry, sucking sound. "Do I want my throat cut, you silly bastard? I only came to keep you from ratting me out."

Jack spat. "And for the money."

"Yes, the money." The cop choked. "A few stinking dollars, what does that mean? It's little enough with Stoker's teeth at my throat."

For a few infinitely long seconds, silence lay between them. Jack pondered. He could hear the nervous puffing of the cop's breath. It was odder than odd. True, the Stoker was a deadly man, but Jack knew this cop—a thick-brained basher who'd once cleaned out a saloon-ful of Whyos, spitting teeth all the while. He was callous-headed, normally too stupid to be much afraid. But he was afraid now. Maybe that meant his information was good. Maybe it meant something else. Jack decided to throw him a wrinkle.

"Half."

"Half?"

"Half the money, and you tell me what these goddamned names are." If the cop was genuinely scared, this wouldn't make him happy— a cheap price for a long coffin. Maybe he'd back out, or try to.

The cop hesitated, but not for long. His big brogans thumped and rustled as he shifted from foot to foot. "Half," he said, his voice sick with bitterness. "You want to screw me down, screw me into a hole."

"Come on, come on."

"Fine, then. After what I've done for you. Take it, then, and I hope your guts rot and roll out your rear end."

"I'm impressed. What am I buying?"

"Missing girls, like you asked. Comfortable ones, or their parents are. Ruth Cruger's on there, and five others."

"Thrillin'."

Money changed hands, and a piece of paper.

A shape moved in the darkness. A garbage can lid slid and crashed with a metallic rattle. Jack and the cop jumped, colliding, and Jack could feel the meaty body quivering. Sensing a doublecross, he reached out to grab the cop's sleeve, came up with a handful of gun barrel. The round metal froze his palm. He waited for the hot gunshot, the thump of pain, the spouting geyser of his own blood.

"You smiling bastard," the cop huffed. He was wrenching and twisting the gun, trying to break it from Jack's grasp. To get a clean shot? Jack squeezed his fingers, tried to get his body braced to push off and run.

An animal scream echoed off the hard, damp walls.

"A cat," said Jack, breath gusting. "A goddamned cat."

He felt the cop relax, sag. And Jack took a chance, cut loose his grip on the gun. No shot. The cop humped forward, his shoulders falling, hands on knees. Jack leaned forward, too, gasping out the tension, shivering from the clammy sweat crawling up his body, trying not to show the ragged remains of his fear. Just like the cop.

The cop recovered first. He wheezed out a long sigh, pocketed the revolver, started to move off.

Jack didn't have the whole thing figured yet, so he tried one last sally, to see what kind of response he'd get: "We'll meet again."

The cop's baritone reverberated from the weeping alley walls. "On a hot stone in Hell."

The whole exchange is in our reports now, catalogued under "Ruth Cruger," tucked into a file drawer, gathering dust, wedged in with all the information on the case. Taken together, the file shows many things about myself, about Whistle, about our police force, about our city, that make me grind my teeth. And one of those things is this: The cop turned out to be right.

CHAPTER SEVEN

GRACE AND I, DRESSED WARMLY against the chill evening, stepped from a cab at West End Avenue and West 76th Street and looked up at a massive, lighted pile of a mansion—four stories of angular granite hung with ivy, topped with plunging expanses of roof tile, the third and fourth stories embellished with jutting pillars hefted on the shoulders of stone cherubs and surmounted by carven lions hiked up on their front legs and looking as belligerent and haughty as if they owned the place themselves. I had lifted my face into a raw wind to examine its sweep and heft, and I could hear the air whistling through my molars as my jaw sagged.

"Nice job, being the Chilean Consul," said I. "Or, if it isn't a nice job, at least it pays well."

"He is the *former* Chilean Consul," said Grace. "But he also has mines, ranchland and other business interests in Chile and elsewhere. He lives grandly, but is generous with social causes and treats his employees well."

"He does, does he?" I asked, as we stepped briskly up the stone steps that angled down from the front door. "I wonder if he has any openings?"

I pressed the bell, and there was a moment there in the cold when I was looking about, thinking vaguely and not minding my tongue.

"How do you know all these men?" I asked. My words registered then—I'd put it more personally than I'd meant.

Grace's face was obscured in the darkness, but I thought I could detect a quizzical tone in her reply. "In Chile, José del Campo was an exporter. Before my father passed away, José did business with him—paper products and wine—and consulted him on real estate investments in this city." I composed my face in an expression of fascination, though the warm flush I could feel on my cheeks would have ruined the effect in better light. Fortunately, Grace was sweeping on. ". . .after Howard and I were married in Peru, he hosted a party for us in Santiago."

A butler cranked the door open at just this moment, and I was very glad of that. As the servant led us up a spiral mahogany staircase, I kept my face to the front, pretending deep interest in the glittering chandeliers, the polished statuary, the gilt-framed mirrors. At last we reached del Campo's parlor, a rich treat of green velvet, polished parquet, shining crystal. The walls were hung with shadowy paintings —a bare-shouldered woman placidly stroking her chest and gazing upward, a smug troubadour in fancy dress leaning on his mandolin, a wild landscape dominated by broken mountains and wind-torn trees.

José de Campo, savoring a slim cigar, was hovering near a blazing fireplace topped by a 17th Century Baroque mantel of Verona marble. But as soon as his black, sparkling eyes fell on us, he shipped the cigar into the blaze and approached eagerly, swinging his fat little body with the controlled hip-hop of an expert fencer.

"Mary Grace!" he exclaimed, capturing Grace's hand gracefully and massaging it with his lips—a gesture that was, I'd say, a touch overdramatic. "I have been devastated by your absence from my life." Obviously, he liked dramatics of every flavor. He turned to me, clapping his hands together with satisfaction. "Of course, I would hesitate to approach you abruptly in the street, given your escort. Yes, indeed. Your ferocious friend might club me from my shoes."

I smiled weakly, forcing myself to show as many teeth as I could, though my lips were stretched to the edge of pain, while Grace laughed at del Campo's antics. "José, this is my chief investigator, Julius Kron. Kron, meet the gallantry champion of the Americas."

I snapped up his paw, though I was afraid my own might absorb an overdose of cologne. He squeezed, and I was surprised to find a coiled-spring strength bracing the pudginess of his palm and fingers. I re-examined his face, saw the bone forcing the jaw outward, noted the sharp look in the sparkling eyes, recalled his swift, sure pace. Perhaps he was a fencer, in fact, and in more ways than one.

Del Campo ushered us over to the fire—a crackling conflagration, the wood popping and snapping in an orange swirl of warmth. My skin began to thaw and I was glad of the heat and glad of the drinks that arrived shortly—Merlot for them, whiskey neat for me, with the taste of smooth, old wood at its bottom, and a thump in it that set my belly and lungs as pleasantly aflame as the crackling pine and hickory. I concentrated on that feeling, since Grace was handling the main affair, and since she quickly came to the point, describing the jewelers, the tale they had to tell, and their constant contact with young women.

"Ah, yes," said del Campo, firing up another slim cigar. "The scenario sounds familiar, though I have no direct knowledge of Carlos De Souza or Ricardo Alvarez." He took a long, sensuous draw at his cigar, and blew the smoke out in an aromatic cloud. "Missing girls. . .a distinguished-looking older man. . .a good-looking younger man, who presents himself as titled and wealthy. . .a thin business front."

He involved himself in another long inhalation of tobacco smoke, another magnificent exhalation. "This sounds to me very much like the Uncle Game."

Grace looked at me and set down her wine glass.

"A swindle?" she asked.

"Worse than that," said del Campo. "A vicious criminal enterprise —white slavery."

I saw Grace's eyes darken. "White slavery, indeed? I am quite familiar with that."

"Yes," del Campo said. "From your work at the People's Law firm."

"Young girls tricked and forced into houses of ill fame," Grace said. "Hungry waifs lured from railway stations. Little French girls, poor and hopeless, smuggled here, told of fine jobs waiting for them in factories or theatrical productions, then sold and ruined." She paused. "But the young women who are missing are far from destitute."

"The trade in women is like other commerce," del Campo said. "The price of a virtuous woman fluctuates. There are commonplace goods, and there are items for the special taste." He paused, and looked away. "The opportunity to degrade a woman with delicate sensibilities, one used to a soft life, can command a high price in the market for souls."

His gaze returned to us. "And, of course, these women have jewels and money they can be induced to bring with them."

Jewels and money. My mind went to something Ruth Cruger's parents had said: Ruth had a "secret fund."

Grace was calm. "Tell us."

Del Campo placed his cigar in the silver ashtray on the intricately-worked coffee table. He composed himself, placing his hands palm to palm, tenting the pressed fingers under his chin. "The traffic in wealthy American girls has been going on for years." His eyes turned inward and his lips contorted with what I read as true feeling, not his usual over-drama. "Young girls. . . The method of abducting them is well known." He sighed. "It involves an older man—the Uncle—who comes to an American city from Latin America with several prepossessing young men, called the Hooks."

He paused. "It can be worked by just two men, an Uncle and a Hook, if they are fast operators and pluck girls who are not close friends." His sigh was contemplative. "In this case, of course, the young man must be very smooth and particularly seductive."

Grace nodded wryly, apparently dwelling on a recent memory. I didn't like the look of that very much, it seemed to imply more than I wanted to know about what had passed between Grace and this bogus Count. But, be that as it may, this was an investigation. So I gulped my whiskey and let it kick my stomach about, serving as its own distraction as del Campo's lecture flowed onward.

"The man meets a girl of the desired type and courts her with delicacy," del Campo was explaining. "After he has secured her love, he says he must go to South America. This, of course, requires a cover story, and he has a ready one. He says he cannot marry her in the United States because he would be disinherited under the laws of his country."

That was rich. I snorted, trying not to let my nostrils vibrate any more than the well-bred atmosphere called for. "And the girls fall for that?"

Del Campo waggled a hand in the air. "A young woman in love is prepared to overlook many discrepancies. The naive are very sure of themselves in circumstances that seem obviously dangerous to those of us who have achieved a hard-earned cynicism. And, of course, in matters such as this, the Uncle helps greatly."

"How so?" asked Grace.

"The Uncle 'discovers' the love affair and objects strenuously to the marriage. He is furious, demonstratively forbidding it in the presence of the young lady involved. At length, though, he relents. It is a marvelous performance, the way he allows himself to be won over bit by bit, until he grudgingly approves the match and agrees to act as chaperon for the couple on their trip to South America."

Grace leaned forward. "Does the girl elope to prevent her parents from interfering?"

"Often, but not always. This is one of the most upsetting aspects of the whole business. Sometimes the parents encourage the match, blinded by the young man's title."

Grace's chin rose and fell, acknowledging a familiar story. "Yes," she said. "That's the nature of sophisticates, or those who assume that attitude. Charlatans like this false noblemen, who would be unmasked at once in the most rustic rural town, are catered to in New York, where it is considered worldly to be blasé. But please continue."

Del Campo regained his cigar and took a short puff. "On board ship, the young man continues to treat the victim with respect. This is an approach that tends to impress her deeply, given the fact that courtship by her own young countrymen (del Campo glanced at me) tends to be rather rough-and-ready."

A smile flitted across Grace's face. I wasn't sure what that was all about, but it made me uneasy. I lifted my own eyes to the crystal chandelier and kept them there as del Campo, involved in his story, rambled on. "The respectful attitude, of course, is insurance that the young woman will not catch onto the game and seek aid from her fellow passengers," he said. "Indeed, in the case of an 'elopement,' the young woman sometimes pretends to be traveling alone, as insurance against inquisitive family friends she may encounter. She may even book her passage under a false name. But the pretense is dropped as soon as the ship makes port. Then the young woman is sold, quickly, for anything from three to five thousand dollars."

I took more whiskey, but Grace's wine sat forgotten next to her hand, and her face was drawn up in a look I had often seen—a resolute, determined expression—whenever she was confronted with a tale of some innocent taken advantage of. Her lips parted with emotion. "Do not the police in the country of destination try to break up this brutal practice?"

Del Campo smiled apologetically. "You are well-traveled in my part of the world, Mary Grace," he said. He rubbed his thumb on his pointer finger. "You are familiar with the *mordida*."

"The payoff."

"Yes."

I lifted my glass, stepped in. "And the American cops, don't they do anything? After all, these are women from wealthy families. Their relatives can raise a holy stink."

José del Campo recovered his cigar, puffed at it, waved it in the air. Then he released a long breath, his lips twisting into a world-weary smile, his wiry shoulders shrugging expressively inside his finely tailored coat.

"They can, if they are sure of themselves, but they are not. Is a particular disappearance a crime or merely a family scandal that has not revealed itself? The families do not press the police, and the police may be subject to other forces." Del Campo smiled wryly. "I believe the *mordida* is a custom that travels well."

CHAPTER EIGHT

HAPPY JACK WAS IN THE outer office when Grace came in at 8:06 a.m., a few moments before I arrived from a breakfast meeting with a poker-room manager who had his motorcycle serviced at Cocchi's place. Grace didn't flinch at Jack's nature-butchered features, a reaction he told me later made him feel comfortable with her immediately. The problem was that he made a mistake that embarrassed him down to his toes.

"Good morning," she said, as he braced up in a bentwood chair. "Are you waiting for me?"

"For Kron," said Jack, his usual instinct for defiance making his reply short. A nerve twitched in his left cheek, causing the smile etched into his facial muscles to twist and contort. "I got a report."

"You may deliver it to me."

"I'm sorry, Miss. It's too important for the secretary. That fancy young fella in there awready tried to get me to spill. I told him no."

"I am Grace Humiston."

The flat cap came off Jack's head in an instant.

"Excuse me, Ma'am."

The doorbell jingled as I pushed in, stopped when I saw the scene, read lack of understanding in Grace's face. "If he hasn't told you already," I said, "this is Happy Jack Mullraney."

"Mr. Mullraney," said Grace, inclining her head, "Your courage has put us in your debt."

The three of us were settled in the inner office: Grace at her desk, examining the piece of paper, Jack sitting, twisting his cap in his hands, me leaning forward, taking it all in. "I apologize it's so little," said Jack. "The copper was spooked worse than I've ever seen."

Grace continued to read. "Still, there's enough here to be useful. Names and addresses of the missing girls—we can move quickly with these." She looked up. "Do you have any idea how this list was composed, who wrote it and how he or she got the information?"

"That I don't," said Jack, "The copper was on the jump the whole time and circumstances wasn't something he gave attention to."

"I see." She let this drift. "Have you seen this policeman's writing before?"

Jack's crusty pointer finger made a little jab at the paper on her desk. "That's not his writing there, I know that. He's give me messages in the past, an' I could barely make 'em out. Not like that one, that looks to be a fine hand, don't it?"

Grace's eyebrows came up. "Indeed it does." Her face changed. "A fine hand and good information. And you have put yourself at some risk to get it, have you not?"

Jack looked at his cap and his strange smile tilted slightly—an odd change, perhaps his version of a real smile. "Me life's been at risk since my mother borned me. The streets is risk, it don't mean nothin'."

Grace considered the reply and Jack's ragged clothing, and her eyes gentled. Grace wasn't one for sentimentality, she knew the con games and deceptions of the poor as well as those of the rich, but everyone was human to her. "It means something to us. And we need solid allies. We would like to keep you on retainer, pay you some regular sum until we need you again, in addition to your fee for this job."

The cap twisted. "Don't need to do that. I'll work for you when I can, but there's other things I can do to keep me belly jammed and me heart thumping—some of 'em legal."

He looked up. "Almost forgot." He reached into his pocket and withdrew some currency. "I screwed the copper—excuse me, Ma'am— I took the copper for half what I said. Here's the dough." He got up, shuffled to the desk, crisply stacked the bills, totting up the total as if delivering tribute.

I made my right shoe go rat-tat-tat on the floor, as if I was impatient with this display, but I was just playing with him. "You're going honest on us, Jack," said I. "That's a bad sign, for it's a practice that will throw you off your game."

Jack jerked his jaw at me and would have given me the half-arm salute if there hadn't been a lady present. Instead, he made as if to flip his wool cap in my face, but kept his grip on it. "Call me honest again and I'll give you a third eye," he said, plenty of sand in his tone. "Mind you watch yourself."

Grace tapped her desk, spoke in a smooth, measured way. "You are brave and honest."

Jack glanced at her, looked down, said nothing. But he brushed with careless unease at his hopeless hair, his color deepened, and the rosiness of the blood flowing to his cheeks added health to his papery skin. Though his head was ducked, I detected something else about his appearance, too. A bad sign, I had said in jest, but perhaps it turned out to be a bad sign, indeed, for he was showing the kind of honest emotion—gratitude, pleasure—that the street grinds to dust. Once again, his strange smile tilted.

There were five names, in addition to that of Ruth Cruger, on Jack's list. They were Maria Greene, Victoria Ingley, Nancy Leonard, Barbara Dunston, and Amelia Karcher. The list gave Grace two full two days' work, and at the end of those two days, the answer to the riddle of Ruth Cruger's disappearance seemed obvious to me. As it turned out, the answer did not seem obvious to Grace, but I discovered that only much later.

Grace and I proceeded to destinations that turned out to be

comfortable and sometimes posh. The servants and their mistresses were put off by my appearance, even in my best suit, but they readily accepted Grace and I kept my silence. I saw my share of polished mahogany stairways and cleverly-worked fanlights, of brocaded lamps and wall tapestries, and I tasted a good deal more tea, coffee and sherry than I am used to. We visited dignified brownstones on the upper West Side, rambling homes on Long Island, a country estate in Connecticut. All five interviews followed a pattern, and it appeared that this was the pattern that Stoker McCullagh was trying to cover with his screen of blarney, viciousness and smoke. I begged off on the last one, a visit to a Tudor mansion out on the Island. I'd had entirely too many high-toned liquids and too much dignified chat by that time, and Grace harmonized with these people far better than I did. So I waited outside as Grace went in alone to speak with Adelanta Karcher, widow of a wealthy factory owner.

Grace entered the house at mid-afternoon, and word of her mission was quickly transferred by the butler to Mrs. Karcher, who, the butler implied by his manner, was recovering from illness. A quarter of an hour later, Grace and Mrs. Karcher, a heavy, rubber-skinned woman rouged severely to color up her flagging spirits, were settled down in the living room taking refreshment from a Colonial tea service.

Around them, bulky, awkward furniture pieces loomed like draft horses shouldering each other in a narrow stable. Mrs. Karcher's face was drawn tight about her blunt cheekbones, her eyebrows peaked with pain, her bulbous lips stretched to a thin, quivering edge. She handled her bone-china cup as if the duty of drinking was too much to bear. She sipped a few drops, tiredly plucked a water cracker from a tray offered by the butler, put it to her lips, put it down. She surveyed Grace, tossed her head, looked away. "You are a lawyer," she said, "and you have some questions about Amelia. Am I to understand, then, that you represent her?"

"No," said Grace. "I merely wish to ask about the circumstances of her disappearance."

Mrs. Karcher's face fell, but she issued a long scornful sigh. "I do not know the circumstances of her disappearance." She considered this, biting her lips. "Amelia simply packed her things one day and was gone, leaving not even a note. I suppose she left just to spite me, to torture me." Suspicion crawled in Mrs. Karcher's tired eyes. "You are not withholding information, are you? That is the way of lawyers, always seeking some advantage by telling or not telling, something that will earn them a fat fee. You are not here to negotiate a sum so that I might be allowed to see her again?"

Grace kept her own voice soft. "No, certainly not. Please believe that I would not hide her whereabouts if I knew them, would not deny you a reunion. No mother should have to undergo that kind of treatment."

"No mother—" Mrs. Karcher's ungainly fist hopped to her mouth, intercepting a sob. "The girl is always so difficult," she exclaimed. "We never agree." Then the sobs broke free, the torrent flowed, her shoulders heaved and rolled. "Why, why, why? Why did she do it? Have I been such a bad mother?"

Grace shook her head. "I'm sure you have not. You must not think—"

Mrs. Karcher did not break off her sobbing, which she now was trying to blot with her left hand as her right fist pumped at the air, driving her next words. "It makes no sense, none. What is her motive? There is plenty of money here in the states, plenty of money, is there not?"

Grace hesitated, perplexed. "Most assuredly," she replied at last, "though—"

Mrs. Karcher flounced up and began to trundle about, emitting piping sobs and rough-edged sighs, sounds that seemed to express the very extremes of tortured anger. Her pacing carried her back and forth among the gargantuan furnishings—the cane-back Queen Anne sofa covered with velour cushions, the medallion-backed cane wing chairs of antique mahogany, the walnut coffee table, the Duo-Art reproducing piano.

She marched and wept, marched and wept. "Why has this

happened? How can it have happened? I had chosen a fine young man for her, things were going extremely well. Roger Marley...Farley... whatever his name is. His father owns half the garment district." She paused once again, and her fist began again to pummel the air. "Clothing is a very fine business, very fine. It is very lucrative, isn't it, Mrs. Humiston? Yes it is, isn't it?"

"Yes, indeed."

Mrs. Karcher flung herself about, red-faced, her hair all down about her eyebrows. "Then why did she have to go chasing after this Count What's-His-Name? Why, in God's name? What is left for me? Do you realize I have only one daughter?" She wept and stormed and moaned. "Who is there for me now? Who is going to take care of me in my old age?"

"It is too soon to give up hope," said Grace. "Perhaps I can help, I have some experience in that line. If you will supply me with details, tell me about the Count, about what happened shortly before your daughter dropped from sight."

Mrs. Karcher flung herself back on the sofa, swiped vigorously at her nose, policing up the salty flow of tears and mascara that had painted dark, smeary thoroughfares on her cheeks. She sighed a long sigh, recaptured her breath. "Amelia had been seeing this young man. She said he was rich. Argentinean." Mrs. Karcher coughed wetly, half-lifted her arms, dropped them. "Are Argentineans really rich? Who knows? They are so far away they could be anything."

Grace picked up her tea cup and drank, letting Mrs. Karcher find her own way.

"He never came to the house, and she was even reluctant to tell me his name. But I went through her things—doesn't a mother have a right?—and found his signature on a love note. 'Ricardo.'" Mrs. Karcher's lips vibrated derisively, her teeth clenched. "Not a good name, not a trustworthy name, not the sort of name I am used to."

"You never saw him?"

Mrs. Karcher took up the water cracker again and snapped at it, her teeth crunching and crunching, as if she had the Argentinean between her molars and was giving him a good grinding. "She always claimed he wanted to meet me, he and his stuffed-up uncle," Mrs. Karcher snorted, her tears receding. She swept a hand at her wet cheeks. "But there was always an excuse not to. He was up to something, that one, but she couldn't see it, she doesn't have the brains of a chicken."

Mrs. Karcher fell silent, her face working into an expression of violent rumination—an attitude that intensified for a few moments, then began to recede, her upflung chin falling, shoulders collapsing, teeth nipping nervously at her lips. Grace drew a breath, released it slowly. "How long has she been gone?"

Gone.

The one word had an effect denied to all the others. By degrees, the harsh scarlet of the big woman's face went away. Slowly she whitened, and all the structures of her face—her pine-knot eyebrows, sweeping cheek ridges, bulky jaws—seemed to crumple like tissue, curling and fading. Real tears came into her eyes, replacing the angry ones—big, clear, round tears, swelling and swelling until their surface tension broke. Down they flowed, washing away all the pretension, the petty fury, the selfishness.

"Eight months," Mrs. Karcher whispered. "Eight months, and not a word." Her voice caught. "I listen for the phone, sometimes think I hear it ringing, but that is only in my mind. I watch for the mail, go through it, look for her hand in each address, tear the letters apart. Nothing. I find nothing. I hear nothing. Why doesn't she contact me? Why?"

"Perhaps she will."

The answer was haunted by a different tone from all that had gone before. "She won't. She's gone."

Mrs. Karcher looked at her half-eaten biscuit as if it had appeared suddenly in her hand. Slowly, she put it down, folded her hands in her lap and looked at them without recognition. She spoke, and her voice was dull.

"A week ago I had a dream. It was dark, I could hear a ship's bell tolling, and I seemed to be on the water, far from land. Very faintly, I heard her calling, beseeching me as she used to do when she was a little girl, long before my husband died, long before all the fights. I strained to hear, as hard as I could, but her child's voice changed into a baby's cry. Then her voice faded, and all around me was the sea-mist, below me was ocean. I came awake feeling. . .alone."

Mrs. Karcher looked up, her fleshy face hollow now, her eyes large and dark and deep and overgrown with pain, like ruined stone fountains in a forgotten garden.

"When I get angry with her, it feels as if she is still alive. But she isn't. She isn't anywhere on this earth. She's lost."

CHAPTER NINE

WE HAD GATHERED PHOTOS OF the missing women. So it was that Grace had likenesses of three of them in her handbag on her train-and-taxi ride back from Long Island. And that led her, on impulse, back to Cocchi's shop just as the chill shadows of evening were lengthening among the buildings of Manhattan, cutting slices of night across the paving-stones, turning alleys into black pits that smelled of the leavings of humankind.

Grace had used the long ride to ruminate on what we had found, sometimes playing her fingers over the surfaces of the photos as she did so. She was using them not as a psychometrist does, to try to pick up images from the spirit world, but to open her mind fully, to try to glimpse the gauzy outlines of her own hidden thoughts, to make creative connections. Grace never strangled her instincts. She used them—as she used all tools at her command—to their fullest, though in so doing she knew she was laying herself open to the charge of hunch-playing.

"Every time a woman does make a discovery, somebody pipes, 'intuition,'" she told me once. "It's a way of saying that women must pluck ideas from the ether. In reality, logic has its place, and so does instinct, whether the well-trained mind is male or female. Playing logic and instinct together, making them mesh—that is the key to successful detection."

So it was that as the taxi made its way through the bumpy streets, its hard-rubber tires catching here on a misaligned seam, slipping there on a manure-slickened cobblestone, she was straightforwardly examining what the parents of the missing women had told us, but also opening her mind to floating scraps of information and observation.

The stories had been similar to Mrs. Karcher's—each young lady had said she was seeing a rich young Argentinean, had mentioned the uncle, had said little else—not surprising, since in each case the parents had opposed the relationship. Perhaps, in time, the wealth of the young man might have weighed into the situation and changed their minds. But there had been little time. The period between the meeting and the disappearance had been short—sometimes as little as a month, never more than two. Afterwards, the police had failed to turn up anything of note—indeed their lack of success and their obvious lack of interest were striking, even given their normal incompetence. The families had been confused and upset, but also embarrassed. None of them wished to broadcast that their daughters had fallen for a disreputable man. Perhaps, in the end, all would turn out well. Perhaps, perhaps...

The taxi jounced once more on the cobblestones, jolting Grace from her thoughts. She glanced out the window, caught the stark black letters of a sign for 128th Street and realized she was only a block from Cocchi's shop. Something tugged at her mind, and she redirected the driver.

The line of investigation concerning the De Souza pair seemed to be proving out quite neatly, Grace herself said later. That in itself was not a surprise. Once a detective gets on the right track, information tends to accumulate quickly and point clearly: There are not really so many branches in human events. To the sleuth who has spent some time in the business, the world seems a predictable place. The great problem in detection, she noted, is not to assume too much, not to outrun yourself, not to get careless and scant the evidential links.

In this case, De Souza and the Count seemed clearly to be the mysterious Argentineans who were wooing and luring away New York beauties. But none of the families had actually seen them. Indeed, the Cruger family had so little knowledge of the "foreign young man" who had taken their daughter's fancy that the De Souza link was tenuous. To make a case in court, or even to push the probe aggressively, would require eyewitness identification. And so: Cocchi.

Grace stepped from the cab in the half-dark, her shadow bisected by the falling glow of a street lamp. The gray streets were sparsely traveled, the few pedestrians clutching themselves tightly against the frigid evening, their feet ringing sharply on the sidewalk, their pale faces set with dinnertime purpose. Cocchi's shop was not fully lighted, but a small lamp glowed within, and Grace glimpsed vague movement beyond the glass.

She pushed the door, heard the bell click and jangle, felt her feet scrape the floorboards. At the back, Cocchi's gnome-like body merged with a mechanical shape that gave him the look of a robotic Centaur— his torso emerging from a vivisected motorcycle. His wrench made a tock-tocking sound as it ratcheted a nut into place. His concentration was strong—he seemed not to hear the bell—but then his form went rigid. Up he glanced, his eyes vacant of recognition, seeing—she thought—only her silhouette, and she imagined that shocked him. His nostrils flared, eyes gaped in the smeary, spilling lamplight. Then he sucked breath, and his eyes came back, focused, and air came out of him in a long, lingering whoosh. He jumped up, his silly teeth going every which way in a smile that split the darkness as he wiped his hands hastily on his coveralls, thickening the smears of grease on the cloth stretching over his hard little chest.

Around his feet, strange, disconnected spare parts lay like segments of a chicken being prepared for the pot. "Brake job," he said, in a wheezy half-whisper. His hands made a quick, dismissive pass in the direction of the machine. "The police, they always want everything done quickest." Then, as if frightened by his own voice, he glanced at the ceiling, where his wife's footsteps were crunching heavily, sporadically. Grace, mimicking the gesture she had seen him display on her visit with me, put a finger to her lips and moved forward silently.

He oozed a grateful look as she stopped at his counter.

"Greetings, lovely lady," he whispered, straining forward through the half-light. The move brought his face within inches of Grace's, and his moist eyes bulged.

"Greetings," said Grace, withdrawing three photographs of varying sizes from her purse. She arrayed them in a line on the splintery counter, delivering them for Cocchi's inspection. But his eyes stayed on her face as she did so, and his mustache trembled slightly as his nose wriggled, drawing in her perfume. He seemed enthralled, alone in some state of private reverence. Sensing his preoccupation, she shot him a direct look. That did the trick, and his gaze dropped to the business at hand.

With a languorous intake of breath, he examined the photos of Victoria Ingley, Barbara Dunston and Amelia Karcher. "The pretty girls," he sighed, reaching out a tubby hand and passing it over each face as if he were touching living flesh. "Yes, I know them, I see them all." He waved a hand. "Back, back in time."

Grace's tone was businesslike. "Where did you see them?"

He dropped his chin, using the reply as an opportunity to force his face closer to Grace's, drawing attention to the fragrance of his mustache, redolent of onions and garlic. He put a grubby digit to his lips as he replied, and his tone was conspiratorial. "They go to the Spanish. Over and over, they go. Sometimes, couple times a day."

Grace drew back. "Two or more together?"

Cocchi cocked his eyes upward, thinking, allowing his hand to stray inches closer to that of Grace, which lay near the photographs. "I think—" He paused, drawing out his reply. "—never together." He leaned forward, and patted Grace's fingers to drive the point home, nodding as if more certain of his memory. "No, no, never together. One girl come, stay in the shop for a while, then come out, face all pink and warm." He paused, reflecting. "She move with a little wriggle —mmmm, oh, I can't help but watch." He sighed. "She leave. Then another one come, some long time later."

His own memory had impressed him in some private way.

70

Something liquid and warm burned in his eyes, his pocked cheeks stretched sharply, and his tongue played about his lips, saliva glowing on its tip, highlighting the cobbled, reddish organ that tastes delight and eases hunger.

Grace was watching every detail of his face and expression, trying to fathom the feelings that drove his reactions. "Did either of the men ever escort these girls past your shop?"

Cocchi's expression of pleasure was transformed instantly. Disgust turned his lips inward, his chin trembled and his eyes radiated heat. "That young Spanish," he said. "He walk them—take their arm, right there on the street." He bit off his words, and for a moment his mouth fought for expression as his eyes, growing wary, seemed to signal that he was struggling against the urge to speak. But the mouth won. "Something bad about that fancy one," Cocchi spat, his eyes drawn suddenly to the pale image of Christ on the wall, the body disfigured, the nail-marks in the hands burning red as infection. The repairman crossed himself, shivered, the contortion of his muscles fluttering his shabby clothing, blurring his image in the half-light. "I get a fear for the girls when I see that one."

A bell jingled suddenly behind her, and Grace turned. Cocchi's front door scratched, the bell on its string still quivering. A tall man with aquiline features pushed in warily, stood stiff as an exclamation point. He was of the moneyed class. That was obvious from his fine beaver hat and his pinch-back suit of black cassimere worsted. He dropped his eyes sheepishly, perhaps ill at ease because of the late hour. Perhaps personally shy, too, because he looked from Grace to Cocchi several times before he cleared his throat and said distinctly: "A monkey wrench."

Cocchi gave a quick, irritated shake of his head, tilted an apologetic smile at Grace, and turned to deal with his customer, shuffling down the counter as he did so, drumming his hand in the direction of his merchandise boxes. "Which grade, what?" The customer hovered, seemingly perplexed, and Cocchi's right hand jumped out, made a come-come gesture as his voice went low, too low for Grace to hear.

The customer, though, was still a few steps from Cocchi and his reply was distinct. "Uh, fifteen-dollar," he said, shambling forward quickly. His hand plunged inside his coat, slipped out again clutching a wallet of delicately-worked leather. He spread it, demonstrating a sheaf of bills, plucked two, handed them over. Cocchi took the money, jammed it in his pocket, thrust a boxed wrench at his customer without even a pleasantry. The man took it awkwardly, cocked it under his arm, hurried out.

Cocchi turned huffily back to Grace. "Always a bother, when I'm busy," he said.

Grace smiled, glad he was keeping on track, resumed the interview. "These women," Grace said, "You say that when they visited, they followed each other at intervals—first one for a while, then another?"

Cocchi's nose screwed up, and his eyelids sagged, mouth pursing as he composed his face in an imitation of Grace's serious expression. "Intervals, yes. That's what they come—intervals." He thought. "One come a few times. Then gone. She never come back. Another one come."

Grace began to collect the photographs. "Was that also true of Ruth Cruger?" A long silence. She picked up the photos, placed them in her purse, looked at Cocchi. He was regarding her carefully. "Yes," he said. "That Cruger girl. The same."

I lived simply in those days, in clean, serviceable rooms over the Boar's Head, a saloon between Second and First Avenues. The place had a view, you might say—my living room window gave on a large illuminated cross suspended over a Catholic church a half-block away.

On wet nights, the cross seemed to shimmer and weep. A Christian, which I was not, might have read something into that. God was grieving for America, which was inching towards war. Yes, war was on the way. Many said it, and no doubt it was true. How else to explain the sudden infatuation with peace? There were anti-preparedness marches every weekend now, the well-meaning ladies swathed in white fluttering their banners on the avenues, the cops out in force to keep the peacekeepers in order.

Oh, it was coming, all right. German saboteurs had blown hell out of Black Tom Island out in Bayonne the previous July, disrupting a major shipping point for munitions bound for Europe. They did it right—bridges over the East River shuddered, shrapnel was flung into lower Manhattan, and windows from the Battery to 42nd Street cracked and fell, sprinkling glass-daggers on the pavement below. The country wouldn't put up with that kind of treatment forever. Gen. John J. "Black Jack" Pershing, hard as a leather strap, was chasing Pancho Villa down in Mexico, warming up to hunt the Hun. Society matrons were taking pistol practice. Men—and women, too—were drilling with wooden guns on Governor's Island in New York Harbor.

Woodrow Wilson was having a hard time stretching his professor's face around the words that would send thousands off to the butchering fields, but the wise men downstairs in the Boar's Head, their faces a-sweat with alcohol and good fellowship, were telling me he would soon get the job done. I believed them. Why not? If you want the real low-down on world affairs, don't ask a statesman, ask a drunk.

Grace entered the Boar's Head shortly after nine p.m., while I was communing with a mug of beer. I caught sight of her in the mirror over the back-bar, and moved quickly to intercept her. The only women who normally crossed the portals of the Boar's Head were gangsters' girls or women who were gangsters themselves, like Roaring Maggie, a 300-pound terror who once chewed a man's nose off in a bar fight ("You couldn't get that good a cut of meat at Delmonico's," she often said later.)

As I moved, the clatter of conversation around me slowed or dropped to a murmur. Grace had style, and it showed off in here like a diamond in a garbage dump. Her face was flushed from excitement—there was high color around her cheekbones, where the alabaster skin was tight-knit—and her dark eyes made my stomach jump and melt.

"Making a late evening?" I said.

She tossed her head, though I didn't think it had been a bad sally.

"I am here on business," she said.

"As always," I said. "Come upstairs."

Up we went, ascending creaking mahogany stairs that I supposed many a man had come rolling down in past decades, pockets turned outward and his hair in his face. Through the years, the Boar's Head had been a sometime brothel and roll joint, though my own sojourn there had calmed the trade—I had a reputation for rectitude because I got my sleep and seldom ruined my clothes with vomit.

We slipped down a hallway grim with flocked wallpaper, the baseboard scuffed by the flailings of rude boots. I reached a paneled door—it was pine, but stained to look like mahogany—fumbled a brass key from my watch pocket, snapped open the lock. "Aren't you afraid for your reputation?" I asked Grace, trying for a joke.

"I am here on business."

"So you said." She didn't smile, at least I didn't think so, though the light was against me, and I could have been wrong. The room was close, and I could smell the perfume of her through her many layers of proper clothing. I let the dark linger a split-second before I popped the string on the overhead bulb.

The room flashed into sight. The bed was neat, the small writing desk carefully organized, closet doors closed. I ran a clean ship, otherwise I never would have let her in. One corner held a small ice-box, another, a walnut wardrobe. Two pine bookshelves held a Shakespeare, some European history, tabloids rich with old murders. The only chair in the room was an office chair in front of the triangular writing desk.

"You do not require much," Grace said.

"I do not have much," I corrected. "Take the bed. It's not luxurious, but it doesn't roll around all of a sudden, as the chair is prone to."

She didn't get coy, as some might have. She gave me a measured look, sat quickly, flung off her hat, used a pillow to prop her back, and spread her purse on the window-pane quilt. Her hand fluttered inside, drew forth photos. She lined them on the bed in a neat array.

"Victoria Ingley, Barbara Dunston, Amelia Karcher." She drew a breath. "Do you have the others?"

I fished in my suit coat, came up with two photos of my own, added to the display. "Maria Greene and Nancy Leonard." I'd missed one, and my fingers went back to get it. "Ruth Cruger."

Grace took Ruth's photo and regarded it. "The case has gone far beyond the fate of this poor girl," she said. "Cocchi identified the Misses Ingley, Dunston and Karcher as having visited the De Souza shop." She paused, mulling things over. "And Ruth...Ruth must have gone to Cocchi's shop to get close to Ricardo Alvarez, to cover her intrigue with him from the eyes of her parents."

I could feel my face drooping, and put a hand to my jaw to brace it up. Unaccountably, I felt left out. A man should enjoy his work, should get some satisfaction out of detecting, when the rest of his life consists mainly of beer and the odd tumble on a race-horse or a hand of poker. I cleared my throat. "Why didn't you wait for the photos I was collecting? Aren't we in this together?"

Her eyes were bright. Her dark hair, cut free of the hat, was a long wave that might have floated a racing sloop. "Of course we are in this together," she said. Her lips were parted, and the coming and going of her breath made them pulse slightly. They were very red. "But we need to move quickly."

"I'm as eager to move quickly as you are," I said. I was suddenly aware of my body, of how heavy it was, and awkward, of how it smelled of bay rum, beer and tobacco, of how I'd gone since an early dawn without having changed my union suit. I thought of her husband. He always looked as clean as a fresh-dipped sheep, and he never smoked. It was unhealthy, he said. Unhealthy. Who'd ever heard of such a thing?

Grace rose restlessly. "That is good, speed is important," she said, "because all evidence indicates that José del Campo has called this correctly. There is an ongoing scheme to kidnap young women and sell them into sexual bondage. It is going full force, and we are the only ones who stand in its way."

I fought to get my thoughts back on track. "Given our lack of friends downtown, that makes us vulnerable," I said. I shrugged, cut her half a smile, knotted up my forehead, moved to the office chair and sat down. I pulled forth a short cigar, flamed a match, touched off the smoke. The warmth sank into my lungs, spread through my chest, liquefied my limbs. "And it makes you particularly vulnerable."

"Why is that?" she said, looking out the window at the lighted cross. The dark sky had clouded over, and a leisurely rain descended, pummeling the hard stone with a soothing sound, soft as breath. The cross shimmered and wavered through the plunging stream of water.

I waved the cigar. The movement seemed false, made up, but she didn't seem to notice. "Because this Carlos De Souza and Ricardo Alvarez, or whoever they really are, know what you look like. And they know your reputation."

A gust of wind swooped suddenly through the rain, flinging a rippling curtain of water against the window glass in front of her. "I am not afraid."

Right. That went without saying. She often perplexed me, frustrated me. I was afraid, plenty of the time, and not just of getting my ribs split like firewood. "No," I said. "But, from a standpoint of tactics, I can't allow you to be taken out of the game."

She smiled. "What do you propose to do—frog-march me everywhere under shotgun guard?"

"I am a fair hand with a shotgun."

"I will not be intimidated." She sat abruptly on the bed and began to collect the photographs. "Men count on that with a woman. That's why these girls are so easily taken."

She took up her hat, arranged it on her head. The room seemed closer, rain gurgled and dripped on the window pane. She rose, and I did, too, looking for some way to keep the contact for another half-hour. "An ugly night is shaping up. Allow me to escort you home."

Her eyebrows went up, and I feared that my emotions were clear in my face. Then I became convinced of it, for her next words were soft, and she preceded them with a conciliatory gesture, half-extending her right hand. "I will not be seen to be guarded," she said. "It will give our enemies aid and comfort." She smiled. "But I will take the loan of an umbrella."

I moved to the wardrobe and extracted one—old, but well-kept. She took it, opened it suddenly with an athletic, one-handed movement, then slipped it closed with equal skill. "Ah," she said. "A familiar model."

She moved to the door. "Good night," she said softly. "You are a good friend."

I sat for a long while afterward, looking at the closed door. A good friend. Women have a way about them, being nice in the most damned vicious way. She should have just driven the point of the umbrella into my chest—eventually that wound would have stopped hurting.

CHAPTER TEN

AS I SULKED IN MY room, as Grace made her way downstairs through the crowd in the saloon and out into the rainy evening, death was on the move. If Woodrow Wilson had been less resolute about keeping us out of war as long as possible, if shipbuilding had already been burdened with wartime needs for steel, if Grace had already been asked, as she later was, to make her own donation to the cause, she would not have been alive twenty minutes after her leading foot struck the sidewalk. I don't suppose you know that at that time the corset industry used 15,000 to 20,000 tons of high-grade steel each year. Well, it did.

Grace had hoped to hail a taxi upon leaving the Boar's Head, and it appeared at first that she would have no trouble doing so. As she emerged, she saw a cab—a Ford machine—quivering and squeaking toward her a block away on the correct side of the street, its flag up, indicating it was free. Her ride home was seconds away. But the cab was just out of hailing distance, the rain had begun to fall more intensely, and Grace wasted a crucial few moments snapping the umbrella open and perching it above her head before raising her hand to beckon the driver.

Just as she did, the cab suddenly put on speed and swept by her, its tires cutting through the rain puddles and flinging a hard spray that splashed on the cement with a sound like ripping silk, dousing her skirts. She caught a glance of the driver's face—a white smear inside the shadowed windshield—and of the silhouetted passenger, oddly shrouded, as the cab's gears clashed, pumping the machine forward at an even greater pace, whirling it down the street and around a corner, leaving behind a mystery. The cabbie already had a passenger, so why had he left his flag up?

The unsettling oddity of that was overwhelmed by her pique. Grace jerked her umbrella in frustration, sizing up her options and not liking them. She could re-enter the Boar's Head and call another cab. If she did, she would be faced with the necessity of waiting in my room —an uncomfortable prospect, given our recent exchange—or in the bar itself, where the rough revelry would be even more unpleasant. Or she could walk to the nearest subway station.

The second option would normally have seemed quite attractive. The subway was not far—down one block and over another. In the absence of the rain it would have been a comfortable stroll, even relatively safe. The neighborhood was coarse but not typically violent, and the retirees and workingmen's wives who lived in the apartments that lined the street kept good watch.

The rain changed things. It was less likely that there would be ruffians hanging about, but it was also less likely that anyone would be keeping an eye out to ensure the safety of a lone pedestrian. Well, so be it. Grace, never faint-hearted, and now feeling pugnacious as she looked forward to the battle with the slavers, dismissed what she considered to be a minor erosion in her prospects for personal security, and set out on foot.

It was by now 9:36 p.m. Not a late night yet, but a gloomy one, with an insistent wind—the kind of night that makes country places seem wild, that deadens footfalls on city streets. The rain, sheeting down, deepened the darkness and iced the air. Grace proceeded briskly, clutching her umbrella upright against the downpour. In my mind's eye, I can see her now, a damp, resolute figure dark against the night, showing in detail as she moved through the yellow pools of illumination eddying from the street lights. Above her, the cold concrete buildings rose, their patterns bisected by alleyways and narrow streets. Far off, she could hear the grumbling bustle of more heavily-trafficked neighborhoods, but here the only sounds were the rain whispering on the cement, the gurgling of water in drainways, the sodden stamping of her own footsteps.

At the corner, she paused under a cigar-store awning to re-orient herself. She looked to the right. A block away, the iron-and-glass subway entrance crouched pagoda-like over the passageway that led down to the world below—a dark opening into the dry, clean, rumbling belly of the great city. She turned toward it, and vowed to make better speed.

As she did so, she heard—behind her, and still at some small distance—distinctive footfalls rapping out a rhythm that was deliberate, measured, sure. She turned. A hundred feet away, pressing close to the shadow of a wall, a figure moved, spreading and dark, its wide-brimmed hat pulled low. Some kind of cape wrapped the silhouette, obscuring it, though the wind tugged and twisted at the enveloping cloth. On came the form, its leather soles tocking on the slippery sidewalk—certain, centered, aimed at her. It was twenty feet away now. Striking distance.

She turned to run, to find a place of refuge. Too late. Behind her, the footfalls rattled faster, sped, grew frenzied. The brick wall to her right at least would protect her back. She braced against it, facing the danger as the dark figure took her. Its left hand snatched her dress. Its right flashed a blade, sullen and hard. She stiffened her legs as the blade rasped into her left arm above the elbow—she felt its ice in her flesh, then the sickening flame of pain. She coughed, her throat catching. She tried to think, to push out, but the attacker's empty hand caught her. She smelled a man's cologne, musky with the odor of almonds.

He threw her against the wall, and a protruding brick struck her just below the rib cage. She gasped for air. Her knees began to give, and she felt herself sag. Her muscles were twitching, lungs laboring. But she stepped to the side and put room between herself and her assailant. Then she threw up the canopy of the umbrella—an awkward expanse of fabric and curving steel—buffeted her assailant and blocked his attack.

His blade was trapped. He fought to get it free for a deadly slash. She gasped in a lungful of damp air, and parried once more with the umbrella as the attacker lunged, spinning him into the wall as she stepped away. She immediately reached up the shaft and seized the catch, collapsing the canopy. Now she had the equivalent of a short, blunt pike in her hands: The umbrella's point was hand-forged and sharp. She retracted her weapon to gain momentum, and stabbed hard at his neck. She was hoping for a lucky hit, bruising his internal carotid artery, snapping off blood to his brain. No luck. Her stroke went wide. Even so, she'd done some good. The attacker grunted, clutched at the wound.

Then he growled something animal and low, and spread himself. Grace tried to rally, but now she couldn't make her muscles respond. Weariness flooded her. She heard a ringing in her ears, felt her blood mixing with the falling rain on her arm. Her attacker was centering the knife, coming for the death thrust. She readied, to turn it aside if she could, to take it bravely if she couldn't. She got her umbrella point up, but it wavered and trembled. Her attacker flipped it aside, plunged the knife into her torso just below the left breast. Fire and breath-sucking pain exploded in her heart.

Down the street, a shout echoed. Footsteps came drumming, splashing through far-off puddles. She was too tired, too done, to lift her head. But suddenly the attacker was gone. Out of the corner of her eye, she saw him take four quick strides and merge with the dark of an alleyway. A hard little shadow sped after him. Grace caught a glimpse of her savior—a whippet body in ragged clothes, a pale, twisted face snapped on top with a flat cap. Happy Jack.

Grace moved against the wall for support, gasping. She cupped her left arm over her stomach, trying to hold her insides in. She looked down at the arm. Blood pulsed from the wound, infusing with crimson the wet wool of her coat, the black cotton of her blouse-sleeve. She moved the arm experimentally, gritted her teeth, but saw the forearm and hand move naturally, felt nothing leaking from her chest. Gingerly, she tugged at the place where the chest wound should be, caught a flap of dress, of steel-reinforced corset. The blade had sliced the corset, but the steel mesh had held. Six months later, Grace and thousands of other women would donate their corsets to the war effort, to increase the stockpile of scrap steel for shipbuilding. Perhaps that dollop of steel in Grace's corset would help build a ship that would save lives. It already had saved one.

Jack was suddenly back at her side hopping about, frantic with anger and concern. "Missed the bas—" he began. "I'd of had him, one more jump. The sonova— Sorry, Mrs. Humiston. Lost him in the dark. Let's get you to a hospital now."

Happy Jack and I hovered about as the surgeon on duty finished his work. The wound was clean, doused with disinfectant, swathed in bandages, and the young doctor—who sported a shaving-brush mustache and an air of royal superiority—was adjusting a cloth sling over Grace's shoulder.

"You won't want to put any strain on that arm for at least two weeks," he was saying. "I can answer for the repairs, but not for the consequences if you decide you just have to bake a cake or knit some booties."

Grace smiled warmly. "If I knit anything it will be a gift for you." He smiled foolishly, and preened. "An ego-warmer, if I can find enough wool. I imagine it would take a great deal." The doctor's smile jerked right off his face.

Grace slid from the examining-table. Jack and I moved in solicitously, but she waved us off. "I've had all the nursing I need," she said, "Let's talk strategy."

At her direction, we made our way to one of the hideaways she maintained in various parts of the city—in this case, the back room of a cigar store on 111th Street and Broadway, which she used as an alternate office when danger threatened. She even stopped on the way to summon Whistle from whatever night-time activity occupies a fledgling lawyer—probably practicing Valentino moves, or pleasuring himself with thoughts of Theda Bara. He hadn't gotten to bed early, that was sure, for he was dressed neat as a pin in a $30 blue serge suit (how did he afford such extravagance?) and his blond hair was well-coiffed and clean, his eyes alert. As we arrayed ourselves around a rickety card table yellowed with the light of brocaded lamp, he had his little notebook propped in his hand, his head cocked to one side like a robin expecting a bread morsel.

As it turned out, Grace had a morsel for all of us. "I'm afraid this is evidence that Ruth Cruger is dead," she said. "I've had that as operating theory, now it's more. No-one kills to prevent discovery of an abduction."

Whistle didn't comment, and Grace didn't pay any special attention to him, for which I was glad. She was always carrying on about him, fancying herself his mentor or some such—I don't know exactly what she imagined, but whatever it was it didn't make the business move forward any quicker, that was sure. I sucked a healthy draught of sambuca—the cigar-store owner had supplied refreshments —and put in my two cents.

"It was a considered decision," I told Grace, who was pacing, highly charged with the adrenaline that had pumped her heart during the attack. "You were followed for some time, probably all the way from Cocchi's. One of the jewelers spotted you—that's my guess— maybe even caught sight of you showing Cocchi the photos, and that was enough for them to know you had to be dealt with."

Grace waved her free hand. "If so, why didn't Jack see the shadower?"

Jack's cap rotated nervously in his hands. "'Cause I wasn't following all that way," he said. "Kron came downstairs just after you left, picked me out of the crowd at the Boar's Head and told me to keep an eye out. You'd got a good lead on me by then, and I had to cast about some. And the hacker come out of nowhere."

He lapsed into confused silence, his lips twitching, eyes dropping, shoulders slumping. Grace went to him quickly, shaking her head, patting his arm. "You have no reason to rebuke yourself," she said, lifting his jaw and giving him a warm smile. "I believe the knife-man was dropped by a cab near the attack point. So he really did come out of nowhere, and if it hadn't been for you— It was a timely rescue."

Jack took a breath, and his little chest swelled. "For the fella that cut you, it was," Jack said. "You was doing him, looked like. Giving him hell."

Grace was thinking carefully. "Not quite that, but I did give him a thrust in the forward part of the neck, just here, on his right side."

I clubbed the table with my fist, making the sambuca glasses jump and slop. "Then that little Spanish bastard has the wound on him— Ricardo. I'll grab him, make him rattle, and find that proof bleeding from his fine young neck. He'll squeal like that monkey his Uncle is so proud of."

Whistle cleared his throat. "That monkey is an animal," he said. "We should not emulate its behavior." Grace turned to him immediately, as if he were royalty ready to spit out some gobbet of wisdom. Her eyebrows were up and her eyes were eager—all for this little bird in his over-rich suit, his too-neat locks and his Italian silk tie. Really, I wondered about him, sometimes. He was always hovering about, not really contributing, but always showing interest in what we were doing. Too much interest, I thought, even for a clerk. But Grace couldn't see that, so I let it go.

"What Kron suggests is a churlish move," Whistle continued, folding his legs one over the other, "And a stupid move, too. The young jeweler wears an ascot, which would conceal any neck wound. Kron would literally have to attack him to examine him, and without a hint of real evidence." He put a hand to his mouth. "Can you imagine the risk? Captain McCullagh would have Kron taken for assault and battery, and horrid things might happen to our detective under lock and key."

Oh, don't worry your blond head about horrid happening to me, I thought. Now you on the other hand—if you were to go into lock-up — I examined Whistle, and my smile was thin.

Grace set down her glass, from which she had barely sipped. Jack waited attentively for her next words. "McCullagh. . . Yes, he might play a role here, but I doubt if it would be quite that obvious," she said. Whistle reddened a bit—he wasn't used to Grace cutting across his silly speculations. But he didn't say anything, just licked his lips and shifted his bottom. "For a brute," Grace was saying, "McCullagh has been quite subtle. I feel his presence everywhere, though he stays just out of sight, just off-stage. It was, after all, McCullagh's statement about the missing girls that started us on the line of inquiry that led to this attack."

She looked up at me, at Whistle, at Happy Jack. "And the linchpin in that inquiry was the policeman who passed the names to us." Her eyes settled on Jack. "Would you contact him again? He may be the key. His reaction, I think, will tell us."

I fancied that Whistle was taken aback by this idea. His shoulders shrugged inside his fine suit, and he swept his golden hair with one hand as if something up there wasn't exactly in place and he had to make it so. He even put out a finger as if to make a point, but his mouth stayed shut.

Jack saw none of this. His eyes were all for Grace Humiston. He put on his cap like a soldier suiting up. He touched the cap, stood up. He had a mission now, a purpose in life, and he looked richer than Andrew Carnegie. He said nothing, but squared his shoulders and turned to go. As he swept through the door, I envied his thoughtless courage, his loyalty and faith, his resolution. And I continue to envy them to this day, despite the result.

Chapter Eleven

THE NEXT MORNING, THINGS TOOK an interesting turn—not that they hadn't been interesting up to that point. I was summoned to Grace's office to meet a woman I soon judged to be the best-looking I'd ever seen, and the least truthful.

She was about 23, I estimated, with all the juice of youth, all its possibilities, all its dangers. And she looked Hispanic, with an olive cast to her features and black curls pirouetting above her smooth forehead, her eyes moving with dark eagerness, shaded by some strange hurt. She sat dressed for the street in a navy-blue velour coat with the collar and flare cuffs trimmed with synthetic beaver fur. Where the coat opened, it showed a black, embroidered dress encasing a body that curved easily and fully against the cloth.

"This is Consuelo La Rue," Grace was saying. "She has a story to tell that is of some interest. For my part, I would not mind hearing it again."

Exuding the scent of attar of roses, the woman extended a smooth paw, the wrist curved downward with practiced elegance. I took her fingers, and they were some of the best fingers I'd ever gripped—I had to make an effort not to roll her fine-grained skin beneath my thumb as if I were savoring a rich cut of cloth.

Consuelo La Rue. . .all right. The goods were there on the surface. Below that? Well, we would see. Miss La Rue seemed uncertain. She glanced at me, turned to Grace. "You have believed me so far, surely?"

87

Grace smiled—an expression both sympathetic and wry. "I am easily convinced in these matters," she said. "Kron, however, is a man not to be trifled with. You must keep your eyes on his face very carefully as you talk, to see if your words are striking home."

The invitation was enough to cause Miss La Rue to focus entirely on me, aiming her best parts in my direction as I strolled restlessly around the room, looking her over carefully, trying to keep my mind on business.

"I have escaped from white slavers!" she said, with a hesitant glance at Grace. I took this to mean she'd begun her first telling with just such a pop-off, and was now checking to see if it played as well the second time around.

Grace's expression gave her no clue as to that, and I busied myself with the bric-a-brac on the mantelpiece, pretending disinterest so as to goad Miss La Rue to her best effort. I judged that would be an excellent effort, indeed. Still, as she continued, she seemed subdued.

"They took me to a cellar on an irregular thoroughfare in Harlem."

I shot a look at her, made my voice mechanical.

"Address?"

"It was 542 W. 127th St."

Cocchi's address? I felt my mouth split in a disbelieving smile, looked quickly at Grace, but she was keeping her expression as neutral as glass. She had her own thoughts, but she didn't want them to affect mine—she wanted me to give the woman the full treatment, so we both could factor the results. I looked back at Miss La Rue. "What lies above that basement, on the first floor?"

"It was dark when they brought me in, but I smelled motor oil."

"Really?"

"Yes." She paused. "I wish I could tell you more, but I—" She dropped her eyes. "I believe I was drugged."

I marched across the room, scooped up a wooden chair, whipped it around and smacked it down on the floor. I sat in it reversed, looking over the back, peering at Miss La Rue like a cop looking over a back fence into a garbage-filled alley.

"Drugged? Really?" I plucked at my lower lip, made my face innocent. "And was that a fresh experience for you?"

She blushed. "Certainly it was."

"And a terrible experience, too. Drugs can ruin your powers of observation, can't they? They can even put wild things in your head."

Her back stiffened, and that put her front into an even more delightful perspective. She tossed her head. "I don't like what you are insinuating."

"Don't worry about it. I don't like what I'm insinuating, either." I thumbed my right cheek, drew the nail down it in a long, meditative pull. "Tell me—you escaped from this cellar?"

"Not exactly."

I smiled. "Not exactly. No."

Miss La Rue ignored the irony. "They took me out sleeping. I awoke in a passenger waiting room down by the docks—they were preparing to put me on board a liner."

"And of course they left you for an instant, and you slipped away."

Miss La Rue looked at Grace with anxious desperation. "They did."

Grace spoke soothingly. "Just tell your tale. Don't be afraid."

I ping-ponged Miss La Rue back to me. "And you had no idea where the ship was bound for?"

Miss La Rue dipped her eyes, turned them full force on me. They were magnificent. Shapes moved in their dark depths like a shadow ballet. "South America," she said. "The Argentine."

"And how did you know that?"

"They were quite open about it, the Count especially."

"The Count?"

"The Count de Clements, Ricardo Alvarez."

Well, wasn't this easy? I had begun to feel a bit sorry for the vicious son-of-a-bitch we were chasing. The evidence was piling up on him like a load of slag from a Pennsylvania steel mill. People walked right in off the street to lay the goods on him. It was like having evidence catered. I questioned Grace with a look, but she did not respond, so I turned back to Miss La Rue. "And this Count, was he alone?"

"Carlos De Souza was his colleague. Alvarez called him Uncle."

Whack! More slag. The rumbling of its descent was unsettling my stomach. I rose, shook my head. "Let's start over. Where did you meet these two?"

"I met the Count at my dressmaker's, Madame Lagrange, on West 58th Street. One day when I was looking at some sketches of a gown Madame was designing for me, I heard her address a very handsome young man as Count de Clements. She later told me he was a member of the Spanish nobility. I told her I would like to meet him."

I pretended shock. "What?"

Miss La Rue looked defiant. "I know it was very unconventional." She dropped her eyes. "Lately I have been living an unconventional life."

I said with contempt: "And so you. . .met. . .this Alvarez? And later stepped out with him?"

"Many times," she said easily, then hesitated. "Always in public," she added carefully. "At restaurants, museums, sometimes at Van Cortlandt Park to ice skate."

"And you went to his home?"

"I never went to his home."

"He never invited you?"

The young woman bristled. "He invited me. I did not go."

My sneer was pronounced. "I thought you were unconventional."

Consuelo La Rue turned to Grace. In her voice was both anger and supplication. "Is he here only to torture me?"

Grace shrugged. I couldn't read her any more than Miss La Rue could. "Bear with him a little longer."

I was back on the attack in an instant. "Describe this cellar where you were held."

Miss La Rue glanced once more at Grace, then at me, and seemed on the point of breaking off the interview. Then, abruptly, she continued: "It was sumptuously furnished in Oriental style—divans, little cot beds, deep-piled carpets, softly-shaded lamps." She paused—a tactical pause, it seemed to me. "There were two beautiful girls there. I promised to go back for them, but I didn't. For this, I deserve to be punished."

I laughed richly, slapping my thigh. Perhaps I overdid it a bit, but it's best to make the point clearly. "You have a great gift," I said. "The moving pictures need someone like you. I saw one of their shows the other night, and it was terrible—no imagination."

I turned to Grace and spoke to her as if Miss La Rue had evaporated. "I've got a couple of things I need to check out, since there's nothing new on the case. I'll be back at noon." I snapped up my hat, brushed by our visitor without even looking at her.

Grace caught up with me in the outer office. Her forehead was ridged with thought. "What do you think?"

I rotated my eyes upward. "How did she get in touch?"

"She says she read about the Cruger disappearance and Cocchi's shop in the newspaper, recognized the address and called the Crugers. They provided my name."

I smiled without mirth. "A publicity seeker. She's rattle-brained enough."

Grace considered. "Her story is so bad that it is interesting."

"If you want bad stories, I can get a barrelful."

"She knows about De Souza and Alvarez."

"Sure, and she says Cocchi's cellar is tricked out like a Parisian bawdy-house."

"Have you seen it?"

"No."

"Have you seen any police account of what is there?"

"No."

"Perhaps we should find out."

CHAPTER TWELVE

THE LITTLE CAFÉ ACROSS FROM Cocchi's shop and De Souza Jewelers was as it had been: curved-iron chairs, marbled table-tops, the clinking of cutlery and china issuing from beyond the padded, swinging doors to the kitchen. A pleasant smell of fresh bread and hot coffee. Consuelo La Rue drank her coffee black, in great quantities, and with gusto. I looked across the window table at Grace, and her lifted eyebrow showed me that she, too, had noticed the incongruity. For a woman who held herself out to be a cultured product of Spain, it was strange that Miss La Rue drank coffee like a dock worker.

"Please, can't we go and see if my companions in misery are still being held?" Miss La Rue importuned piteously, taking another hard shag at her coffee cup.

"In good time," said Grace, with her eyes on the jewelers' shop. "You know we might be denied admittance."

Miss La Rue sighed. "We might, indeed, but at least we'd be making an effort. What are we waiting for?"

Grace took a sip of tea and looked at Miss La Rue placidly. "As yet, we don't know what we are waiting for. But whatever it is, it will come."

Miss La Rue flounced and sighed impatiently. "You speak so obliquely, you are almost tiresome."

Grace's gaze remained on the street. Down the block, there appeared a young man in clothing of European cut—the coat nipped

93

at the waist, shoulders padded, pants full and straight, a peach-colored ascot clutching his neck. His features were razor-like, lending him a dangerous beauty. "Surveillance often is tiresome," said Grace. "We simply are watching for any comings and goings that may inspire suspicion. You must keep an eye out for anyone you recognize."

Miss La Rue followed the young man with her eyes. "I will," she said. "But it's such a bore."

The young man, without glancing our way, passed Cocchi's shop, turned and entered De Souza Jewelers. An expression of agitation flitted across Miss La Rue's features, and she quickly caught up her cup and drank. This proved to be an especially long drink, but when Miss La Rue once more put down her cup, she appeared more composed.

"My God, the drugs have muddled me so," she said. "Surely, that was Ricardo Alvarez."

"Surely, it was," said Grace. "Now it is time for us to visit Mr. Alfredo Cocchi."

As we entered, Cocchi was in an ebullient mood, dirty as ever, but glowing with satisfaction. His face was daubed with grease, but a fresh red bandanna was knotted tight about his neck. His smile was so bright I fancied he had grown dozens of extra teeth. "Mrs. Humiston!" he boomed, practically giggling, "You will be the first to know! A man is interested in my Ferris wheel! A manufacturer!"

He turned out from behind his counter, wiping his hands on his bandanna as usual. From a pocket in his overalls he produced a sheaf of bills, swished them around as if he were fanning himself. "He has given me money! A promise of his good intent." In his excitement, he looked over Consuelo La Rue perfunctorily with no flicker of recognition, but his eyes clouded as his look settled on Grace's bandaged arm.

"Lovely lady, you have had some hurt!"

"Merely a matter of some carelessness with a knife," said Grace. "But your news is wonderful! Is Mrs. Cocchi happy?"

Cocchi always seemed to have better control of his mouth than he did of his eyes. His lips retracted, and now he seemed to have doubled the number of his multiplied teeth. But his eyes weren't quite as lively as his tone. "In good time, I tell her," he said. "When I got the whole pile."

Grace smiled. "An excellent plan, I think."

She turned. "May I introduce Miss Consuelo La Rue? You know Kron, of course." She hesitated for a moment as Cocchi moved to greet the newest lovely lady. "We have come on business," Grace said, "but we would not want to trouble you."

"What trouble?" said Cocchi expansively, as he kissed Miss La Rue's hand, fondled it, caressed it. "Anything you want, we do."

Grace's face grew serious. "Though our inquiries appear more and more futile, we are still investigating the disappearance of this poor girl, Ruth Cruger." She paused, as if upset at what she had to ask. "Really, we are simply going through the final motions, making sure we have done everything we can." She paused again.

"Mrs. Humiston," Cocchi said, taking her free hand. "I don't like to see you like this. You have something you want, you ask me. I do. I do anything."

Grace still hesitated, plucking a non-existent thread from her coat sleeve, then releasing a long breath, looking up from downcast eyes as if she feared her request would be rejected. "We would like to look at your cellar."

Cocchi's reaction was all one could ask. He ran his eyes over us, not neglecting Consuelo La Rue, then smiled widely. "Of course, of course. The police have been there, but you have not." He shook his head. "You are very right—the police are not to be trusted."

He waved a hand, beckoning us to the rear of the shop, pausing just before the door to the alley. To his right, stairs led upward to the living quarters. Directly at his feet was a battered metal ring in a recess in the floor. He bent, clutched the ring, heaved upward. A section of the floor rose. He propped the door open, dropped downward through the hole. His voice, slightly muffled, issued from below. "Careful on the stairs—I make a light for you."

Illumination flashed up from the hole, and I glanced at Miss La

Rue for her reaction. Had she expected things would go this far, that we would take her immediately to confront the truth? Or had she been pushing a bluff with her showy efforts? I saw her draw herself up slightly, as one does to face an unpleasant prospect, but she caught me looking, and loosed a weak smile. I swung a hand at the opening. "Don't you want to lead us into that fancy room down there?"

She moved her lips in a way that was more Gallic than Hispanic and resolutely moved to the hole, with Grace and I close behind. Down we went, with the smell of raw earth enveloping us and the dull light of a dusty bulb washing the damp, splintered steps over which we passed. The stairs turned and ended. Cocchi stood across from us, eagerness and chagrin mixing in his face, like the host of a shabby restaurant greeting important guests he knows he cannot hope to impress.

In a few seconds we stood arrayed on the floor of hard-packed earth in a dank cellar notably bare of Oriental splendor. There were no divans, no cot beds, no fine carpets or lamps, and the air smelled of rot and mold and motor oil. The only furnishings were old free-standing cupboards lining the walls, deep and bulky, with doors warped and out of plumb and legs cracked—no doubt from being shifted occasionally with no regard for the oppressive weight of their contents.

Cocchi, after a brief hesitation, began hastily to move from one cupboard to another, opening their doors to reveal stores of battered tools, cans of motor oil and grease, bins of sprockets, spare gears, washers, screws and other supplies, and the reserve stock of the shop's small inventory of products: among them, seat covers and several stacks of boxed monkey wrenches such as were piled on the counter in the shop above. "No girl here," Cocchi said solemnly. "I showed police. Now I show you."

It was close in the cellar, despite the chill day outside—Cocchi's face was beading with sweat. The bandanna about his neck must have been hot, for suddenly he clutched it and undid the knot, freeing the strip of cloth, revealing a neck as grease-stained as his face. Grace looked searchingly at him, and then at Miss La Rue, who turned her eyes away. "Thank you, Alfredo," Grace said. "You have aided us greatly."

CHAPTER THIRTEEN

IN FIGURING THINGS LATER, I decided it was no accident that Happy Jack arranged to meet his informant in the Stag Cafe on West 28th Street. The place had tradition, cheap beer and the kind of people that Jack was most comfortable with: grifters, cutthroats, boosters, pistol men, and degenerates of all kinds.

The clientele had left its mark. Half the chairs were broken and unstable, old cracks showed in the back-bar mirror, and the mahogany top of the bar itself—usually a sacrosanct place—was scarred with carvings of nicknames, favorite parts of the female anatomy, shamrocks, hearts, even outlines of dogs and cats.

The place had been known as the Cafe Maryland several years before when it was run by Chick Tricker, a lieutenant of the major gang leader Monk Eastman. Tricker had bought it from Dan the Dude in an effort to establish an outpost in the Tenderloin, a sedate area compared to the Lower East Side, where Eastman's gang made its home.

Tricker's reign at the Cafe Maryland had not been peaceful. One of his comrades had the bad grace to reach deep into the territory of the Gophers, Jack's old gang, and extract a juicy trollop named Ida the Goose, who had been the consort of many Gopher captains. One night, Ida was sitting at a table with her newest protector and several of his friends when five Gophers pushed through the swinging doors, slaked their thirst with beer at the bar, then produced two revolvers each and settled down to work. Four of Eastman's men went down in the ensuing fusillade, including Ida's latest lover, who tried in vain to hide behind her skirts.

There were bullet holes in the floor, a water stain on the ceiling from a pipe that had broken 40 years before, peeling walls, and air thickened with cigar and cigarette smoke. In fact, the smoke was so strong it lent substance to the air: if you'd have knocked the walls down, the exact shape of the place would have remained, occupying the same address—a saloon-sized smoke statue.

I had never spent much time there myself. I do what needs to be done, but there's no point in letting courage get out of hand. This was a deadfall, a drop place, a last stop for the hell-bound. That, no doubt, was why Jack picked it as a rendezvous. Among the fish-belly eyes, the slack jaws, the putty-like skin, the rank smell of alcohol-pickled bodies, anyone healthy—any visitor from the real world—stood out in sharp detail, was easy to recognize. A stranger would have been no problem to spot. But his motive might have been.

Even in the feeble light of the cheap chandelier, I could see the apartment was unbelievably messy. The covers on the single bed were carelessly thrown back, and the top of the nearby dressing table was disfigured with a welter of perfume bottles, makeup pots, stray pills, combs, brushes, and opened lipsticks, all dusted with spilled mascara, daubed in places with spills of nail-polish.

Gowns, shirtwaists, and hats were heaped in piles or flung carelessly across chairs. A barely washed cup in a cracked saucer waited on a table near a gas ring. The gas ring, heating water for tea, hissed beneath a tarnished saucepan. Near the cup and saucer, a jade earring was caught in the fabric of the tablecloth; a bright sash hung from the chandelier like a hangman's rope.

I paced to the window, pulled back the drooping curtain and looked out. The view was of a brick wall twelve feet away, and in the moonlight even the bricks looked tired. Behind me, Grace spoke abruptly: "A poor showing for a young lady of substance, I'm afraid."

I turned. Consuelo La Rue sulked on the sofa, curling back into its awkwardly piled pillows. "So what?" she said. She scooped a cigarette and a kitchen match from a lump of possessions on the cheap coffee table, snapped the match into flame with a thumbnail, and fired up the tobacco. She inhaled vigorously, and let the smoke stream out. "I should get the cops in here," she said. "You two aren't supposed to go busting into places."

Grace said: "You invited us in."

Consuelo La Rue drew herself up for legal argument. "I only did that to find out why you followed me home." She pointed a finger. "But when you go around checking labels in my dresses, and looking through my drawers, that's invasion of privacy." She flashed a contemptuous glance at Grace. "And you're supposed to be a lawyer."

I moved to her gas ring, snapped it off, continued on to the closet and began to riffle through the contents. Miss La Rue half-voiced a protest, then fell back hopelessly. She turned to Grace again, and this time her lower lip trembled slightly, bouncing the cigarette in her mouth. She snatched it out and looked at the floor. When she spoke again, her voice was small. "And not only that…they say you look out for people."

Grace's eyes were determined. She gathered her arms to her bosom, rocking slightly, seeming to gather her strength for what she had to do. Then she spoke, her voice low and intense. "Out there, someone is seizing young women from their homes, and I have not the slightest doubt that at least one of them is dead. I mean to have the killers in my grasp." Instantly, she was next to Consuelo La Rue. "You have been playing a dangerous game with us. Now you have two choices—tell us the truth or face prison. Because, by Heaven, I will find a way to put you there!"

Miss La Rue looked up, pushing herself backwards on the sofa, her eyes misting over, her mascara appearing to melt. "You can't—"

Grace Humiston spoke quietly. "You do not know what I can do, what I *will* do if pressed. Even *I* do not know. Talk."

Miss La Rue dissolved in sobs, pushing at her eyes, lacing her fine hands into her long, dark hair. I said coolly, "You can start with your real name."

The sobbing continued for a few moments. Then Miss La Rue began to recover shakily, keeping her left hand over her streaming eyes, extending her right—asking for help. I pulled my handkerchief, took two steps, handed it over, hoping the repair work wouldn't take too long. Fortunately, it didn't. After a short session of tear-blotting, she gave one last convulsive sniff, and muttered, "Luisa Clary."

I looked at Grace and she flicked a hand, a signal for me to continue the interview. I did, keeping things to the point. "From?"

"Los Angeles."

"And your game?"

"It's the con."

"Why am I not terribly surprised?" interposed Grace. "But this is a very unusual type of confidence game, isn't it? Misleading private investigators?"

Like congealing plaster of Paris, Luisa Clary now began to harden again. Her shoulders stiffened, her back bracing her attitude. She was a quick one with the moods—an oddly attractive trait, if you like a bit of off-balancing. Dry-eyed, though the tear-marks still spotted her make-up, she said, "I guess."

I hovered over her, close enough to smell her perfume, which was tinged with sandalwood. "We are not going to dance the two-step with you," I said. "You had better start spilling. And go easy with the imagination."

Luisa Clary took an over-long pull on her cigarette, her long-lashed eyes hot and bright, then blew the smoke out with an aggressive puff. She leaned back, looked to the side, pushed at her hair, and emitted a short laugh. "Why not? This town has done me anyway. I had a decent stack and four trunks full of top-grade clothes when I got here four months ago, and now here I am in this badger-hole with you two barking at me."

She took another drag at the cigarette, more naturally this time, and let her long, slim body drift back resignedly against the pillows, arraying herself with sensuous languor. "De Souza and his snaky little friend cut me right out of my own game, and didn't even know it," she said. Her full lips twisted—an expression that would have ruined lips less tasty. "We were shopping for the same marks, and they carried off all the bargains."

She paused for a moment, and the composure returned to her face. When she spoke again, the rancorous edge was gone from her voice, replaced by a thoughtful tone. "My con is pretty simple, but it does well enough. I work the fancy dressmakers' places and meet young women with plenty of money." She smiled wisely. "Usually I break down sobbing in front of the modiste when a good mark is in the shop. I let them squeeze the 'truth' out of me—that I've ordered a dress I can't pay for."

She tossed her head in an attempt to show how heedless she was, but it didn't come off as well as she'd have liked. "If the mark is soft-hearted enough, she takes me aside and I treat her to the whole story —how I'm from a rich Spanish family, but got infatuated with some low-life who brought me to New York and then tossed me out. How I'm out of money. And how my family won't have anything to do with me now."

Luisa paused. Her eyebrows flickered uneasily, but her tone was sardonic. "They love the romance of it."

Getting no response, she continued. "Generally it doesn't take me long to land a spot as a companion with either the mark or one of her friends. I live with them, feed their hot little fantasies about men, and get introduced to their rich men friends, who soon start having hot little fantasies about me."

Now her smile was more natural—she was enjoying the memories of her own allure. "From there, it's an easy jump to a soft landing in the middle of some man's bank account. And if things don't move quickly enough, I just arrange to have a confederate snatch some of the female mark's goods." She abruptly leaned forward, ground her cigarette into an ashtray. "We sell them off, and I move on."

"Tell us about De Souza and Alvarez," Grace said.

Luisa grimaced, made as if she were composing a retort, then shrugged. "They cut me out twice, that's all. I was just getting started with two different women, Victoria Ingley and Barbara Dunston, when the marks dropped off the globe. I never met De Souza and Alvarez, but the marks had told me enough so I was able to figure out what had happened."

Grace examined her. "And now we arrive at the charade with Cocchi's shop."

Luisa smiled. "Yes, don't we?" But the thought apparently did not please her. Instantly, she grew morose and thoughtful, though she retained an aggressive edge. "I'd read about the shop in the newspapers—they said that was where the Cruger girl disappeared." Luisa stroked her chin meditatively. "I didn't know it was right next to De Souza's, but I'd heard both shops were in the same neighborhood. And I thought there probably was some connection, because the Cruger girl would have been a prime target for the slavers' game. I wanted to damage De Souza and the Count. I couldn't do it myself, but somebody like Grace Humiston could. So I cooked up my story about the cellar, and brought it in to you, all hot and fresh."

Grace sat down on the couch and fixed her eyes on Luisa's. Grace did not speak, but watched the young woman's face, listened to the gradually accelerated pace of her breathing, allowed the silence to develop, to press in. Luisa had put up a hard front so far, but now her pallor grew more distinct. The life of a con artist is not always an easy one. Perhaps she was recalling life in some place of confinement, where all faces are pallid.

Grace said, "But you must have known we would search out the lie."

"Yes!" said Luisa—an explosive release.

Then her face dissolved in agitation and her words began to tumble.

"I thought I would just say it was a mistake about the cellar but that it was still true about the slavers." Her hands shook. "I'd say the cellar I'd been kept in must have been somewhere else, and you'd believe that, and you'd take me on as an assistant and I'd help you and. . .and we'd get the slavers anyway, and I'd get my picture in the papers and I wouldn't have to worry about finding rich men, they'd be all around."

At last, she seemed to have let it all out. Her body vibrated under the rush of words, her hands jerked to her face, genuine tears spilled loosely from her luxuriant eyes, and she tried to bury herself in the comfort of the handkerchief. Into this steamy cauldron, Grace dropped an ice cube of doubt. "You had no chance. Why take such a risk?"

Luisa's reply was a thin, wild wail, an exculpation, an excuse to absolve all treacheries.

"I was broke!"

CHAPTER FOURTEEN

WHISTLE STOOD IN THE DOORWAY of Grace's office, his eyes raccoon-like from lost sleep, a shadow of unshaven beard blunting his crisp jaw. The subservience of his attitude was unusual: He dipped his head.

"That Mullraney fellow called last night."

The words, falling as they did on a weary tableau, did not elicit an immediate reaction. I was slumping haggardly in a chair near Grace's desk. Grace braced herself carefully, her skin tight and pale. "Did his informant appear for their meeting?" she asked, pulling a legal pad toward her in the event that she needed to make notes.

Whistle tugged at an ear. "Another fellow did."

My sagging body straightened. Grace rose, alert as a foxhound. "What?"

Whistle cleared his throat. "At least that's what I understood. Mullraney was speaking in code. He had to, I suppose, because he said his 'new pal' was right there, buying him a drink. He called me Julie, asked whether his little girl had gotten the bandage off her arm. I gathered he was talking about the attack on you. He'd made a toy for his little girl, he said, and perhaps it would make her feel better, she'd always liked animals. He knew she'd wanted a blue dress, he said, but he'd looked all day and hadn't been able to find anything good in blue. Then he cut off. Haven't you heard from him?"

I exploded upward. "You know damn well we haven't!"

Whistle put a hand on the doorjamb, as if gripping it for purchase in the event it proved necessary to fling himself from the room. Still, he spoke defiantly. "I don't know any such thing. I expected him first thing this morning."

Grace said quickly. "Where was he?"

"The Stag Cafe," said Whistle.

"Did he describe the fellow who met him?"

"No. He couldn't, I don't think, even indirectly. Except he said he hadn't found anything good in blue, meaning, I'm sure, that the man was not his police informant."

"Did you try to call me?" Grace asked.

Whistle looked aggrieved. "I knew you would be out late, tracking and interrogating Miss LaRue."

Grace studied him keenly. "Yes."

I scorched Whistle with a look. "Jack's not the kind to drop down so quick. I'm heading for the Stag."

Grace said, firmly, "We will all go."

Nothing inside the Stag, so we checked the back. Morning light slanted down from above, glancing crookedly between the grotesque buildings elbowing each other like bums fighting for breathing room in a flophouse. The floor of the alley was still damp with dew where the sun had not touched the concrete, and diffused light lay here and there in soft patches like carpets worn to the threads. At first we saw nothing amiss. Then my eyes fell on a woolen flat cap hanging on a splintered board sticking from a battered garbage can. Its perch was odd, as if someone had hung it there out of the way so that it would not get blood-spattered in the carnage that followed.

Jack sat against the flaking plaster of the back wall of the Stag Cafe, propped up as if to enjoy a last smoke before bedding down amid the muck, broken bottles, and rain-driven garbage. His usual smile had relaxed a bit in death, as if the ultimate passage had freed him from his hopeless mask of gaiety. He had died hard. His collarless shirt was scored with a dozen slash-marks where the knife had penetrated the flesh of his chest and back, and dried blood formed lines of rough red-black powder on the edges of colorless gashes on his hands and forearms, cuts incurred as he had tried to fend off the blade.

Of the three of us, only Whistle gasped—a choked sound that ended in a strange gurgle. I held back for a moment, trying to control my breath, as Grace hurried forward and fell to her knees on the right side of the body. She closed Jack's blank eyes and a tremor went through her. She'd attended corpses before: When you work with the poor, you are called upon to deal with those who come to bad ends, but it's brutal work. She looked up at me with wide eyes in which the tears sparked, but she didn't raise a hand to stem them and I knew she wouldn't let them fall. At last, I stepped forward and knelt on the other side of the body. I reached out and straightened Jack's awkwardly-angled left arm, stupidly, as if I could somehow make him more comfortable. That was something I couldn't do for him, but there was something that I could, that we could. We settled down to a close examination of the body.

I turned out Jack's pants pockets, began an inventory. "A Barlow knife, three smokes, half a pack of matches and 39 cents in change." My voice was steady—I don't know how I kept it that way.

Grace took the knife, unfolded the blade, ran her hand down it. It was dry, clean except for a few errant slivers of wood. I followed her thoughts, spoke them for her. "No blood. He never got it out to defend himself." I returned to his pockets. "There's a stub of a pencil here, but nothing to write on."

Grace took the pencil, turned it in her hand. With a fingernail, she dug at the little brass clamp that held on the eraser, teasing free two white threads that had clung there. "This is the pencil that hung near the telephone inside the Stag," she said. "There was a piece of white string tacked to the wall next to the phone, next to messages written on the wall in graphite. The end of the string had been snapped off."

"You didn't find any message from him on the wall?"

"No." Grace considered, her face drawn. "But he might have had time to scrawl a message on some scrap of paper while his companion was distracted. If so, he'd have hidden it on his person." Grace unbuttoned Jack's shirt, and gently ran her hands around the area where the belt cinched the pants to the body. "Nothing."

Her eyes surveyed Jack's legs. And his shoes. She put out a hand, touched the fading leather.

I said it first. "He stuffed his shoes with newspapers. It's worth a look."

We worked quickly, I with one foot, Grace with the other. A few moments later, four substantial scraps of newspaper lay on the alley floor, crinkles still showing where it had been impossible to smooth them out. We scanned them intently, and I thought I noticed something. "Is there something in this headline? It looks like somebody has scratched a line through it."

Grace seized the scrap, turned it so that the early-morning light fell on it at a different angle. The headline read, COAL-MAN BUYS MONTANA RANCH. The word RANCH appeared to be struck through. She examined it closely, sighed. "No, it's not a line, just a tear in the paper." She released a long breath. "Still, it's an odd place for a tear, away from the edges of the clipping. And it's ragged, as if someone made it by pushing a thumb or finger through." She twitched the scrap, and on the edge of the tear, reddish-black dust fell away.

Whistle, his face damp and pale, forced himself in for a close look at Jack, then stumbled back, bracing himself on a garbage can, his eyes rolling. He bent as if to vomit, then straightened with swallowing sounds. "I— Should I call the police? I'd better call the police," he croaked.

I didn't even look up at him. "Yes, you'd better," I said. "That's what you're good for."

Footsteps stamped on the concrete at the end of the alley, and Grace said, "That won't be necessary."

A booted policeman stood there gaping. I glanced at the news scraps, then at Grace. I asked: "Are we finished?" Her hands moved swiftly, tucking the papers into her purse—and the knife. Her eyebrows came up. "For now, we are."

For a moment her mission—the one thing that held her firm—was over. She rose and took a few steps down the alley away from me, toward the rising sun. Her hair was bright with the fresh light of the new day, and she made no sound that I could hear. But suddenly her head dropped, her fists came up to meet her forehead, and her back-muscles tensed and convulsed violently, shaken by grief like an awning quivering in a hard wind.

Stoker McCullagh arrived with the homicide detectives in their nondescript suits, their splashy ties. He took one look at the body with disdainful interest, then backed off and let his detectives work. They moved quietly around the scene, giving voice to none of their usual grotesque comedic patter.

Grace watched them intently, as if the manner of their investigation held as much interest as its result, while I confronted Stoker. "You should have stayed in bed," I said. "There's nothing on him worth stealing."

Stoker raised an eyebrow, showed me plenty of teeth, turned his head to the side. The line of his chancily-shaved jaw was a sharp and rough, like an overused razor, and his eyes were shrewd and indifferent. "You've been through his pockets, then? That's obstruction of justice and a bagful of other things. That's worth a tampering-with-evidence rap, if my mood turns ugly."

"Go to it," I challenged, my voice husky. "Take us both down, me and Mrs. Humiston. I've no particular friends, but you know hers. Justice Charles L. Guy, of the New York Supreme Court, for one. We'll have a story for the front pages, and Judge Guy will be glad to lend moral support."

The bone of Stoker's jaw seemed to expand, stretching the skin so that high, white points showed. He nodded at Jack's body, which the coroner's assistants were scooping onto a gurney for transport to the waiting van. Jack's head, lolling back, struck the edge of the gurney and bounced. "That one thought he was onto something, and see what it bought him." The cop opened his mouth in something like a laugh. "Don't think he took the last place in Hell. They've got a rock down there just your size."

I measured the distance between my curling right fist and the point of Stoker's jaw, feeling the blood pumping in my arm, building up the heat that would fuel the punch. I shifted my feet slightly to get the platform right, lowered my left shoulder to get some sling-shot effect. And then Whistle grabbed the arm.

"Come! Mrs. Humiston says..."

Bad timing. I torqued my pulsing arm hard into Whistle's clutching hand, turning furiously at the same time, and the flow of energy caught him off-balance. He reeled backward, tangling his feet, falling with a wail to sprawl on the alley floor. My right leg trembled as I managed—barely—to restrain myself from launching a finishing kick. Then I turned and marched away, my head feeling hot and light, Stoker's laughter following me out into the street.

Grace caught up with me inside the Stag, where I was bellied up to the bar. I'd removed my hat, placed it over a bar-carving featuring an amorous zebra and a chorus girl, and had ordered two mugs of beer. The beer from the first mug was dripping down my neck and pooling under my collar, the beer in the second was moving speedily down my throat.

Grace sat next to me. The bartender, a ladder-high Polack with dirt-encrusted knuckles, his striped shirt drawn up with sleeve-clips, moved forward with a surly look. "We don't serve women here," he said, a bit of his native country's accent slurring his words. Fatigue deepened the frown-lines around the bony scoops of his eye-sockets, made his meaty lips sag. "It's rough trade."

Grace nodded her understanding. Then she removed her hat, surveyed the bar carvings, placed her right forefinger on the image of a woman being romanced by a baseball bat. "You won't have any trade at all if I close you down for an obscenity violation." she said. "This is quite artistic, but not the kind of thing countenanced in the municipal codes." She smiled wispily. "Beer, please."

The bartender looked as if a donkey had kicked him in the forehead. His jaws clenched and reddened. At last his expression resolved itself into a belligerent look. He held it for a few long seconds, but it couldn't stand against Grace's return gaze. He shrugged, drew the beer.

We sat for a long time, sipping, our eyes on each other in the back-bar mirror. Grace finally opened the show. "Whistle is a very competent young man," she said. "In his own way, he is as committed as you are to the pursuit of justice."

I hunched over my beer, examining the foam, seeing my reflection repeated many times in the bright, wet bubbles—all the little faces looking back at mine, with dullness in their eyes. "He's a weasel."

"You, of course, are without fault."

I thought this over, stirred the foam with my thumb to make the faces go away, then drank them all down, feeling them pinging off the inside of my throat and richocheting off the lining of my stomach. They hurt, every one of them. "No, if I was without fault, Jack wouldn't be sleeping in that meat wagon."

"That is my responsibility." Something in her voice made me glance sideways. Her face in profile held the cold promise of a sharpened axe—the brows drawn up, the cheekbones peaked. Before, she had been determined, now she was on the hunt, and she would make short work of it. A chill ran through me, and my stomach settled. I pulled my handkerchief, mopped my neck. She was leaning forward now, examining the welter of carvings in the top of the bar, her right pointer finger tracing the outline of a freshly-cut shamrock. Her lips made a clicking sound. "Do they do this every night?"

"What?"

"Carve these pictures on the bar?"

"I suppose, there are enough of them." I surveyed them. Right before me, amid a whirling, slanting mass of lines were cupid's hearts, revolvers, even a rendition of Sando the Strongman. Plus a goodly collection of zoo animals, all strung out in a line that drifted on down past Grace's seat. She examined them briefly, brushed some woodchips away from a carving to my front, seemed to lose interest. She lifted a finger at the bartender, and he took his time sliding over. He heaved a bored sigh. "What?"

"A man has been just been found murdered in your back alley."

He scratched at a raw fever-blister on his nose. "So?"

"Were you working last night?"

This was a tough one—he had to consider it for quite a while. "Yeh."

Grace's tone was patient. "Perhaps you saw the victim. His name was Jack Mullraney—a small man, woolen flat cap, striped collarless shirt, baggy pants, old brogans. His face was strange—always set in a smile."

The bartender mulled this over, looking about for inspiration. As he did so, he discovered a spot on the bar that needed his attention. From under the bar, he produced a rag, began to wipe the invisible spill, grinding the rag in. At last he shook his head. "Nah." He went back to his rubbing.

I spoke up. "That bar's clean enough."

The man lifted his head, surprised. "What did you say?"

I leaned over the bar, gathered his shirtfront gently, then compressed my hand, drawing him six inches closer to the bar. "I said if you don't stop cleaning and start talking, I'm going to pull your face off and make you blow your nose in it."

Quietly, Grace said, "Now you remember the man."

The bartender, astonished, said, "Yeh."

I released his shirt, turned back to my beer.

Grace lifted her chin. "What do you remember about him?"

The bartender laid a finger on his diseased nose, looked unhappy. "Not much. He came in late, ordered beers." His eyes drifted to the surface of the bar, then up at me. "Sat where this fella is sitting."

"Alone?"

"Some fella came in later, sat with him. He had beer, too."

"Describe the man who came in."

The bartender glanced again at me, looked sorrowful. "Lady, I can't. It was busy, half the Tenderloin was in here last night. He was just a fella bundled up, muffler around his neck, hat down. I hardly looked at him."

"But you remember Jack. Why?"

"Don't know." The bartender yelped, jumped back. "What the hell —?"

Grace had moved suddenly and the Barlow knife was in her hand, the blade inches from the bartender's chest. His hands were up in self-defense, tongue slurping at his lips. Grace' thumb caressed the blade. "I know."

"Know what?" the bartender croaked.

"Why you noticed him," said Grace. Her hand relaxed, letting the knife fall to the bar top. "He was carving on the bar with this knife. There are wood-chips on the blade similar to those from the bar. And he was doing more than that. He was pointing out to you what he was carving."

The bartender hiccuped, fearful and uncertain. "How do you know that?"

Grace's eyes moved from the bartender to me, then back again. "Because you had half the Tenderloin in here last night, but you still remembered Jack. When you said Jack was sitting where Kron is now, you first checked the surface of the bar. You saw a carving there that jogged your memory." Her eyes dropped to the scarred and whittled oaken surface. "Which one?"

The bartender's hand was resting on the bar. Suddenly, it jerked spasmodically, skittering across the gouged oak, leaping along the backs of the carved zoo animals, until it came to rest on one of them. The filthy fingernail of his forefinger quivered on this one like a dowsing stick, flickering over the curled body, the tiny ears, the long, looping tail. Pointing out the monkey.

Chapter Fifteen

WE GAVE JACK A GOOD burying at a little graveyard up in Queens where the wind shushed through the branches of the spruce and poplar trees and footfalls shuffled by on the sidewalk, echoing off the high buildings. There was a playground not far off, erupting with the sharp, joyous yelps of children. Jack's last place was a city place—I hoped it was comfortable for him, and supposed it was, for he had always been a city man.

There were not so many of us at the graveside, but how many does it take? Grace, her husband, Whistle, and me. And a priest to say the words, his shoulders bent with many years, his voice rising into the wind, his black cassock puffing about his ankles. Grace made as if not to cry, and she held up pretty well, but her husband had to clutch her close a few times. It made me a bit uncomfortable, seeing that, because I would have liked to have clutched her myself, to have done the husband's duty, and I didn't like myself for having those feelings, because they didn't fit the occasion. There was no dignity in them, that was the simple fact, and they intruded on my grief for Jack's passing. That was a disservice to him who had laid down his life for me and Grace, so I vowed to make it up to him, however I had to.

The monkey carved on the bar seemed to point clearly to Carlos De Souza, who favored monkeys and their images. It wasn't proof, not yet, but we would get that. It was clear enough to me what had happened. Word had got back to De Souza that Jack was doing our bidding, squeezing information from the police reports. A dirty cop could easily have let that leak. De Souza would have figured that Jack—a crook and a lowlife—would be the perfect double agent, that he could turn him to find out what Grace was doing. Once De Souza made the approach, Jack would have kicked back on him, unable to hide his loyalty to Grace. At that point, De Souza had exposed himself. The only solution? Murder.

There was the scenario, but the police weren't going to help us prove it, just the opposite, so we did the only thing we could do. We pushed harder.

Grace and I were out early and late, following Alvarez and De Souza wherever they went, for the ice skating at Van Cortlandt park, to fancy dress balls at Fifth Avenue mansions, to the bootmakers, to the men's shops. And it was my luck that I made the first strike, as I lounged with a racing newspaper in my grasp in the lobby of the Hotel Metropole, having followed Ricardo and a classy lovely there for an afternoon tryst. During the shank of the afternoon, she emerged on her own, and I let her go, waiting for Ricardo to pop out of his hole. He didn't, but she returned a couple of hours later, dragging plenty of boxes and bags with her. It was odd, her sudden shopping trip after a bout of lovemaking, and her apparent aim of caching her new treasures in a hotel room. It put me in mind of Ruth Cruger, who had gone out in the middle of the day with no traveling clothes, but possibly with a secret bank account to supply her money for a trip. A trip from which she'd never returned.

Grace looked pale and peaked when I reached her office, and she held her slashed arm awkwardly, though she'd dispensed with the sling. In fact, she was strengthening the arm—and her concentration—with the .32-caliber Colt Pocket Positive. As I stood silent and unnoticed, she raised the pistol, aimed at the death mask, snapped the hammer, lowered the pistol. I held my silence and she repeated the process, over and over. A few more moments of this, and I coughed. This stopped her in mid-stroke, and her head popped toward me.

Drily, I asked, "The reconstruction of a crime?"

She turned back to the task. The pistol rose, snapped, fell, rose, snapped, fell. "Target practice."

"Time is growing short," said Grace. "We may have only a few days." Her practice session over, she was presiding now over a council of war. Whistle and I, pointedly not looking at each other, watched her. The huge clock on the wall, with its white face and grotesque-deco hands, ticked in time with her pacing. "We need to find out who the young woman is, gain her confidence, and try to convince her parents that their daughter is in deadly danger."

I stirred. "That is going to be some piece of work."

"Yes," said Whistle. "She is enthralled by this young man Alvarez. If we approach her directly, she will not believe us. Further, she will tell him all that we have done. Our plans will be exposed."

Grace's gaze settled on him for a few seconds. "Something tells me our plans are not perfectly masked now."

She appeared to shake off some troubling thought, then hurried on. "Jack's role in our work, for instance, was discovered by our enemies. Of course, the man who attacked me might have seen him coming to my aid. And his appearance is such that he is very well known. Finding his usual haunts would have posed no problem."

I didn't know quite what to make of this, but Grace seemed to be concentrating this spiel primarily on Whistle, so I kept my eyes on him, too, and I thought I saw his lips droop, his eyebrows elevate in apprehension. What was that all about?

Quickly, Whistle said: "But we must keep focused on our immediate problem—the young lady."

One last, long look, and Grace said, "Indeed."

She touched her lips. "Since we cannot approach the young woman directly, we must do so indirectly. We need a duplicitous confederate, and we need her right now."

I bent forward and rested my elbows on my knees, tipping my head forward so I could knead the muscles at the back of my neck. I pumped hard on them, but I couldn't get the spasms to release. Slowly, I said, "I'm afraid I know who you're talking about."

When I knocked, Luisa Clary had most of her possessions packed. One glance through the opening door told me things had not been going well. The mussed and scattered bedclothes showed she'd slept very little, and her arms and legs sagged wearily. Her face was thin with hunger. She'd gone without breakfast, I supposed, and had little hope for lunch. I gave her a significant look, stepped past her into the room, and there I found a third cause for her distress, lying on the floor with its insides spilling.

It was a large fabric-and-leather suitcase with tarnished brass locks, scarred by the sharp corners of park benches, stretched by hard use, scuffed by railway terminal floors. It looked like the type that normally would bulge to accept whatever load it had to bear—second-hand dresses in bad times, stolen dresses in nefarious times—but this time the suitcase had fought back. Luisa had no doubt pushed down on its top vigorously with her small, shapely arms, had tried sitting on it to smash down the contents. But the technique of closing a suitcase by sitting on it requires a friend who will actually close the case once you have compressed it with your bottom. And Luisa had no friend to do so.

The suitcase had not yielded. Despite her best efforts, it had remained obstinately—smugly—open. And this last frustration had broken her. As I watched uncomfortably, she sank onto the suitcase and wept.

I didn't know what to do, so I went and stood over her, trying to compose an appropriate speech, something gruff and comforting to get her back on track and complete the business I had with her. But she carried on and on with piteous, keening sobs and wails, so that her distress just ruined her face, though her little hands came up to protect the work she'd done with the mascara and the face powder, the floods sweeping all her handiwork away in rivulets that trickled through her fingers.

Then the worst possible thing happened. She got her legs under her, rose, reached out blindly and clutched the front of my English Roll grey suit, pressing her pretty head against me, her sobs buffeting my breastbone. And this was too much, for her smell of attar of roses went right through to my brain and started the canaries singing, as I felt her breasts warm and full on my chest, noted that her small ears were like masterworks of German china.

"Here, now," I said, at first lifting my arms in an effort to comfort her, then desisting, not wanting to paw. Logically, the thought occurred to me that I should push her away, but somehow that did not seem to be a humane option. At last I circled her carefully with my left arm, trying to be matter-of-fact about the firm, neatly-cut shapes of her shoulders, led her over to the bed and sat her down, thrusting away all thoughts of swinging her at length among the pillows and sheets. I coughed hard to get my thoughts back, pulled a clean handkerchief from my breast pocket and held it out. She took it with a trembling hand, placed it over her nose, and, thank God, summoned an authoritative honk.

"There," I said with relief. "Christ, I thought you were going to go on like that all day." I straightened, shook myself and looked around the place, lonely and cold and littered with the scraps of departure— wire hangers angling across the floor, discarded underclothing sagging from the edge of a wastebasket, empty boxes tipping their tops like awkward swains. I blew out a long breath. "Who were you running out on this time?"

This brought another desperate wail of sorrow, choked out between a renewed round of sobs. The handkerchief wavered in front of her face, limp and awful, flipping about like a drenched flag. "Everybody was running out on me!"

Horrified at how rashly I'd gotten her spigots going again, I ordered, "Now stop that!" I went to one knee in front of her, hoping to enforce my command with the scarred expanse of my face (it usually had that effect), but only getting myself into further trouble. At this range, the pitiable, dripping mood of Miss Luisa Clary made her eyes shine more attractively, enhanced the allure of her strong cheekbones, brought into sharper perspective the richness of her lips. Breaking every rule that had enabled me to survive for more than three decades, telling myself I was only doing it as a technique to calm her down, I leaned forward and touched her lips with my own.

For a few seconds, she helped with the technique. She seemed to be familiar with it. Then I regained some semblance of good sense. I broke off, stood up, turned away and said, "Well, now!"

I could hear that she was no longer sobbing. I took that as a bad sign, a very bad sign. I stretched my neck and rolled my shoulders, trying to loosen my muscles, to brace for whatever might come.

At last she said, "Why did you do that?"

Now there was a question that went to the heart of the matter. I coughed, clamped my hands together, toothed my lower lip, examined the door, which I now wished I had a good reason to make use of, tried to think how to answer her. Why had I done that? Why, indeed?

"We're offering you a business proposal."

"Oh?" I could hear the smile in her voice. "Is that how you usually do it?"

I rounded angrily on her, but my blood pressure was up for a reason that wasn't anger and my stomach was going soft, for now she was even prettier, with the devilish light playing about her eyes and her lips compressed and wry. I forced my eyes away from her, pretended I hadn't heard.

"This business proposal wasn't my idea," I said deliberately, cracking my knuckles to emphasize the words. "It was Mrs. Humiston's. I argued against it. In my book, women like you are always a mistake."

The bed creaked as she leaped up. "And just what are women like me like, anyway?"

"Trouble," I said, knocking my fists together, already feeling more in control. "Give you a break, and you'll try to work your way around into something you don't deserve."

The tear tracks on her cheeks were barely dry, but you'd never have known it from her attitude. She picked up a face-powder pot as if she meant to throw it, smashed it back down on the table. The contents flew. "Really?" she said. "Really, now? So you are an expert on women? And choosy, too? A church-going type, I suppose you are, a psalm-singing slab of meat in a nice suit. So I guess you have your pick of ladies from the Women's League of Virtue?" She paused, seething, casting about for a really saw-toothed verbal sally. "Funny, I would have thought your women would be the nickel-a-dance kind."

In two steps, I was in front of her. "You've got a dirty tongue." She stuck it out at me. Actually it was rather clean and inviting, a reversed ruby teardrop, but I tightened my jaw, summoned an expression of righteous disgust. "That's something a kid would do. Grow up, why don't you? Christ, you don't have any dignity."

This shot went home. Her angrily raised hands slowly fell, and her face paled and quivered, the shapely nose drooping, her chin going out of control. She didn't cry, though. I wish she had cried. That, at least, I'd learned to deal with. But she simply whirled away from me, all her muscles trembling, and spoke, her voice husky.

"I've got dignity," she said, with terrible softness. "Everyone tries to take it away from me, but I've got it."

She remained with her face to the bed, the fists at her sides tightening gradually as she spoke, her body growing rigid as a sentry box. "I've been on my own since I was fifteen, ever since my stepfather tried to do things to me and I wouldn't let him, ever since my mother stood around stirring the soup and pretended everything was okay. I've got my dignity."

Her voice rose a bit. "I've worked in hash houses, shirtwaist factories, offices where the boss hired you for one thing and expected you to do another. I've been in cheap plays where I had to do the last act pretending I didn't know there was a piece of rotten tomato on my skirt, but I've got my dignity." She looked at me. "I've stolen from people, lied to people, made them think I was a friend, then sold them out. I've been locked up, done in, put down, but I never worked the streets, there are some things I won't do, I've got something inside that's still my own." She paused, and her neck straightened, her chin came up, and all the pugnacity in her face and voice was gone. "And I've got my dignity."

"Yes," I said, keeping my eyes as ironic as I could, which I suppose was not very ironic. "And now you've got a job."

Chapter Sixteen

THE YOUNG WOMAN I'D SEEN with Ricardo Alvarez came out of De Souza Jewelers exactly at 2:04 p.m., hair mussed, lipstick uneven, looking as if she had been entertained vigorously with the kind of parlor games seldom played in polite households during the afternoon.

No doubt the tryst had taken place in the quarters Alvarez and De Souza occupied above the store. That didn't overly surprise me, except that Alvarez had for some reason earlier found it necessary to rendezvous with the woman at the Hotel Metropole. Probably he did so on the pretense that he had to hide their intimacies from his "Uncle." The uncle was out today—Grace had observed him earlier, getting into a taxi outside the store, his monkey—as usual—on his shoulder, and had followed him I didn't know where. With the old man out of the way, the young folks were taking chances at home. The young woman's cheeks glowed with the salubrious effect that athletic sex has on blood circulation, and her step expressed energy and verve as she also hailed a taxi.

"She's had a nice roll," said Luisa, lounging next to me in our rented Ford Center Door Sedan. "Let's hope it's put her in the mood for some more shopping."

I straightened behind the wheel and said, "Try to speak like a lady —that's part of your act."

Luisa wiggled on the seat, thrusting herself sideways so that her body came close to mine. I gave her an irritated look as she patted my arm. "But I don't have to act with you, hey Kron?" She giggled deep in her very deep chest. "I can be right-and-ready Luisa, girl of the streets, ace con-human, as long as it's just you and me?"

I kept my eyes on the mark, refusing to look at her. "Try to act professional."

Late afternoon. I steered through light traffic down Fifth Avenue, my concentration so intense that once I had to brake sharply to avoid hitting a man running to catch an open-sided trolley. At last the taxi ahead swooped through pedestrians, jerked to the side of the street and dispensed the young woman, who spent a few moments at the driver's window, issuing instructions and cash.

"She's sending him home with the goods, so she can go and collect more," said Luisa. "If I was on my own, I'd make some excuse to stop the driver half a block away and get in, and I'd cop some little goodie before I got out again."

"You're not on your own," I said, "and we've got business at hand." I jabbed a finger at the young woman, who was entering the portals of a white granite shopping emporium, drifting past a window display of women dressed in fashionable style. In the last two hours, our mark had concentrated on small shops. "Here's the first store that's big enough to give you room to play," I said. "Get in there and lay on the con while I relay a message to Mrs. Humiston."

Luisa slid to the door. "Oh yes," she said, "Your boss." She paused with the door half-open. "Very pretty. I'll bet she always acts professional."

"Yes, she does."

Luisa leaned back across the seat, far more than necessary, projecting her very attractive torso into my danger zone. "It's a mistake to be on the job all the time," she said. "You miss out on the fun."

I noted that her eyes changed when she talked like this and her skin breathed perfume. I managed to control my own air and temperature and said, "We've got work to do."

126

She pooched out her lips. "Aren't you going to encourage me?"

"I'm not in the encouragement business. And you shouldn't need it, anyway. You're getting paid."

"Not the same way the boss pays you, I'll bet." She flounced out the door and was gone.

For part of the time Luisa was stalking her mark, I observed her—at first by myself, then with Grace—but I wouldn't have known her exact method if she hadn't explained it to us later, in a debriefing we used to enhance our detecting. It took Luisa the better part of an hour to spring her trap, using her knowledge of human psychology and women's fashion.

The set-up was subtle. From behind a purse display, Luisa noted the type of perfume the quarry was purchasing at a nearby counter, then moved into the woman's wake and sprayed herself with that same scent, known as Evening Ecstasy. Luisa didn't neglect the detail work. With careful calculation, she used an excessive amount, just as—her sensitive nostrils had told her—the other woman had done. Then, using her knowledge of upper-class female shopping behavior, Luisa contrived to move just one stage ahead of the quarry, so that when that young lady arrived in the shoe department, Luisa was already busily engaged in treating an overworked shop girl rudely—a performance she knew would instantly mark her in her target's eyes as upper-class and right-minded.

Luisa abruptly broke off the encounter before the quarry was fully on the scene and hurried off to lingerie, where she expected to close on her mark as a buyer closes on a house. Luisa wasn't wrong about the nature of shopping patterns—the target arrived a few minutes later, right on schedule. By this time, Grace and I, role-playing a married couple having a miserable time (wife dragging bored husband out to buy a promised blouse) were covertly watching from nearby, and we got to see the climax of Luisa's performance. Pretending to be unaware of the target's presence, she clutched two fluffy chemises to her bosom, expressed a piteous moan of frustration, turned suddenly, came face to face with her quarry, and blurted, "Oh, can you help me?"

The young woman already had seen Luisa in action, had noted her expert skill at handling the help, had been tremendously impressed. So it was that the target, whose own technique for humiliating shop girls was so awkward as to sometimes go unnoticed, was flattered that this ace shopper would call on her for anything. And, furthermore, her nose told her that this was a creature with wonderful taste in perfume —at this range, Luisa's Evening Ecstasy blended with her own. Still, the mark was mindful of the danger (and worse, the social impropriety) of speaking with strangers. She said, cleverly, "What?"

"Can you help me?" Luisa repeated. "I've got a terrible decision to make." She held out the chemises, one in each hand, as if they were two of her babies, one of which she had to give up for execution. "I'm shopping for an ocean voyage, and I can only take one of them."

Luisa saw a deep wave of sympathy washing over the mark's face, practically drenching her eyebrows. No doubt the mark had often faced just this agonizing dilemma herself, for her eyes actually grew misty, recalling the rapier-like prod of anxiety. She laid a hand on Luisa's arm, and said, "Of course."

With that phrase, she bit down firmly on Luisa's hook and the rest of the operation ran on rails. Quicker than you could cash a stock dividend, Luisa had pumped several choice bits of information out of the young woman, including her name—Miss Jane Pilkington—her snazzy address, and her plans to sail to Bueños Aires with her husband-to-be in just four days, on board the liner *Calpurnia.* This last gem stunned and delighted Luisa, who breathlessly blurted that, by some fantastic stroke of chance, she also was sailing on that very ship on that very day.

Within a few minutes, arms linked, Luisa clutching a box containing her new chemise—bought with our cash advance—the two new friends were going off for tea, petits four, and a cozy chat about the most fulfilling methods of grinding the poor further into the dirt.

A few steps away, Grace took a turn before the mirror in the white crepe de chine blouse she was trying on. Given the price of the blouse and our surroundings, it appeared to be the height of fashion, with its flat hood narrowing to a triangle-point in front, embroidered on the turned-up edge in a color matching its robin's-egg-blue lining.

I will say this: Grace looked fine in it, though she would never buy it, it being an extravagance. I had a sudden urge to offer it to her, even put a hand to my wallet before I realized what I was doing. I drew in a long breath, hoping she hadn't seen me. She hadn't. Her eyes were on the reflected image of the blouse, her thoughts on Luisa Clary.

"She is very professional, isn't she?"

I bit my lip. "A professional thief."

CHAPTER SEVENTEEN

ON FIFTH AVENUE ABOVE 57TH Street, the sidewalks were narrow—the fine houses pushed close to the street like beefy gentlemen thrusting themselves to the fore in a theater bar, eager to display their prosperous shirt fronts.

"They speak a different language up here," I said, edging the car to the curb.

"It is a language with which I am quite familiar," said Grace, adjusting the front of her visiting outfit. "It's high language, but it genuflects in the presence of titles. They love their kings, dukes, princes and earls." A smile twitched her mouth. "Unfortunately, in this part of New York, a Count counts for something. We can only hope for the best."

"Do you want me to go with you?"

"No," said Grace. "I had better keep you in the background for the next few days." She put a hand on my shoulder. "If I have to fall back on my desperation plan, your identity will have to change. It is best that few people see you as you are now."

With that, she was out of the car and moving with purpose between two fierce carven lions lounging on either side of a bank of marble steps that led upwards to a white granite mansion. I watched her ring the bell, saw the butler who answered—a tall man, narrow and old. Over the stone steps, his voice clattered in clipped, parched tones, as if he controlled his saliva to keep his dignity dry. "Whom shall I say is calling?"

"Mrs. Grace Humiston." Her voice bit clearly at the chill air, impeccably precise as the visiting card she now placed on the silver plate he offered. I saw the movement of her hand, knew—though it was too far off to see—that she had turned down the corner of the card to show she was there in person, not just plying the empty round of visiting-card distribution. He gestured her in, they disappeared through the door, and she was off to face the redoubtable Mrs. Eileen Pilkington, subscriber to the opera, member of the congregation of Grace Church, owner of a country house, giver of balls and parties.

Grace told me later that she could gauge the daunting nature of her task from the stiff, chilly furnishings of the house. After a suitable delay, the butler reappeared, descending the stairway past helmeted suits of armor, and ushered Grace upward to a living room thick with tapestries and furniture. The pieces were Cinque-cento Italian—ample walnut tables with an age-given patina, wide-back chairs with curiously-carven splats, torchieres with twisting, gilded columns.

Mrs. Eileen Pilkington, who apparently had taken up the newest vice for women, was smoking a Sweet Caporal, knocking the ashes abruptly into a silver ashtray fashioned in the shape of a small elephant. Like the room's furnishings, Mrs. Pilkington was heavy and excessively draped. She rested on a spreading bottom that apparently had resisted efforts to shrink it in hot saltwater baths—a common nostrum, for all that its success rate seemed to be vanishingly low. Mrs. Pilkington endured Grace's salutations without comment, waved her to a chair. "I knew your father, Mrs. Humiston," she said. "A great man." A Niagara of smoke gushed from her mouth and she whirled ashes across the Oriental carpet. "I doubt he would have approved of your current work."

Grace smiled graciously. "What aspect of my current work would have most displeased him, do you think?"

Mrs. Pilkington's eyes grew heavy-lidded. "This sordid business of mixing with criminals, of course. Though I doubt he would have been amused by your equally sordid penchant for legally trumpeting the whining of the poor."

"Though few knew it, my father was quite generous to the poor and to those falsely accused," Grace said. "A man may enjoy wealth without crashing it down on the less fortunate."

Mrs. Pilkington absorbed this, her lids drooping even more, her fleshy wattles twitching like irritated amoebae. She smoked and thought, smoked and thought, knocking ashes onto the elephant, the table, the carpet. "Very well," she said at last. "What have you come for, a donation for your gutter folk?"

"Actually, it is the other sordid aspect of my career that has brought me," Grace said. She paused, drawing out Mrs. Pilkington's anticipation, and was gratified to see the older woman neglect to knock away her cigarette ash, so that it grew perceptibly longer as the seconds ticked away. "I fear your daughter is about to be taken off to Argentina by white slavers."

Mrs. Pilkington's laugh rasped like iron filings cascading down a wooden chute, continued spasmodically for several moments, then tapered off into a series of little barks. "What melodrama!" she said, grinding her cigarette into the little elephant's back, then instantly firing up another smoke, drawing in a long gust, releasing it with a long, luxurious gasp. "I'm afraid you are wide of the mark this time," she said. "My daughter is to be married to a Spanish nobleman."

Grace kept her temper. "He claims to be a Spanish nobleman," she said. "I strongly suspect otherwise."

"Strongly suspect? And what do the police say about your strong suspicions?"

"The police are not always reliable in these matters."

Again, the cascade of iron filings, the little barks. "And you, Mrs. Humiston, are you always reliable in these matters?"

"We are speaking of your daughter's life."

"Oh. Well." Puffing, ash-flicking, an expression of resigned pique. "Jane has pretty well arranged her life without any help from me. She takes after her father in that. Frankly—and I don't know why I am being frank, possibly because you are showing some interest, however misguided—Jane has such an unhealthy interest in sex that this match may be her only chance to save herself from disgrace."

Grace said, in measured tones, "One girl who fell prey to these men is almost certainly dead."

On the couch, Mrs. Pilkington's bulk shifted and rolled like a ship making through heavy seas. She rotated her eyes upward in profound disgust. "Oh dear," she said. "Do you think I would actually allow my child to go abroad by herself and marry if I hadn't thoroughly checked out her betrothed myself?"

Grace blinked. "You have?"

"Of course I have," came the reply. "With the Argentine ambassador in Washington." Mrs. Pilkington propped her cigarette on the elephant's back, and leaned forward, almost tipping off the couch, to rummage in a stack of correspondence on her heavy walnut coffee table. She extracted a telegram, waved it with ironic triumph.

Grace rose, stepped forward, took the paper, unfolded it and read: "No adverse information about either Señor Carlos De Souza or Señor Ricardo Alvarez has come to my attention. Please accept my congratulations on your daughter's engagement." It was signed, "Romale S. Naon, Ambassador of Argentina."

Grace looked up in disbelief. "This is simply a form reply," she said. "Do you think that the ambassador actually made any effort to probe the backgrounds of these men?"

Mrs. Pilkington's eyes were hateful, haughty, dismissive. "Of course you wouldn't understand," she said. "Señor Naon is a personal friend."

Well, it had come to this: All of us—Grace, Luisa and I—had been set on a course from which we couldn't deviate. We were being carried along by events and had to hold on tight. I had the nagging feeling that were being carried along in the wrong direction, and from what I later learned from Grace, that belief was more than a feeling with her. Still, the die was cast, and, for Grace, it was time for a major confrontation with her husband.

Grace, as I have said, was the type to plumb human psychology, to think deeply about the meaning of everyone's actions, including her own. And she was constantly gathering evidence about herself, about her obvious motivations and those not-so-obvious. Howard Humiston was no great psychologist, but he had been married to Grace for a good while and had some powers of observation himself—otherwise, he wouldn't have been the effective attorney that he was. So you couldn't discount his analyses, and Grace didn't. Perhaps if she had discounted them, things would have gone more easily. Or perhaps not.

We were close, Grace and I, and in the years after this affair, we became much closer. So it was that I eventually learned the details of the head-knocking time she'd had with her husband just before we launched off on the adventure that was to end in two deaths and the solution to the riddle of Ruth Cruger.

As usual, Grace's bang-up with Howard took place in their apartment, in the normally relaxed time after dinner. Howard reached for the coffee pot and poured himself a cup. His simple meal of beef stew, toast and applesauce had disappeared so cleanly that his crockery now looked fresh from the sink, but as he looked across at his wife's meal, he noted that her food was still intact, having spent a long time cooling. She stared fixedly above her fifth cup of coffee which, like the previous four, she had drunk in silence.

Abruptly, she said: "I am going to Argentina in two days' time."

He was silent for a long time. "Very well," he said. "You have made all the arrangements?"

She shook her head abstractedly as if her thoughts were elsewhere. "Oh yes—tickets, packing."

He stood up, took up his cup of coffee, stumped over to the Spartan mantel with its collection of dusty Germanic figurines, its broken clock-under-glass. He thrust one elbow onto the mantel among the bric-a-brac and sipped from his cup. "No," he said. "I mean the arrangements if you don't come back."

She looked up, stunned out of her distraction. She said, "Why wouldn't I come back?"

He shrugged his elbow off the mantel and began to pace on the simple, scarred carpet. He slumped slightly, as tall men do when they do not want to intimidate with their size. His pacing was measured exactly, up and down, up and down, the length of a jury box. He chose his words carefully.

"This has been a particularly dangerous investigation, I know, though out of respect for your nature, I do not ask you questions. You were good enough to tell me recently—when you came home with a bandaged arm—that you had been attacked with a knife." He sipped his coffee, spread his hands wide. "Perhaps you are under the impression that it is no great matter for a husband to go off to work in the morning knowing that his wife is being followed by people with knives."

"Howard—"

"No. Let me finish. You now propose to go off to Argentina. If you disappear on this adventure, I will not even have the comfort of knowing the details of why you died, nor will I have the slightest clue to aid me as I set out to avenge you."

"Howard," she said softly. She drew him to the sofa, set his cup on an end table, held him as best she could. He was a huge, ungainly bear of a man who could never take a step without appearing in danger of a stumble. Only in court, with his voice swelling with the certainty of his cause, did he move with grace, sweeping a deposition from a table and swinging fluidly toward a witness, flinging back his head to launch an objection, pounding his fist in rhythm on a jury box to drive home a point. "I have never deceived you about the work I do, have I?" she said.

His chin resting awkwardly against her head, he said, bleakly, "We used to do the same kind of work."

He pulled back, his chin tightening, the fire coming up in his eyes. "And there still is work to do, don't you know that? There still are poor people being thrown out of lodgings, feeble-minded people imposed upon for experiments, immigrant girls in the garment district working in appalling conditions. Have you forgotten the Triangle Shirtwaist fire?"

She said tightly, "I have not forgotten."

Six years before, 146 young women, mostly Italian and Jewish immigrants, had died in that fire, many leaping to their deaths still clutching their pitifully small paychecks, one of the two exit doors barred to keep them from sneaking off with spools of thread. He sighed. "Only lawyers can prevent such atrocities, lawyers willing to badger the sweatshop owners, lawyers who sacrifice, lawyers with steel, like you."

She pulled out of his arms, rose and began to pace as he had, up and back, up and back, trying to find words to convince the most difficult jury of all. She said, softly, "So many injustices."

"Yes."

"We spend ourselves on small things, while the larger evil goes on around us."

"Yes."

"But we cannot allow ourselves to be diverted by our inadequacy —having taken up the weapons for a good fight, we must carry on."

"Mary Grace—" he said. He rose from the sofa, powerful in his lack of style. He looked down, away, and whispered, "I am fighting for your life."

She went to him, held him, laid her head against his chest. She said, "For your sake, I would choose the smaller danger, if I could discern it. Where lies the most deadly danger? In the sharpness of knives, or in our own fear of evil men?"

He placed his hands on her shoulders, and left her. "I pride myself as being one with fine words," he said, "but you can always best me there." He turned, and she could see something about him had changed. "So I will not trade fine words with you. I want you back— back from the alleys and the cells and the autopsy rooms. You do not fear evil men. I do. They will kill you." He sighed ironically. "And what will I have, for all my high-sounding crusades? Will I have a woman to sit with me in the evening, to share my bed, to think of when things go well or badly? No. I will be a dead man walking."

Grace looked at him, anguished. She loved him, but she also loved the hunt. There were others who could love him, only one who could press this hunt.

She rose, clenched her hands. "I must close with these men," she said. "Six girls missing, Jack dead in an alley ripped with a dozen wounds, his only legacy a pitiful clue carved on a bar. This dead man, these ghosts cry out to me."

She drew herself up and inhaled deeply. "All are set against me— these killers, the police, the wealthy parents in their blind vanity, even you. And still these ghosts! And I the only one who can give them rest!"

Howard Humiston went to the sofa and slumped down. Weariness enveloped him, his large hands moved and stopped, he closed his eyes. "You have a beast within you, Mary Grace. It consumes the unjust, but it consumes you, too. Its fangs are close to your heart, and it is always hungry." He opened his eyes. "I can live with you," he said. "But I cannot live with the beast."

CHAPTER EIGHTEEN

WE STOPPED ON THE SIDEWALK and looked up at Luisa's apartment building. Grace put her face near mine. "From now on," she said, "all is secrecy and deception." My mouth was dry. Her face was so close that I could make out individual brush-strokes of powder on her cheeks, feel the warmth of her breath. "What do you mean?"

Her eyes were as certain as a marksman's. "The fight is joined. Now I must do what I can to maneuver our opponents into a slip. I must harry them and force their hand. And I must do so in an arena where they cannot get help from the police."

I said, "The ship."

She nodded. "There are relatively few liners routed to Argentina, and at one time or another, these two must have tried them all. I will go aboard, ostensibly conducting a general investigation of the disappearances. And we shall see what we shall see."

"What will my role be?"

Grace put a finger on my chest. "An excellent choice of words, for you will be playing a part. Is there some con man of recent memory who has dropped from sight and might credibly reappear?"

I parked my chin on my right fist and thought. "Swifty Blitzer's gone, but everybody knows he's dead—he got a send-off with flowers. Oakie Comstock comes and goes. That would be tricky—he might pop up anywhere, including on the ship. There actually was a fellow around for a while who pretended to be a Rumanian nobleman. He was deported." I knuckled my forehead. "Count Raflasky—that's what he called himself. A nasty character."

Grace smiled. "All the better. Count Raflasky it will be." She pointed up at the apartments. "Luisa is not to know." She nodded. "And no-one else is to know." Her face was stark, the breathing measured. I felt the pulsing of her breath, and it mesmerized me. She repeated: "No-one."

Grace said casually, looking out Luisa's window into the air shaft, "It is entirely possible that someone may die on this voyage. These are desperate men."

Luisa paused in the middle of repacking a suitcase, holding a simple white chemise in her hands. She glanced at me as I sat stolidly on the couch, pretending to leaf through a copy of *McClure's*, and she laughed shallowly, with a nervous little edge to it. "I suppose your detective will protect us."

I looked up, feeling my face flush, but Grace shook her head. "Kron is needed here, to press the investigation. You and I will be alone."

Luisa laughed again, but the laugh didn't carry much weight. "Suits me," she said, carelessly tossing another chemise. It banked off the suitcase, fell to the floor, but she didn't immediately stoop for it. "I'm used to being alone."

I lowered the magazine, noted again how clean and picked-up the apartment was now—the magazines symmetrical, the dust gone, the dishes put away. It was not Luisa's normal living style, even though she had paid the rent with her retainer from Grace and might easily have resumed her former ways. It was as if, even before hearing the final word from Grace, Luisa had readied herself for departure.

Grace had pressed her hands together, thinking. "How have you left it with Miss Pilkington?"

"I'll get together with her on board," Luisa said. "She'll introduce me to her catch and his uncle."

"No contact until then," Grace ordered.

Luisa shot her a glance; it could have been one of rebellion, anger, apprehension. "We had planned to have lunch tomorrow."

Grace said carefully, "We will all three go to a telephone. You will call her and beg off. You will say you have a last-moment appointment that had slipped your mind."

Luisa looked at Grace and slowly wet her lips, but she held her silence.

"From now on," Grace said, "all is secrecy and deception."

There was something about this departure that seemed more final than most, and as I watched Grace packing a few work essentials—legal pad, witness statements, fountain pens—into a pressed-leather briefcase, I tried to put my finger on just what it was. The office was as usual, perhaps a bit more dust in the corners—the Italian girl who cleaned the place had a good heart, was industrious enough when she arrived, but had a weakness for chianti at midweek. Grace was put together as I often saw her—dressed in a conservative gray wool dress, high collar, her hair drawn into a soft wave. Her complexion, though, I suppose, was a touch paler than usual. She hadn't looked at me much in the few moments I'd spent with her getting last-minute directions.

She started to push a sheaf of documents into the briefcase, turned distractedly, as if looking for something she'd forgotten. She released a long sigh, let it all flow out. Her shoulders dropped fractionally. "I believe my husband intends to leave me."

My heart got big and my brow grew humid, I went for my suddenly-tight collar and wrenched at it. I'd hoped for this, but not expected it, and somehow her telling me about it this way, just blurting it out, took the edge off me, made me uneasy.

"I tell you this as a friend," said Grace. "Tonight is our last night before sailing. Something must happen tonight, or Howard and I will be changed forever."

I opened my mouth and cupped a throatful of wind, ready with some brilliant reply. But, really, what reply was there? There are times when speaking is exactly the wrong thing to do, and I'm not too nimble at it at the best of times, so I trapped the words, let them lie where they were, down there in my chest.

Grace pulled open her desk drawer, inserted the documents, slid the drawer closed, plucked up a brass key and clicked the drawer's lock. She continued to hold the key for a few moments, as if uncertain what to do with it. She looked around. The polished wooden desktop was empty now except for the bust of Caesar with his carven eyes. The file cabinets were snapped shut, the unused straight-back chairs ranked against the wall. Grace rose, marched to the door to the outer office and opened it.

"Whistle."

She turned instantly and returned to her desk, wheeling about next to it. The young man entered, slouching slightly, trying to look casual, I thought. There was a wariness about him these days, a ducking attitude like that of a back-alley dog that's taken too many kicks. He'd been like that since Jack's murder. I'd probed him, trying to define his mood, giving him a few verbal belly-shots to see how he'd react. His reaction had been subdued, he'd only growled unintelligibly and gone on with his work. Now he made his way a few steps into the office and stopped, waiting sullenly.

Grace examined him. "I did not want to spoil your weekend by calling you in today, but Kron and I are suddenly summoned to Boston."

Here, now, was a development. Why wasn't she telling him our true destination? And why wasn't he asking for some follow-up, instead of just nodding, as he was doing now, and letting his mouth loosen with something like relief, saying, "I see."

Grace put a finger to her cheek. "We leave early tomorrow, and our mission may take several weeks. We will be completely out of contact, for this is a clandestine operation. You will open the office each day, take messages, but put off any clients who come calling."

She forced a smile. "I know you are a great one for security, so I have locked all the sensitive files."

Again, I wasn't sure what this was all about. But perhaps he knew. His face grew very still, and his eyebrows seemed to prickle with some suppressed tension, his shoulders tightening so that the well-tailored lapels of his suit coat splayed awkwardly. I saw a bit of movement in his sensitive young lips, a stretching of the skin about his ocean-blue eyes, a blushing of blood around his pointed cheekbones, and I supposed for a moment that he was on the point of bursting out with some display of emotion, though I couldn't for the life of me tell why that might occur.

In any case, it did not occur. He stood as he was for a few long moments. Then he made a little shrug, brushed some imaginary lint from one sleeve, shook himself out and smiled, though his eyes never really got into the act.

He said only one word. "Good."

Chapter Nineteen

CARS LESS FORMIDABLE THAN THE four-passenger Oakland Model 43 sedan I was commanding shrank aside as I slammed down the accelerator, geared up and down and pivoted the steering wheel, sweeping expertly down Ninth Avenue. Quite a car, though it harnessed only four cylinders. A highly placed friend of Grace's had lent it to us, and I was a bit surprised that she'd accepted, for she liked to go simple, but I had no such scruples. This chariot had that nice tone of exclusiveness, with its wide doors, silk curtains and built-in dome lights.

And it carried some weight, which I was flinging forward as best I could. To my front, an aging two-cylinder Stanley Steamer quivered out of my way like an enfeebled Rockefeller, a Mercer Raceabout ducked to the curb, a six-year-old Buick "Bug" skittered for safety. We were running late, and I was making up time, my driving foot heavy.

There had been a hang-up at Luisa's apartment—a matter of some female supplies she hadn't packed and had to search for. I'd groused in the corner as Luisa rummaged first in this cabinet, then in that cabinet, finally finding what she needed tucked, in of all places, behind some matchboxes on top of the icebox. Grace took this all in stride, showing only some intensity in the knit of her eyebrows. That seemed odd, for we'd have to push to make the ship's departure, possibly creating a bustle at the on-boarding that we wanted to avoid if possible. The *Calpurnia* sailed at 9 a.m., and by the time Luisa, sweaty-faced, came up with her necessaries and threw them hastily into a carry-bag, we had only twenty minutes to race across town to Pier 54.

I wheeled from Ninth Avenue onto West Fourteenth, the clamor of creaking traffic and the sporadic blatting of car horns echoing off the granite facades of the buildings. To my front, a Hudson Super-Six Speedster slid in front of me, joining itself cheek-by-jowl with a Lexington Minute Man Six touring car. "Christ!" I cursed, feeling a squeezing sensation in the nerves serving the top of my backbone. "The traffic in this city is incredible."

Grace looked over from the passenger seat, and waved a hand, dismissing the matter. Her attitude was serene. "There is no need to take the name of the Lord in vain," she said. "We may need Him before this is over."

Luisa laughed thinly from the back seat, where she was lounging among her bags and cases. "Good luck with that. He's always out when I come calling."

I sighed and tried to ignore the chat. To tell the truth, I was glad that Grace wasn't hectoring me about driving too fast, as she often did. I supposed that, despite her nonchalant approach, she felt that making the ship was her Number One priority. It certainly was mine.

I jerked the Oakland past a street car, whipped onto Twelfth Avenue, and headed toward the tip of the island, with the city rising to the left and the hulks of the ships at anchor looming like white castle walls to the right, luxuriating in the morning sun. Then, once again, the cars in front stuttered to a slow-down, the traffic crept forward, and we crept forward with it. My concentration was all on breaking through it, finding a fender to evade, a slot to zip through. Nothing. We were dragging, hardly able to move. And then, behind me, a motorcycle siren keened and moaned.

I looked back, saw flashing lights and a high-booted police officer triumphantly bearing down on us. "Christ!" I ejaculated again. "Stoker's sent a cop to try to head us off, keep us off the ship. He's tied to this damned Uncle game, and this proves it." I hunched, clutched the wheel firmly, and readied myself. There it was—an opening! A Packard Twin-Six spurted forward, propelled by its powerful V 12 engine, and split a breach in the wall of traffic. I pumped forward on the steep grade, but Grace put a hand on my arm. "Stop," she said. "Perhaps we can dispose of this policeman quickly."

This made no sense. "But we weren't speeding!"

Her look was enough. She didn't have to repeat herself, though I groaned as I slowed and stopped, saving my brake by tapping it in alternation with the reverse pedal and the low-speed pedal. Grace turned to regard the ships as if they were the most important thing in the world as the cop swished up behind, twisting his machine into a flashy stop, then taking his time strolling up to me.

"Fine day," he said, smiling, lifting his goggles from his eyes. He was a self-important little man with sharp eyebrows—Billy Eynon, an officer of no great repute. I was fairly sure he did not know me. He slapped his ticket book on his thigh, looked Luisa over with great interest, noted the hand luggage. Grace was still turned away, apparently leaving this whole embarrassing transaction to me. Eynon cleared his throat. "In a great hurry, are you?"

I ground my teeth. "You're damn right we are."

That jerked his chain. The car had misled him, its richness giving him to believe there'd be soft folks within, a compliant chauffeur, not some red-faced thumper like me. I saw his eyebrows pinch and rise, his lips begin to flatten, his eyes pull back in his head. His jaw jutted. Then something made him think better of his attitude and he rolled his shoulders, lifted one, throwing off the anger. The smile came back, edgily.

His ticket book remained along his right thigh as he began a casual tour of the car. He strolled to its left front forequarter, kicked the hard-rubber tire, ran an eye over the hood. "I suppose it takes a lot of tools to keep a car like this running." An odd remark, I had no idea what was he was getting at. And he followed it with an even odder act, fishing in his pocket, jerking a small card at me. I grabbed it, didn't bother to look, threw it on the floor next to the gas pedal. I'd run out of patience with this badge biker. We had eight minutes to make the ship, and had wasted three on him. "Listen, you silly bastard," I said very clearly. "Give me a ticket or let us go. Whichever you do, do it right now or I'm going to make your weekend the liveliest one you ever saw."

Grace half-turned, gripped my arm to check me, and suddenly the cop caught a view of her profile.

"Mrs. Humiston!" He moved back, threw a hand up, his eyes going all which-a-way. There was shock in his face, dread, puzzlement. And no interest in giving out a ticket, not any more.

I didn't know why he'd reacted that way, but I didn't care. I snorted at him, threw the car into gear, jammed the accelerator. As I winged down the street, I caught one last glance of Eynon in the rearview. Another cycle cop had come up on him and was pitching his arms about, giving Eynon hell. Crazy world. I scarcely noticed as Grace reached down near my feet and retrieved Eynon's card.

Short minutes later, I let Grace and Luisa out of the car around a corner from the pier, made my false goodbyes, whipped the car around, and tooted impatiently through the other arriving traffic. Only now, right at departure, was the clot of people on the pier beginning to break up, as their hand luggage disappeared up the gangplank in the hands of heavily-tipped longshoremen who weren't supposed to get paid for the service at all.

I found parking for the car near a warehouse three blocks away. Out of the back, I snagged a small bag containing a dark raincoat, a peaked hat, and a false beard and dark glasses—an amateurish disguise, but good enough to get me on board. I did the quick-change and ran, huffing heavily. I rushed the few blocks back to the ship in world-class time, then slowed to make a more-or-less dignified entrance with the last of the passengers. We stumbled across a handrail-equipped gangplank dazzlingly lit from above by sun-flashes, dizzily poised over gurgling water below. Its sucking waves flipped and jerked with flotsam —scraps of wood, straw from barges, bottles, boxes, paper.

On we went, treading on a huge, bristly doormat as we passed through the ship's shell plating into the paneled interior, glowing with electric light. The master-at-arms gave me a sharp look, I thought, but perhaps that was only my imagination. Certainly, I got no special once-over from the heavily starched, brass-buttoned stewards and bellboys. They were bubbling, practically elbowing each other at the prospect of a voyage filled with tips.

I didn't waste time loitering about. No reason to give Ricardo or Uncle Carlos a chance to spot me in my thinly laid-on personality. Instead, I made straight for my stateroom, thrusting myself through passageways, jostling with passengers and drunken visitors. Once in the cabin, I sagged, threw my bag on my bed, huffed out a few ragged breaths. Then I relaxed, composed myself. What with all my frantic haste, I'd made it with still a few minutes before departure. I looked about, inhaled deeply. This was my first ocean voyage since the smelly, claustrophobic trip I'd endured as a kid with my parents, and I spent a few moments marveling at the difference between steerage, where we'd had our quarters then, and this first-class stateroom.

Here there were no bunks laid out in long, anonymous rows for a vast, odorous lot of poor immigrants. Here was a real four-poster bed, real chairs, a bureau, a vanity, a writing table—all in French Provincial style, set off nicely against the oak-paneled walls and the purple carpet imprinted with a pattern of fleur-de-lis. The room was detailed like the interior of a fine watch, with an eye for practical comfort and efficiency at sea. The bureau top and shelves had protective rims to keep items from sliding off. The cabin and closet doors could be secured in an open position with little hooks. A thermos and accompanying glass perched invitingly in wall-hung brackets. The bathroom door had a two-inch sill to prevent water from inside from slopping on the carpet.

I stepped to the porthole and opened it, narrowly avoiding crunching my thumb when the heavy brass window pivoted suddenly as the ship dipped slightly at anchor. The smell of the sea, pungent and yeasty, reached my nostrils, a breeze touched my cheek. Suddenly, my heart thumped and raced. Moments of luxury, even of striking variety, were rare in my life. I sighed. For years I'd kept my head down, on the track of this criminal or that, pursuing this or that scrap of evidence. A beer, a ball game, an occasional turn with a fancy lady—that was the only kind of break I'd taken. Ah, well. I snapped the porthole shut to cut off the temptation of the ocean air, and went to work.

From the steamer trunk that had previously been delivered to my cabin, I selected several bottles of make-up and hair coloring, a suit of a finer and more regal cut than I normally wore, tawny kid gloves and shoes of rich leather.

I laid this finery on the bed, then entered the bathroom and stood at the marble wash basin, bracing myself against the slight cant of the floor. Swiftly, I put down a base on my hands, neck and head, then buried my fish-belly winter face under a fine, false tan, taking care to push the greasy coating fully up into my hair and down below my collar line. My hair was very black—a good thing, because the blond coloring with which I was now dousing it would provide a sharp contrast to my usual look.

Completing my skin and hair work, I stepped back into the bedroom, dressed quickly in my new outfit, and added a monocle to the disguise. Then, for just a moment, I regarded myself in the wall mirror—seeing myself simply as Kron with blond hair, ritzy clothes, a tan, a monocle. None of this meant anything in disguise terms without the final ingredient—the style.

In the mirror, I swelled my chest, contorted my face into an uncommon state of jollity, dropped my right shoulder into the stiff posture in which one holds a body part weakened by an old injury. From the mirror, Count Raflasky looked out, a blowsy bluffer of a fake nobleman—coarse, aging, a man uneasy about his health and wary of the threat of prison. Indeed, he looked out with the tightening of the mouth associated with barely concealed fear, for somewhere in his mind, he knew the cabin had shortly before been occupied by a detective. The shattering blast of the ship's whistle vibrated the stateroom's walls—the signal for all visitors still on board to depart. Count Raflasky sighed deeply. This was it, then. A few moments more, and *Calpurnia* would be under way.

The sound of the whistle. I supposed that it had reached Grace in her own cabin, found her in the state she typically assumed at such a point in an investigation. She could have been tucking her clothes away, gazing out a porthole as I had done, doing many things. But I pictured her sitting before her cherrywood vanity, staring into the glass, combing her hair and thinking. In such a situation, she was a great one for meditation, for composing her mind in Zen terms—she had a feeling for the Zen writings, sometimes recommended them to me. She'd be thinking this, I knew: that all the players were in place, the drama laid out in rough terms, the playing field restricted, that you never got it quite as restricted as this.

I seemed to be with her, thinking with her. A slight worry tugged at her serenity—an instinctive worry. Despite her diamond mind, her sharp-edged logic, her grasp of a murder hunt came mostly from her belly. Life is a messy business, she knew—death by violence, moreso. She'd plotted precisely, placed her agents with great forethought. But that meant events had to be predictable, that she was vulnerable to things unforeseen. Yes, the unforeseen could undo her. And what of Howard's announcement? She hadn't foreseen that, and the not seeing had sharpened the pain. She must put that aside, somehow. She must not fail. She had a gift. If she could not be true to her husband, she must be true to the gift.

Her comb stroked smoothly through her hair, stroked, stroked again. In her mind, she allowed the edges of her sharply cut plan to blur, to feather. It was a Zen technique. To focus on all, focus on nothing—to understand all, allow all understanding to come to you. She relaxed, feeling her body rippling with peace. Now, let it all come: violence, chaos, despair—triumph or failure. Now, all was on the hazard.

And so it was with Luisa, as I was to learn later, though all she was doing in her own cabin was trying on an evening gown to distract herself—allowing the silk to drift, accentuating her high, full breasts with a topping of lace that dipped low enough to show off the sleekness of her shoulders. She examined the dress in her mirror. She examined her beauty—the delicacy of her eye shadow, the precision of her lipstick, the strong bones of her cheeks. It was a ritual that usually lent her comfort. But now, in these oddly empty moments, there was no comfort. Her belly clenched, she was afraid, she bit her lip. Panic tensed her fingers and made her ears tingle and buzz. She had played many roles in order to survive, but this would have to be the performance of her life, for the critics would not be indulgent.

She knew that Grace had strict standards.

And so did Stoker McCullagh.

Chapter Twenty

ON THE *CALPURNIA*, AS ON other liners, a passenger might be granted a seat at the captain's table, but he or she could never ask for one. Those who dined with the captain were selected only after painstaking research by the purser, who often interviewed officials of his company as well as other pursers of the line. There was good reason for this. The egos of the first-class passengers often had collided on shore because of imagined sharp practice in business, social slights, differences over women. Part of the purser's job was to head off such collisions on board, for they were embarrassing and bad for business.

Despite these considerations and her late booking, I suspect that Grace Humiston was passed quickly and efficiently—even a bit eagerly —through the purser's screening process. She had enemies, yes, but her well-known charm tended to smooth confrontations, her wit to enliven them, and her fame to make them seem worthwhile even to those among her dining companions who disagreed with her.

If the truth be told, the purser might have been willing to risk a bit of conflict to push a highly-publicized detective like Grace Humiston to the fore. Luminaries were not nearly as much in evidence on the Latin American leg of the routes of the British Bright Star Line as they were on the New York—Southampton run. Despite this, the cash-insulated travelers on the formidable *Calpurnia* (nearly 900 feet long, encompassing 45,000 tons of luxury) still expected to share the dining rooms and promenades with pulse-quickening celebrities.

So it was no real surprise to me that at 7:34 p.m. on the first night of the voyage, Grace was responding to a special invitation as she descended to the first-class dining saloon on a paneled oak staircase adorned with filigree ironwork, lighted by electric globes held aloft by brass cherubs, and detailed—on its railings and newel posts—with carved flowers, leaves and berries. As she entered the saloon and made her way to her assigned place at the captain's table, a wealthy land speculator from Georgia leaped up to hold her chair.

She stood for a moment as Captain John Wheelwright greeted her lavishly. Eyes around the table rested on her with delight or envious speculation as she settled into her chair (Jacobean in style, upholstered in green leather), then watched as the mid-calf hemline of her loose, straight tonneau-style dress rose just a little, fully exposing her finely-turned ankles. Among those watching eyes were my own, because Count Raflasky's reputation had also survived the purser's scrutiny.

At a nearby table, Ricardo Alvarez sat, and I noted his reaction to Grace, his eyes roving for a moment from the lovely faces of Miss Jane Pilkington and Luisa Clary, homing in on Grace's ankles. His appreciative gaze traveled upwards, tracing Grace's shapely outline, and ran hard aground against her face. His jaw dropped, baring his chisel-like teeth, and his eyes widened, showing slices of white above and below the iris. She looked back at him for an instant with purely professional interest—an entomologist examining a beetle—then turned and smiled at some complimentary remark from the captain. As she did so, Ricardo shot her a malicious look. Uncle Carlos, who sat next to him, half-raised a hand as if to forestall Ricardo's open display of emotion, then let his fingers fall, looking desolate. Poor Uncle Carlos—for once, he didn't have his lascar monkey for companionship, and his human companion was acting badly.

I took all this in with satisfaction, masking my interest by focusing my bogus Continental charm on Miss Susie Bladderworth, an indifferently-styled young lady with formidable buck teeth. Her mother, a shoe manufacturer's wife from Dubuque, Iowa, was glowing at the prospect of a titled son-in-law. No doubt she thought I would add luster to her husband's new line of brogans, a style known as the Shopworker's Special.

Still, I remained keenly alert to the action around Grace, hearing the initial small talk wane as the diners dipped their soup spoons into the Consommé Olga. Captain Wheelwright, too, noted the break in conversation and took advantage of it. He huffed pridefully, sent a glowing look her way, voiced what was on everyone's mind.

"If it wouldn't be an intrusion," he ventured, "I'd like to know about your current investigation."

Grace looked about at the glistening shirt fronts and at the gowns with their fashionable V-cut necks—above which several rather slack bosoms shivered with excitement at the prospect of what she was about to say—and smiled with self-deprecation. "My current investigation is at a standstill," she murmured. "I have been blocked in my efforts to find a missing person—a young girl named Ruth Cruger."

The Georgia speculator leaned over his soup bowl, his courtly attitude contrasting with his display of nose-hair, and a wise look came into his eyes. "Disappeared, eh? And in what direction? Is it possible this Cruger gal may have wandered as far as Argentina?"

"Entirely possible. In fact, she may have booked on a liner such as this one—under a false name, of course."

The delights of the Consommé Olga could not match the deliciousness of this piece of news. Soupspoons froze in mid-air, breaths were sharply expelled, exclamations burst from the diners.

A concerned frown clenched Captain Wheelwright's brow. "I have not followed the case in the American newspapers," he said. "But I would like to help if I can. Do you have a photograph of Miss Cruger?"

Grace looked around the table. "I have one in my purse, but I would be sorry to disturb everyone's dinner by producing it."

Murmurs greeted this sally. "Oh, please go ahead!" "By all means!" "Anything for this poor girl!"

Grace hesitated a second longer, then drew out the gilt-framed photo and passed it to Captain Wheelwright. He took it with suppressed eagerness and examined it closely and at length, tapping his chin with one massive fist.

Wheelwright passed the photo to his left, delivering it into the hands of the Georgia speculator, who scanned it, then shook his head dismissively. "No, she's not the one."

Grace caught something in this. "Not what one?"

"I took this run eight months ago," the man explained. "A gal went over the side. Thought it might have been her. But, nope. Different gal."

Grace lifted an eyebrow. "A suicide?"

"Wouldn't think so. No, wouldn't think so. Big pool of blood, spots all around, like that blood was thrown a distance. Not near the rail, neither. Why, you mind that, don't you, cap'n? You should mind that. You handled it."

Among the table's occupants, a sensation! Chairs shifted on the Royal Purple carpet, feminine hands fluttered over palpitating breasts, polite masculine oaths burst forth. Hardly-touched bowls of Consommé Olga were whisked away by chagrined stewards.

The captain's face—ruddy and British, landscaped with a clipped gray beard and mustache—grew sad and distant. "Yes, I did. A terrible affair." Terrible for him, and terrible for the shipping line, I was sure. His face showed more than one kind of unhappiness.

Grace pressed him. "Her name?"

He spoke heavily, but he was in now, and couldn't see any way of getting out. "She was traveling under the name Julia Grant, but I have to assume that was not her true identity."

"And why is that?"

He sighed. "Because, as far as I know, the company has had no contact with her relatives."

I knew Grace's instinct was to wait until she got the captain alone to ask for details. Even so, she cast a sidelong glance at Ricardo and Uncle Carlos—just out of earshot, but startled by the obvious

156

commotion around Grace—and apparently decided this piece of theater would serve her well.

She said coolly: "I saw no report of this young woman's death in the New York newspapers."

Captain Wheelwright caught the implication of the words—the accusation of a cover-up—and stiffened.

He looked around the table, hoping for a distraction. As if on cue, stewards hurried forward bearing plates of Filet Mignons Lili, Sauté of Chicken Lyonnaise, Vegetable Marrow Farcie. Not one of the diners seemed interested.

Wheelwright shrugged ponderously and plunged ahead. "I made a full report to the company. I assumed they would try to publicize the affair to reach relatives of the victim. Perhaps, for legal reasons, they allowed the police to handle the notification and the matter was bungled."

Grace's eyes were keen. "Are the features of Julia Grant firmly fixed in your mind?"

The captain seemed genuinely sad now. "They are. She was a beauty, with fine manners that were remarked upon by many of my young officers. She did not sit at my table, however. The purser could find nothing definite about her background. And she was traveling alone, though she never wanted for company."

Grace repaired to her purse, brought forth another photo, passed it to Wheelwright. "And is this Julia Grant?"

The captain's eyes fell to the image, grew troubled.

"It is."

He drew a long breath. "And who is this lady, her real name?"

"Amelia Karcher," said Grace, "A young woman of substance. She left a grieving mother on Long Island."

Her look drifted to Ricardo Alvarez and, though he could not hear her words, he grew rigid.

Grace turned once again to the captain. "Amelia Karcher's mother has heard nothing of her fate," Grace said. "It makes me wonder whether correct procedures were followed."

"Certainly, they were!" the captain replied. "I notified the Bueños Aires police. They came on board and conducted an investigation. And they were in communication with the New York police."

The Georgia speculator rapped the table with a knuckle. "Proved it was that deck steward, I bet!" He reached for the photo with a proprietary air.

"They proved no such thing!" the captain said.

The Georgia man was examining the photo and nodding. Grace looked from one to the other of them.

"What deck steward?"

"Anderson," the captain said unhappily. "His name was Anderson —an American."

"And why was he suspected?"

The captain looked as if he was very sorry, indeed, that the Georgia speculator had been invited to his table. Tomorrow the purser would get a good talking-to. Now, however, there was no going back. The captain was dealing with Grace Humiston, after all. What he didn't admit, she would learn. He took in a great breath and released it. "Because he disappeared the same night as did Miss Karcher. His knife was found near that great smear of blood up on the boat deck. And the other stewards had heard him saying Miss Karcher was the sort of young woman he would like to. . ." Captain Wheelwright blushed, but hastily added, ". . .pay attention to."

Grace leaned forward. "And the New York police supported that theory?"

"Well, yes. Or so the Bueños Aires officials said."

"And just what did the New York police say about Anderson?"

In for a penny, in for a pound. "That he had a history of that sort of thing."

"What sort of thing?"

"Paying unwelcome attentions to young women."

Grace brushed aside the euphemism.

"Sexual assaults?"

Several women at the table gasped. Captain Wheelwright

reddened.

"Mrs. Humiston—!"

"Well?"

He bit off the word. "Yes."

The photo passed from hand to hand. "Deliver it over to those two, for sure," the Georgia man instructed, peering at a nearby table. "They was on that trip. Yes, they was."

He jerked his chin at the two men he meant, and both braced up. Uncle Carlos. And his young companion.

CHAPTER TWENTY-ONE

PROMPTLY AT 10 A.M. ON the second day of the voyage, Grace marched briskly from the officers' quarters to a spot on the first class promenade a few feet from Lifeboat No. 8, knelt on one knee, and began an intense examination of the scene of Amelia Karcher's murder.

I'd mingled with the fascinated crowd of passengers watching her performance, though I was admiring it from a different perspective. She had enlisted a helpmate for her mission, and he was appropriate for it—a bewildered but entranced young man, Fourth Officer Archie Kirk, a red-haired native of Glasgow. Fourth Officer Kirk carried in his arms an unwieldy array of rolled-up drawings that, it became obvious from Grace's gestures, movements and clipped orders, diagrammed a scene that in physical reality had long since given way to the cleaning mops and varnish brushes of the crew.

The drawings were the brainchildren of Captain Wheelwright, who had put his British sense of order to work in preserving the details of the crime, the better to make a report to the Buenos Aires police. Grace had wormed them out of him, and now she moved swiftly and certainly, noting—as she told me later—just where the blood had pooled and smeared, where the steward's knife had fallen, where Amelia Karcher's torn undergarments had been cast aside.

She made this a full production, stepping off distances, checking possible witness vantage-points, acting out the incident. And she did this in a preoccupied fashion, ignoring the passengers who had interrupted their shuffleboard games, their brisk walks on the promenade and their deck tennis games to stand sniffing the shipboard air—flavored with the odors of salt, tar, and bilges—and trading low-voiced, thrilled comments as they watched her work.

As interested as I was, there were two other spectators whose interest exceeded mine. And I was about to reel them in. Preening in my morning suit, I moved through the crush as if to gain a better view. Directly in my path were Ricardo, looking whey-faced but nasty, as if he'd spent the night fighting a bottle of whiskey to a draw, and Uncle Carlos, fingering a diamond stick-pin on his vest, watching Grace with rabbity eyes. As Count Raflasky, I focused on Carlos. Clumsily, I blundered into him, turned away with a muttered apology. Then, as Grace turned suddenly, I threw a hand to my monocle, adjusted it, and —as if speaking to myself—emitted one sharp, whispered expletive: "Bitch!" Then I wheeled and pushed off in the direction of the gymnasium.

The ploy was raw, but that was all right. In this business, you have to know your man, and I was sure that—even on short acquaintance— I knew mine. I didn't look back, but I didn't need to. It was all there in Uncle Carlos' face. Despite the fact that he had a traveling companion right next to him, he looked like a man in desperate need of a friend.

It's curious how one can delay exercise for just so long before feeling a powerful need for it. So it was with Uncle Carlos, who looked like he hadn't worked out in decades. Some ten minutes after I'd departed the Humiston watch for the gymnasium, Uncle Carlos pushed through the door after me. He found me, coatless, grudgingly pumping away at the stirrups of a mechanical horse.

We had the gym to ourselves—no shadow boxers, rowing-machine pullers, Indian club hefters, weightlifters. The normal exercisers, apparently, were off watching Grace.

That left us abnormal types. And, for a health enthusiast, Uncle Carlos truly was abnormal—body loose as putty, attitude timid. movements flabby. Gingerly, he tugged at the hand grips on a weighted pulley, made no headway. He smiled sheepishly at me. Hmmph. I sniffed in a hostile Continental fashion, looked elsewhere. But I watched him out of the corner of my eye, leaning on the weights, hardly pretending to work.

Twice, he tried to catch my eye, failed. At last, he grew desperate and shammed a fall, crashing to the floor. I turned my head languidly. He was groaning, clutching a knee, looking for sympathy. So I gave him some, in a heavy Eastern European accent. "You're damned clumsy, you know."

He rose haltingly, gritting his teeth. Apparently, he'd gotten some real bruises. "Sorry," he said. "Such a big noise, such a commotion. This is not the sort of thing I'm used to."

"As the Americans put it, 'You can say that again.'"

"You are not American, then?"

"Rumanian."

Uncle Carlos considered. "Rumanian," he said. "Yes, you have that mid-European manner about you—very delicate, very refined. I much admire it, coming as I do from Argentina, a country with a shorter history of culture. My name is Carlos De Souza."

I shot him a look of contempt, which was real enough, cocked my nose in the air, said briskly, "Count Raflasky."

This took a few moments to register, but register it did. His cow-like face began to form sharp lines of remembrance like a slip of photo paper in developing fluid. At last the image came clear. Uncle Carlos laughed, slapping a thigh so hard he hurt himself and groaned. Recovering, he said, "You old fraud!"

I recoiled at this, getting some lift into my eyebrows, but said nothing. Uncle Carlos abandoned the pulley weights, walked up to me, examined my face. "Raflasky. Of course. I've heard of you for years. It was only a matter of time before our paths crossed."

When I didn't immediately reply, Uncle Carlos grew impatient. "Come, now," he said. "We pursue the same enterprise. I am the Latin American branch of the business and you are the European. You prevail upon rich young American women, take them off to the

Continent for stripping, and I do the same, using my own country as a destination."

For a few moments more, I kept my face empty. Then, at last, I allowed myself to look unhappy but resigned. I glanced carefully around the gymnasium. "So, all right!" I said. "You don't need to send it out for radio broadcast. And I'd appreciate a bit of discretion, since I have a mark in hand."

Uncle Carlos scratched his chin. He sighed, and his eyes grew sly. "One thing surprises me. You are off your rounds, working this part of the world."

I nodded with irritation. "It is the god-damned war. Hundreds of thousands of men are stumbling to their deaths, cities are blowing to the skies, and shipping is being sunk daily. Horrible! One grifter of my acquaintance and two confidence artists went down with the *Lusitania*."

Uncle Carlos's face grew cunning. "I am surprised that violence shocks you. Among confidence practitioners, you are said to indulge in it yourself."

Oh, yes! He was getting to the point, and more swiftly than I could have prayed for. But I had to play him carefully. I screwed my forehead into a great boil of anger, stiffened my jaw, made my eyes hard. Emitting a harsh curse of a breath, I shifted my weight and began to dismount my mechanical beast. Uncle Carlos threw up a hand, spoke hastily. "Please do not take offense. I mention it only in the way of business."

Even as I was progressing, Grace was making headway in unraveling the mystery of Amelia Karcher's demise, which I had concluded was closely linked to the disappearance of Ruth Cruger. For her efforts, Grace had chosen a more pleasant playing field than the sweaty gymnasium. In the Cafe Parisienne on the starboard side of B deck, she was lounging in a green wicker chair and enjoying a cup of tea and a croissant with Fourth Officer Kirk, who, though quite nervous, was thoroughly enjoying her company.

Grace dipped butter from an iced dish, and—with a deft turn of her knife—coated a broken segment of her roll and laid it down. Telling me about it later, she said she felt somewhat embarrassed, because Fourth Officer Kirk reacted to this mundane act with the awe of a ballet aficionado seeing Nijinsky perform a pirouette. But he managed to force his attention away from her beauty, toward her business, and asked, "D'you think it was the steward, then?"

Grace smiled gloriously at him. "I think it unlikely," she said. "Miss Karcher was attacked in an open area with avenues of escape in both directions. And she was young and athletic—the captain remarked on her skill at deck tennis. Even so, she was killed where she stood. That argues the presence of two attackers—one who held her, one who used the knife."

Grace took some tea. "Furthermore, there was no blood smear between the attack spot and the side of the ship, according to your captain's report. That smear would have been there if one man dragged her, but not if two carried her."

Archie Kirk worried his chin with a doubtful knuckle

"Perhaps the steward had help."

Delicately, Grace munched a bite of buttered roll, her head tilted in thought. "Perhaps, but I believe not. I believe he was pursuing Miss Karcher with impure intentions, came upon the attack, and was disposed of. These are only suppositions, of course, in the absence of hard evidence. I would dearly love to have some hard evidence." Grace looked at him. "Tell me, did no-one hear a commotion that night?"

"They all said no."

Grace savored another bite. "Were passengers who socialized with Miss Karcher questioned closely?"

Kirk shrugged. "Hardly, not after the first flurry to find her. The interrogation was left to the police in Bueños Aires."

"Did those two men, Mr. Alvarez, and Mr. De Souza, socialize with her?"

"Yes, regularly. They seemed to befriend her immediately we embarked."

"And did the police interrogate them?"

"I dinna' think so." He paused. "A detective came on board and looked at the blood, but not for long." Kirk looked into the middle distance, trying to recall detail. "He smiled, oh, a great deal, and smoked a black cigar."

Grace took a long drink of tea. "And what makes you think he did not question them?"

Archie Kirk blushed like a man worried he'd said something wrong. "Oh, he took them in a room, all right," he said hurriedly. Kirk nodded twice, quickly. "I was their escort."

Grace smiled once again, winningly. "And did you go into the room with them?"

Kirk looked everywhere but at Grace. "Nooo. But I stood outside the door."

Silence fell, briefly, until Grace prompted him. "And, standing outside the door, you heard something."

A pause. "Yes."

Grace smiled again, and turned one very elegant hand face up on the wicker table. I'm sure Archie Kirk found the gesture attractive, and that pushed him toward a final admission. "What did you hear?"

Kirk wet his lips. Grace lifted her chin just a little, and that is very attractive, too. He gulped, looked at his hands, whispered a single word.

"Laughter."

After dinner, Uncle Carlos drew me away from the crowd in the men's smoking room, offered me a cigar. I took it, lit up. He was jabbering at me, but I ignored him. Instead I peered through my monocle at the Georgian furnishings, the oil paintings, the mother-of-pearl inlay work in the walls, the stained-glass windows. But the man wouldn't let me go. He pawed my arm, continued to patter.

"—Mrs. Humiston. You were surprised to see her here, too, I know. Yes, it's very unusual, very unpleasant. A damned nuisance, her being in the way, with the business you and I might be doing. Running about the deck, worrying about this dead woman. It gets the passengers upset, it gets. . . it gets me upset. I, too, have reason to, ah, be wary of the lady."

His tongue was flapping so loosely it endangered the glassware. Some of the other swells were starting to notice, had even left off harrumphing nonsense about President Wilson and what he should be doing, war-wise. With bad grace, I drew my attention back from a particularly fine oil, dropped my voice and demanded, "What the Devil are you talking about?"

Uncle Carlos looked down, sucked dolefully on his cigar. "I was saying that I, too, have had my difficulties with Mrs. Humiston."

I looked at him as if he'd admitted doing something unpleasant in his pants. Then I blew a gust from my cigar, swiveled my head away.

Up to this point, he had been playing the whipped dog, mealy-mouthing around, looking put-upon, sweating. But that act wasn't all of him. Bringing out his other side just took a little encouragement—my insults, my abruptness. I glanced at him. His fists were subtly clenching, his temples overheating. He frothed and reddened, tongue slashing at his lips. Then, here it came! Uncle Carlos snatched my arm, his fingers biting in, and his overly sauced breath was at my ear, pulsing hot and quick.

"Now listen to me, you overgrown bastard," he hissed. "I know you have something against Mrs. Humiston, because you called her a bitch this morning, and if you have something against her, she has something against you. Well, she is onto me, too, I know it. We both have a problem, and we had better deal with it or she will sink us both!"

I looked at him blankly, but my heart was thumping. All this, and so quickly. It showed how brilliant we'd been in choosing Count Raflasky as a cover. And it showed something else—the depths of the man's desperation.

I took a long drag at my cigar, said, in a very business-like way, "Oh, yes?" Then I paused, I considered, watching Uncle Carlos' face twitch and jump. I took another puff. At last, just when he appeared on the brink of cardiac arrest, I heaved a breath. "Well, perhaps you are right," I said. "What do you suggest?"

CHAPTER TWENTY-TWO

THE MORNING WIND OFF THE water blew briskly on my cheeks as I paraded back and forth on the promenade deck, and the bruise-blue waves marched with a heavy sweep. As I always did when near the sea, I sniffed the air, trying to smell the salt. Once again, my suspicion was confirmed: The sea air has no savor of salt—at least no fresh, clean salt—despite what the writers say. Sometimes the sea smells like yeast, often like wet fur, sometimes—in fact—like pickle juice. But there's no romance in pickle juice. The writers know that, so they fudge it up. They know their business as well as I know mine.

"They have engaged me to kill you."

I said the words while barely moving my lips, cocking my cigar in one hand, brushing back my tight blond hair with the other, noting the sudden, white explosions of fish leaping upward from the deep.

Grace took no note of me. In fact, to any observer, we could have been in different worlds, though we were only a few feet apart. She had paused near me, as if by chance, to re-tie the hair-bow of a six-year-old girl who had wandered away from her mother. Grace clucked amusingly at the girl, spoke without looking at me.

"Excellent. Did both approach you?"

"Just De Souza."

Grace tickled the little girl and made a mischievous face at her, causing her to giggle and jig her arms about.

"You must draw them both into the act. It is the only way."

169

"It won't be easy."

"You must do it."

"What about the Karcher murder investigation?" I adjusted my monocle, shook my cigar-ash over the side and watched it float away in a snatch of breeze.

"Bungled and covered up."

The little girl turned and ran, laughing, back to her mother. Grace rose, smoothed her skirt, slid gracefully away, leaving behind her final instruction.

"Kill me well."

Uncle Carlos was nerved up and so was Ricardo Alvarez. I found that out when I braced them two hours later in the passage outside Jane Pilkington's stateroom. They instantly drew me inside for a palaver. It was a swank place—Louis XVI in style, the wallpaper enriched with fleur-de-lis, figured ceiling-plaster, a crystalline light fixture, a bed set off by curtains of deep purple satin. I noted an oak-paneled door that appeared to lead to a dressing room, and I had a thought—

But my partners in crime were too careless to search every nook and cranny. Ricardo flung himself on the bed with a proprietary air, and I wondered if he had had occasion to visit the room for indecent purposes. Luisa—the close consort of Miss Pilkington—could no doubt have told me about that, had she known I was aboard. I'd played with the thought of approaching her as Raflasky. I might have gotten to know her better, assuming I wanted to know her better, considering she was so tough at the center. If she'd just been a bit softer— Not likely, though, for she was a woman who'd lived roughly. You have to be careful with such women.

At any rate, she'd done what we'd hired her for, moving in close to our marks. I looked about the room for some sign she'd spent time here—a scarf I recognized, a purse, perhaps—but I saw nothing. I was paying a great deal more attention to my surroundings than was Uncle Carlos, who drifted dolefully until he bumped up against a bentwood mahogany chair and, abruptly, sat.

"So, why is this necessary?" he said. "Why do we meet, why are we put at risk?" He tapped his cane on the toe of his polished, Spanish-leather boot. "We have agreed, the proposition is completed, why are you harassing us?"

I didn't answer right away. Instead, I examined Ricardo, noting his supple muscles, the razor-edge of his features, his dark eyes bright with aggression. He wasn't easy to plumb. He could have been the knife-man who had dealt with Grace on that dark, rainy street, he could have been the one who did the slash-work on Amelia Karcher right here on this ship. But that was by no means certain. The Uncle, for all his gloomy facade, for all his signs of age and weakness, could be the blade-master himself. One could never be sure about such things in the absence of evidence. But I was soon to get a clue.

I made a face, answered Uncle Carlos. "This is not harassment, simply caution. The Humiston woman recognizes me, I'm sure of it. That will make things much more difficult." I moved, swept a hand at the air, overdoing it in the grand style. "She did me an injury in the past, but that has been long past, we had little personal contact, and I had hoped she'd forgotten. Today I passed her on the promenade deck. She pretended not to recognize me, but I saw that evil spark in her eyes."

Ricardo spoke from the bed, his voice like static. "You are engaged to remove that spark from her eyes. De Souza says you are a professional, though I am beginning to have my doubts. What is the problem?"

I blew out my cheeks, acting brusque. "You must at least help me, you must carry out the set-up. On my own, she'll never let me get close to her in a dark passageway."

Ricardo released a contemptuous hiss. "You are wetting your pants, you are old, you are sweating. I knew this was a mistake. I will gut her myself!"

So that was the way it was. It wasn't for want of a killer that the Uncle had hired me. It was to protect his personal killer, who found knife work a bit too tasty, who was likely to throw caution to the winds.

The Uncle's shocked whine parried Ricardo's rashness. "No! You agreed, Raflasky. It is your job and yours alone."

I knew exactly what he was thinking. They couldn't kill Grace on the ship themselves without exposing themselves unduly, without raising new and nasty questions about their possible connection to the murder of Amelia Karcher. Grace was a celebrated detective, there'd be no hushing up her murder, no hiding the nature of her final investigation. I moved my chin, tossed my head. "My job? So, I decline. I am a professional. I decline."

The Uncle's voice rose almost to a shriek. "You are so hasty, so hasty!"

I made my face like a stone, waiting. His lips and eyebrows were going every way possible and several times he made as if to speak, but didn't. Ricardo watched, his mouth tucked-in and sour. After a few moments, Uncle Carlos at last threw up a hand, spoke wearily. "All right, all right. We will watch her. We will track her. We will guard her stateroom when you go in. But that is all."

Excellent. An excellent start. I made a rumbling in my throat, let my eyes cloud. Then, distinctly, I said, "More money. I want more money."

"More money! We have offered you a thousand dollars!" The Uncle sighed deeply, the air coming out of him like wind from a squeezed bellows, his sunken chest going in and out. He paced about for a few moments, shaking his head. Then, without looking at me, he flicked a hand at the air. "All right. All right. More money."

"Double terms."

He cast a furtive glance at me, and now his reply was resigned, but quick. "Yes. All right."

"Very well then."

I smiled, took three steps to the stateroom door, pushed my way out. Out here the air was fresher and cleaner than I'd ever known it. I was pretty certain, though, that my departure didn't end the talk of killing. They didn't intend to stop after bagging Grace. My demand for an increased fee had ensured that. They intended to take her out, lay the blame on me, then bisect my own gizzard with a dagger. At least, that was the way I saw it. Ricardo seemed to like that kind of work. I couldn't see him backing off it.

I wondered what Luisa Clary thought about that, about the impending demise of Count Raflasky. By now, I figured, she knew about it. For she had indeed left something behind in the stateroom, and I'd just decided what it was. She must have left it there just before we entered, only seconds before, when she'd heard our voices outside and hopped into that dressing room so she could hear everything we said. I sniffed the sea air again, just as I'd sniffed out her presence in the room. The clue to Luisa was attar of roses, the perfume she always wore, her signature scent.

CHAPTER TWENTY-THREE

LATER, I REPROACHED MYSELF FOR not taking the lead in planning Grace's murder, for my failure to do so cost a life. It wasn't that I didn't have a plan in mind. I did. And I could have laid it out right away, during the war council in Miss Pilkington's stateroom. But I'd hesitated. Ricardo and Uncle Carlos were boiling for blood, and it would have been difficult right then to cool them down, to convince them to wait. That was my aim, though: Stall for days, squeeze them for details as to how and where they'd done away with Ruth Cruger, pass the information to Grace, await orders.

Of course, I needed a strong argument in favor of waiting. And I took my time working it out that afternoon, as I lounged snugly under a steamer rug on a curving wooden deck chair, sipping at a steaming mug of tea to fight off the chill of the sea-breeze, pretending to listen to Miss Susie Bladderworth's descriptions of the joys of Dubuque, cutting quite a figure in my loose-fitting English tweeds. That kind of sturdy outer garb was needed on deck to ward off the weather, even though it absorbed the smell of tar, and I'd have stood out from my fellow passengers without it.

While I exhibited excellent sartorial style, I had an opportunity to focus on the players in our drama. Uncle Carlos, Ricardo, Luisa and Miss Jane Pilkington made a foursome on deck chairs not far from me, and Grace several times passed us by, occasionally alone, sometimes with her new found lap-dog, Fourth Officer Archie Kirk. It appeared she was deliberately provoking our Argentinean assassins. Because of my timetable, that worried me, for it might push them to hurry things. Nevertheless, I determined to play a waiting game, until she counseled me to go another way.

Stalling made sense not only for my personal plans, but for the confidence man I was pretending to be. Raflasky would want to wait to carry out the bloody deed until very late in the voyage, perhaps right on the point of debarkation, so as to take advantage of the confusion and bustle churned up by the departing passengers. I could make a convincing argument to my two bloody friends that this should suit them, too, for it would cut short the period during which suspicion about Grace's murder would attach to them. And some suspicion would fall on them. After all, the crew had noted the close association of Ricardo and Uncle Carlos with the Karcher murder. And their corrupt dealings with the Bueños Aires police might not be enough to save them this time.

Of course, there was a counter-argument. Given time on the voyage, Grace might pin them to the Karcher killing. From her brief message, I felt her prospects were bleak, but they would not know that. They feared her reputation, they imputed special powers to her, they were worried. At least, Uncle Carlos was worried. Ricardo seemed to savor butchering women, seemed to be driven. And from his attitude toward me, I gathered he wouldn't mind spiking my ears to the wall of his stateroom, either. He'd want Grace splashed early enough in the voyage to ensure he had time to do that.

It was complicated, that was certain. And something else was complicated, too—Luisa's attitude. She seemed overly anxious for someone so experienced in the confidence game. Whenever Grace passed her, she kept her gaze downward, as if afraid she would lock eyes with Grace. Of course, that could have meant simply that she feared being found out, but it seemed to be more than that. She was in conflict, feeling guilty.

Later in the day, after a robust luncheon in the skylighted social room, I broke away from the Bladderworths long enough to take a reconnaissance around the deck, roaming fore and aft, feeling the vibrating roar of the engines, sampling the mood of the passengers. Did they have any sense of the deadly game being played out among them? They had none. Except for two ten-year-old boys re-enacting the murder of Amelia Karcher with dramatic whispers and flurries of play-acted violence, the passengers seemed to have lost interest in Grace's investigation. They had turned to more usual, less gloomy pursuits. Cries of laughter mixed with good-natured groans as they competed at miniature golf, engaged in tugs of war, and took part in biscuit-and-whistle races, in which the players gobbled a mouthful of dry biscuits, then strove to be the first to whistle a popular tune through the saliva-sodden mess.

In contrast to the other passengers, my attention was never long away from violence and the prospect of it, never long away from Ricardo and his Uncle. They appeared quiet, but edgy, and the young man's fiercely suppressed energy at last burst forth. At mid-afternoon, Ricardo suddenly leapt up, threw off his suit coat, and joined a novel footrace—twice around the circumference of the boat deck at the top of the ship, down a long canvas chute to the promenade deck, down another to the pool level, down still another to the poop deck. From there, the runners rushed down a hatchway, through corridors and back up to the boat deck via the stairs. I didn't participate, of course. I'm no runner, not when I don't have to be. Just hearing the racecourse described by a steward made my leg muscles tremble.

But I kept an eye on the finish, an eye on Ricardo. He was not the first to finish, but he was among the first, and he strained for the best position, throwing himself along the deck with fleet-footed abandon. It seemed an odd bit of gaiety for him, but perhaps it was not gaiety at all. After the finish, he flung himself once more into his chair, carelessly acknowledging the laughs and applause of his companions, dabbing the moisture from his face with a steamer rug. And he looked at me over the edge of the rug, sweating, exhilarated, scornful. I couldn't read the look, not then. Later, looking back, it was easy to read. His eyes were full of challenge.

Dinner.

Miss Bladderworth entertained me with a recitation of some of the more tiresome attributes of her recent gentleman callers, either to encourage my suit or to put me on the alert that I had plenty of competition and had better get cracking. My attention strayed constantly across the dining room. Luisa—dining with the Argentinean contingent—was looking particularly nice, in an evening dress that did something spectacular with black taffeta. But she was outshone at a nearby table by Grace, who cut a cool, statuesque figure that, I was sorry to see, was not lost on Fourth Officer Archie Kirk.

The young man, in arranging her chair for her, had leaned much closer to Grace than absolutely necessary and once, during the salad course, he had had the temerity to touch her arm. I bristled at that. That, I knew, was a breach of good taste. Should I report it to the First Officer? Or should I surreptitiously thump the fellow in the ribs the next time he passed? The latter, I decided.

My resolve grew stronger at the end of the meal, when Grace and the officer abruptly departed the dining room for places unknown. That made me feel sour, but did not divert me from duty. I had decided that, given Ricardo's edginess, I'd better keep an eye on him this evening. I was free to do so. Just as the dessert course arrived, Miss Bladderworth was beset by a severe attack of mal-de-mer, almost resulting in the gushing return of all the other courses she had ingested. Attended by her mother, she hastily retreated from the dining saloon, leaving me inexpressibly relieved. Attaching myself to a duo of giggling doyennes, I trailed Uncle Carlos' group into the second-class dining room for a performance of amateur variety, to be followed by dancing with the ladies.

It was a long evening for anyone with a refined taste for entertainment. And, for that matter, even for me. Among the offerings —as announced by the program—were a Song ("Danny Boy") by Mrs. Graindofer, Comic Patter from Mr. Fish entitled Mrs. Fish's Boy Jack, a

Dance by Miss Celeste Flight, a Pianoforte Solo by Miss April Zweibeck, some arch Highland buffoonery from Mr. Boggs, and, as a finale, Miss Isadora Bleak's celebrated Whistling Solo. By the program's end, which was some hour and a half in coming, I was longing for the comparative high drama of Miss Bladderworth's Adventures with Various Paramours.

Because of my own reaction, I was amazed to see that Ricardo Alvarez was absorbing the performance with gusto. His muscular shoulders shook with laughter at the predictable sallies of Mr. Fish and Mr. Boggs, greeted Miss Flight's awkward gyrations with explosive applause, and erupted into a fury of huzzahs and hand-clappings at the conclusion of the Whistling Solo.

He seemed in fine fettle. But perhaps he was simply working himself up to something. The performance ended at 10:26 p.m. and, as the dance floor was being cleared of chairs, Ricardo appeared to be excusing himself from his companions. A temporary departure, perhaps to fetch his dancing shoes, or was he retiring for the night? Watching him stalk with fluid purpose past the band tootling through its warm-up, and through the crewmen hastily ranking the chairs along the walls, I felt an unaccountable twinge. It drove me into a sudden, rather rash action. I jumped up, making my excuses to the doyennes, and made straight for Uncle Carlos' table, where the old man hovered between Luisa and Miss Jane Pilkington. He looked stricken as I came on, fearing some familiarity, some effusive greeting that would signal we already were acquainted. But, no fear. I covered myself.

"Count Raflasky," I introduced myself briskly, leering at Miss Pilkington and Luisa. "Pardon my forwardness, but you seem to have cornered the market on beautiful young ladies. Might I appropriate one?"

The Uncle murmured some assent. I hardly heard it, for I was bending down to bestow a smooch on Luisa's extended right hand. Fortunately for what ultimately ensued, I was a more awkward hand-kisser than the real Count Raflasky: My chin, as well as my lips, touched Luisa's creamy knuckles. Almost immediately, the lights went down, the band struck up a lively version of "Alexander's Ragtime Band," and I swept Luisa away across the floor, essaying a daring step known as the Grizzly Bear.

In her stateroom, as she prepared for bed, Grace was thoughtful. Was everything in place, would everything play out as she hoped? She had done all she could; now she would have to wait. She hated this part. She thrived on action, felt certitude when she was moving.

She recalled another ocean voyage. After she and Howard had married in Lima, Peru, they had taken ship first to Buenos Aires, then to England. A few days out, a passenger had fallen ill. There was no physician on board, but she knew the ailment. She'd encountered it while investigating peonage in Mississippi. Reddish spots on the mouth, tongue and the inside of the throat. Muscle pain, headache and vomiting. Fever and a high temperature that suddenly plunged to near normal. Smallpox.

There was the risk of death, and the risk of panic. She couldn't let that happen. She went gone to the captain, told him the situation must be placed in her hands. He had agreed. She had mittens made for the patient's hands, and coverings for his face. She burned the patient's blankets, collected every book, piece of paper and every other possible source of contamination, and burned them, too. No-one else fell ill. In England, the ship was given a clean bill of health.

Contagion on board. She'd dealt with it once; now she faced it again. Murder fever. Uncle Carlos and Ricardo were sick men, and Kron might find it difficult to manage them. For the moment, though, he had handled them well. Still, there would come a time... She glanced at the bureau next to the bed. The pistol was in the top drawer. It would stay there. No reason to upset the service staff.

Someone rapped at the door.

"Yes?"

"Captain wants to see you, ma'am." A brisk, British accent. The day steward serving this part of the ship was American, but now it was night. The shift, no doubt, had changed.

"Oh, yes? What about?"

"Didn't say, ma'am. Urgent." Quiet. Respectful.

"Just a moment."

She quickly drew on a robe. Then she hesitated. What could be so urgent? Perhaps a wireless message from New York? That was it. She had requested that the captain's wireless operator stand by. She undid the latch, began to swing the door back. Before she could get it fully open, it burst inward, crashing back against the bulkhead. Ricardo stormed through like a raging demon.

Luisa and I dipped and swayed across the floor, and I watched her eyes and lips turning down, then quirking, as if she were struggling with some inner problem, trying to work something out. I, too, was puzzling over something. I had scooped her up for the dance so as to confide my identity to her, to get information from her. My feeling was that things were moving too fast, gyrating out of control, and I had better speak to her directly about the intentions of Uncle Carlos and Ricardo, if she'd gleaned anything about them. But there were two things against this course. Most important, Grace had forbidden it. Her thought was to keep my identity known only to her. Second, Luisa was acting guilty. Still, I thought, as her perfume tickled my nostrils and caused my right hand to tighten at the small of her pretty back, that might be an argument in favor of direct contact. Why was Luisa feeling guilty? Obviously, because she knew some deadly information, and was waffling over whether or not to impart it. It might be something I needed to know instantly.

As I debated, I know now, Luisa was conducting her own inner debate. And she was working out some vague suspicion about me. There was something odd about Raflasky, she felt, but what was it? Perhaps she instinctively knew the timbre of my voice, though I'd disguised its accent, or perhaps the curve of my chest, to which I'd impulsively pressed her in the past. Perhaps, too, the vigor of my dancing step and the clutch of my arms showed somewhat more energy than she might have expected of a middle-aged man. The oddest thing of all about her dancing partner was that she somehow felt drawn to him, though his personal habits weren't what they should be, for he'd a smear of shaving cream on his chin. Why did she feel close to him? It was quite strange, especially since she'd heard him, only hours before, planning murder. Something was not right.

But there also was something not right about Ricardo. His long absence worried her, disturbed her. Since the voyage began, she had never known him to be out of Uncle Carlos' presence, the two seemed inseparable, and now he had been gone for at least 20 minutes. She thought back to how Uncle Carlos and Ricardo had worked out the details of their plan against Raflasky after the con man had left Jane Pilkington's stateroom. Luisa sighed. She was clutching the man who needed to be there to take the fall for Grace's murder. If it weren't for that, Luisa thought, she'd suspect Ricardo was off attending to that job right now.

The music ended, the lights came up, and Luisa looked over at Uncle Carlos, who was trying to smile at his dancing partner, Miss Pilkington. Luisa saw that he could not smile, that he wore a look of miserable horror as he turned, compulsively, to look at the doorway where Ricardo had disappeared. Her heart plummeted. Her suspicions about Ricardo were right. Or, at least, they were shared by Uncle Carlos, and he knew Ricardo better than any man on earth.

Now what? What could she do? If she acted on her hunch and was wrong, her masquerade would be revealed, she'd be setting herself up for murder. But what if she was right? Grace would be dead, slaughtered. Luisa's hands clenched, pain throbbed in her chest, and the thought came again—what if she was right? Feeling terribly alone, she sighed and put her fist to her face, massaging her cheekbone with her knuckles. The rubbing sensation was odd, slippery, as if some substance had come off her fingers, had dabbed her face. She examined the back of her hand. Yes, there was a smear, and instantly she recalled how it had come there—it had rubbed off when Raflasky had kissed her hand. And it was not shaving cream. A former actress, she knew this substance—greasepaint. From Raflasky's chin.

She looked at me, and suddenly all the clues came together for her: the voice, the feel of my chest, her sense of closeness to me. Her eyes widened.

"Kron!" she whispered. "Give me five minutes, then come to Mrs. Humiston's stateroom."

To Uncle Carlos, she pleaded illness, and was on her way.

Chapter Twenty-Four

RICARDO'S RUSH CARRIED GRACE BACK into the stateroom and flung her full length on the coverlet of the brass bed. He continued his furious attack, lashing a hard-knuckled fist into the side of her head to stun her, then choking her half-senseless. He shredded a pillowcase, snapped a strip of it into her mouth as a gag, and tied her arms to the upright brass tubes of the headboard. Her cloth tethers were thin, but tight.

This done, he relaxed.

"How eager I've been to meet you again," he said, smiling his rich smile, white bone flashing in darkness. "We are going to have a fine time in the next few minutes—the best kind of time anyone ever has on this earth. Then you are going off to wherever it is women go when they die."

She looked at him impassively, seeking the advantage of bravery. He continued about his business. From under his coat, inside the belt line, he withdrew a Circassian dagger, its blade as sharp as a baby's cry. He made no great show of it, it was merely a tool, a metal crystallization of his anger, and he quickly laid it aside, out of his way but close to hand, next to the bed on the polished oak dresser that held a full water pitcher. Turning her head, she could hear the click of the steel on the wood, could see the way the knife's blade winked and shimmered in the light passing through the pitcher.

He was a cool one. Excellent. The cool ones always gave you time.

He stretched luxuriously and removed his suit coat, flipping it onto the floor. His smooth, bright eyes watched her as he stripped off his shirt to reveal the racing muscles of his chest and shoulders. The ascot, too, sailed to the carpet, and the shirt. The disfigurement of his mind found no reflection in his body—it was young and clean, unmarked from waist to hairline.

He reached out to her, undid the twisted cord of her robe, and spread the heavy, velvety cloth back to reveal her body clad only in a thin envelope chemise.

"What a lovely feast is laid before me," he said, as he scooped up the pitcher and slowly poured the water down the length of her upper body, progressing from her breasts, across her stomach and down her thighs, drenching the light cloth so it clung to each curve. Then he leaped on the bed, straddling her, and smashed the water pitcher on the brass uprights, so that jagged pieces clattered and tinkled together as they bounced on the coverlet. She saw him snatch a piece of the broken glass, noted his quick movement, then felt a glass-point pinching the skin just below her left eye.

Her gaze stayed with him, but her thoughts moved inward, to the words of the Stoic philosopher Epictetus: *Make the best use of what is in your power, and take the rest as it happens.* She was calm, and Ricardo knew it. He cursed, smashed the broken pitcher on the floor and snatched up the dagger.

"You are so much like ice now, but I'll heat you up," he said. "You'll be roasting before I'm through. And now, before the feast begins—a little drink."

The blade edged through the soft skin at the side of her neck, and she felt the warm flow of blood. He bent forward, pressing his chest into hers, and flicking his tongue into the blood, lapping it up. Then he leaned back, his chin dripping.

She used her mind to relax herself, to control the pulse of her blood. His face contorted with profound disappointment, and she felt herself gaining the upper hand.

"You damn bitch," he said, holding the knife up in both hands like a pagan priest readying a sacrificial stab. "Are you so ready to go that you don't want your few last minutes? Shall I stick you right now, take out your heart?"

She thought, *Control thy passions, lest they take vengeance on thee,* and looked at him with complete indifference.

"Cold, are you?" he said. "So you look. But I've seen them like you, women like you. Shock freezes their eyes, but—" He ran a bloody hand down his throat, smiled. "Inside here, the pipe is dry, the fear turns the spit to dust, they can't talk. They try, of course, but their voices catch and shake, and they cry— That's you, isn't it? Of course." He changed the position of the knife in his hands, ran it under the cloth of the gag and chopped it free.

Grace coughed hoarsely—Ricardo's grip had bruised her throat. Her ears were still ringing from the fist that had crunched into the side of her head. She could feel the flow of her blood increasing as it drained from her neck to dampen the pillow and coverlet.

She said, "You are under arrest."

Luisa forgot all other considerations and simply ran for Grace's life. Out of the second-class dining saloon she ran, her tiny feet beating down the passageway to the staircase, up the echoing stairs, into the corridor beyond, where the walls throbbed with the thrumming of the ship's engines. As she ran, a man's face sneered into hers—his eyebrows corded, the eyes snapping, skin boiling with the high blood underneath, the mouth a harsh threat. A roaring filled her ears, his voice raised and thundering, laying out her fate if she disobeyed, and the tears shook from her eyes and trickled, spattering her cheeks, so that she had to paw them away, fling them aside to see her stumbling course. All the time, her chin was up and tight and pointed, her ears and forehead burning as she mumbled, over and over, "You bastard! You thought I wouldn't. You bastard! You thought I wouldn't."

Ricardo knelt over Grace on the bed. She was damp, bloody, with bits of broken glass sticking in her moist hair, but he was the one who looked cold and sick, showing the extremity of frustration. His only joy in life had been inflicting sex, pain and humiliation on women, and now this woman had denied him. The fierceness was gone from his eyes—they were like empty rooms at evening, the curtains drawn, the shadows insinuating themselves into every corner. But there still was resolve in the set of his cheeks, determination in the hardening of his lips. It was as if he were firming himself for duty, steeling himself for what needed to be done.

He raised the dagger, and she saw it sweep toward the center of her chest, where her heart thumped and swelled. She twisted to the left, throwing her right shoulder into the air, causing the blade to glance off that shoulder, cutting a raw slit across her right shoulder blade. Even as the pain burned into her, the thin cloth strip that held her left hand tightened against a wedge of broken pitcher, ripped and came free. With that hand, she punched hard upward into his nose, and he gasped with the shock of it, his eyes flickering, spouting tears.

He recovered, caught that flailing hand, steadied himself. Now the hate came back into his eyes, hot and steady, and he got the knife up into position and readied himself for a sweep that would lay her neck open and rip out the carotid artery, transforming it into a rippling snake spilling and spurting her life all over the floor.

At that second, Luisa burst through the door, weeping and furious with fear. She saw the scene, didn't hesitate. One leap took her right across the room, into the air, thumping hard onto Ricardo's back. And her fingernails tore at him, snagged his hair, jerked his head about. Her knees beat again and again into his kidneys, her teeth cut the flesh of his neck and tightened. He thrashed about, frantic with pain and fury, flipping his shoulders this way and that. And at last his strength told, his muscles squeezed and exploded, and, with one violent bucking movement, he threw her off.

I stood on the dance floor, with the empty ripples of laughter rising and dying around me, the bandleader clowning, a trumpet player blatting out a bad rendition of a popular tune. I wanted to run after Luisa, but I couldn't run. I was frozen there, watching Uncle Carlos' face, seeing it curling in a parody of good fellowship. I looked into that face, trying to puzzle out what was behind it, thinking as hard as I ever had. What should I do? What was right? Grace had said the Karcher investigation was blown—no way to pin these killers with that, so I couldn't falter, couldn't betray my false identity. I had to stay Count Raflasky. I had to. I must trap Ricardo and Uncle Carlos in the middle of a crime, otherwise Jane Pilkington would be sold into white slavery, the murder of Amelia Karcher would go unavenged, no-one would ever find out what these two butchers had done with Ruth Cruger.

But what about Luisa? She was terribly troubled—I'd seen that in her eyes, felt it in the stiffness of her arms. She'd said to come quickly. That could mean only one thing. Danger. Danger to Grace.

Uncle Carlos was standing stock still, his dance finished. His eyes were on me and his hands were moving against his trouser legs, blotting sweat from his palms. I must brace him, I must take the chance. Three steps took me to him as I fixed my face in a brutal Count Raflasky scowl.

"Where is our young friend, eh?" I growled. "He rushes out, he is impatient. What is this about? If he is botching this job, I will have his lungs."

Uncle Carlos put a hand up to me, cupping it in supplication. "He — Sometimes I, I cannot control him—"

His hand came toward me then, but before it was half-extended, I was gone. I'd pumped my right leg hard on the floor to get around him, bent my left to aid with the sprint and was off, my leather soles slipping on the waxed floor, my shoulders shedding dancers, bowling them over like nine-pins as I dashed full-throttle for the door.

CHAPTER TWENTY-FIVE

RICARDO WHIPPED HIS UPPER BODY and sent Luisa flying to the floor, thumping her head on the carpeted wood. Then he came off the bed after her, pinned a knee on her belly, and stabbed her—his right arm pumping like a piston. She got her left arm up as the dagger shot at her face, and the blade ran the length of her outer arm, shooting out a stream of blood in its wake, crooking into the flesh of the shoulder. She wailed in agony, but kept that bloody arm stiffly upright, flailed it at him.

Grace launched off the bed, punching her elbows down into the nerves on either side of Ricardo's neck. He stiffened as a shock shivered him from neck to crotch, but he shook himself, trembled, recovered, and lashed out with the fist that held the knife, his knuckles cracking into Grace's forehead, sending her reeling.

I pounded out of the stairwell and into the passageway that led to Grace's cabin, caught sight of another man turning at the other end. Kirk. Fourth Officer Archie Kirk. What the hell was he doing here? Courting Grace, no doubt, despite the anti-fraternization oath he'd sworn to the Bright Star Line.

He came on, shocked at the sight of me and at the sound of crashing furniture, thumps, and cries issuing from Grace's stateroom. We reached her door together. He hesitated, the fool! I thrust past him,

seized the knob, flung back the door. The scene struck me, struck him
—two women, dewed and smeared with blood, and a dagger-man,
naked to the waist, laying about with his blade. Kirk got the idea then,
a split-second too late, and crashed through the breach with me, his
wide shoulders bouncing me around, tipping me awry, so my feet
slipped at the crucial moment and we tumbled down in a tangle of
arms and legs, a stew of boiling beef.

Ricardo was in among us, then, scuttling and slippery, striking out
with his fists instead of the blade clutched in his right hand. He caught
my nose with a rude whack, sending lights flaming through my brain,
clouted Kirk in the throat, dropping him into a gasping heap. I swung,
of course, got off a roundhouse at Ricardo's crown that should have
jellied his brain. He ducked, and my fist gusted off Kirk's forehead,
fish-bellying his eyes.

There was one long moment in that bloody burlesque of a
struggle when Ricardo had an opening on me. He was down on one
knee, having tripped over Kirk's Number-14 shoe, with his left hand
braced on the floor and his dagger arrowed up toward my throat. I saw
death in his eyes, a readiness. The dagger-point winked, and I expected
to feel it inside my head in the next split-second, fighting for mouth-
space with my tongue.

But Grace fell on Ricardo's back, gave him a push, and he lurched
forward and up. Yes, up and out he went, into the corridor, into the
night—bloody and marked, running free, nothing to lose and a knife in
his hand.

Where does a hunted man flee on a ship at night, a ship cutting
through a wild and empty ocean? Where does he hide? What hope has
he? Ricardo, I think, had no need of hope—he had spent it all at some
point long before, in the hungry streets of Bueños Aires, in the beds
of women Uncle Carlos had selected for profit rather than for passion,
in the bloody spasms that offered relief that never lasted.

Now Ricardo ran on, as strong as before, as wild as before, as human—or as inhuman—as he had ever been before, but doomed. His blood pulsed as efficiently as ever, his lungs pumped powerfully, his muscles rippled and sang, but he was trapped. So what was his object, his goal? It must have been this: one final act of violence, one last explosion to mark himself down, to extend one more inch the vacuum of his life—he intended to share his death with one more innocent life, just one.

He pounded down the passageway, his footfalls making the creaking concussions that echo through a large, engine-driven, water-bound container making its way across the endless deep. He fled up the grand wooden staircase, and the carven cherubs shouldering their electric globes watched him go with blankness in their eyes. The ornamental clock on the top landing ticked and never faltered, its second hand cutting forward and down like the arm of a firing-squad leader descending with the final drop. Then he was up on the boat deck in the hissing dark—on top of the ship, open to the sky. As he turned and sped toward the rear of the ship, he began to hear the sound of footsteps behind him, thundering in a tumbling rush. They were my footsteps, of course, the steps of Count Raflasky—the fake Count Raflasky, he must have known by then, the masquerade Grace had used to play him for a fool. And what could he have thought of that?

Ignoring her own wounds, Grace limped to the bed, threw back the coverlet, seized a sheet and ripped off several strips. Luisa lay on the floor, gasping, her own blood and Grace's spattered on her dress and on the carpet. Grace came to her, wrapped a sheet-strip expertly around Luisa's gouged arm, folded and pressed another rag of the white, thready cloth into a compress and squeezed it onto the wound, staunching the blood flow as Archie Kirk stood awkwardly, his fingers clenching and unclenching. Luisa looked feverish, pale, her lips working with physical distress and guilt. She closed her eyes, her cheeks reddening, choked out two words. "Stoker McCullagh."

Grace put a hand to her forehead, calming the fever that burned there. "Yes, yes," said Grace. "I know. I've known for some time. We recruited you, and he countered. That's over. Now the healing begins."

Grace looked up at Kirk and said, "I have one last mission. And you have your work, too—you must stay with this young lady and keep this compress tight. Don't let her go into shock, keep her warm."

At last he had some orders, something he could follow. Fourth Officer Kirk swept a blanket from the bed, dropped down next to Luisa and covered her. As he did so, Grace rose, wrapping her blood-dappled robe around her, cinching it tight. Two steps took her to her dresser, and she snatched out a drawer and dipped into it, seeking a weapon. She found an appropriate one, dropped it into her pocket, made for the door.

Ricardo was a strong runner, I was not. My lungs were laboring and my thighs felt like putty. Up ahead, heading for the area where the open decks stair-stepped down to the stern, Ricardo pumped along like a whippet in full plunge, his legs seeming to swish through the dark air. I strained, the breath burning in my throat, hoping he'd stumble, hoping he'd run up against some obstruction. There had to be one, had to be. Then I thought of it. Yes. The back rail of the boat deck.

Grace had heard my footsteps rumbling off down the passageway, so her initial line of pursuit was clear. She hurried to the staircase landing, then paused, perplexed. To the left and right, long passageways gave access to the first-class staterooms. Ricardo could have ducked through any unlocked door with me behind him. We might be stalking each other quietly now in one of those darkened rooms, or running through the ship, every step distancing us from the point where she stood. She cupped her ears and bent forward, straining to hear the rhythmical rush of speeding steps. She heard them, somewhere, but the cacophony of the ship at night—the squeaking cables, the clatter of passengers' footsteps below decks, even the distant, brassy wheezing of the band in the second-class dining saloon—confused her. Her sharp eyes swung from one passageway to another, trying to fasten on some clue. She glanced at the staircase leading upward to the boat deck, caught a glimpse of a tiny light winking from a step half-way up. She grasped her robe in both hands, climbed quickly, and bent forward. She scooped at the light, and her hand cupped a tiny circle of glass—my monocle, Count Raflasky's monocle. She looked upward again, toward the door that led out into the night.

The railing loomed up in front of Ricardo. I gasped a lungful of air to press me the final few steps, braced for the collision. But there wasn't to be a collision. The bastard was slippery, an acrobat. He sprang into the air, lighted on that railing, balanced himself, half-turned. The moonlight struck his mocking smile, then he rotated back, balanced and threw up his arms, leaped into the darkness. I pounded the last few steps, feeling a pang, regretting the loss of knuckle time with Ricardo's forehead. Oh, well. He'd done the job himself, jumped for the open deck below, knocked himself silly, or dead. I halted, puffing, bent to scoop my hands onto my thighs, shuffled forward to the rail, looked down.

Christ! The bastard had done me! He'd remembered something I'd forgotten, had taken advantage of it. The canvas chutes from the afternoon's foot race were still tied in place, and Ricardo had slid down one, and was running across the deck below to the next. I cursed, gasped heavily, lumbered up onto the rail. Over I went, floundering, swooping out of control down the chute, canvas raking my backside, my limbs banging together like logs caught in a waterfall, my dinner lurching up my throat.

I was jettisoned from the first chute, vaulted for the second. I got to that one, slid down. Then I was on to the third chute, the one that would deposit me on the poop deck. My body went awry, but I fell into that last canvas tunnel, slid. Even in the midst of my tumble, I caught a glimpse of Ricardo leaping from the end of the chute, drifting between an electric crane and an electric winch past a capstan. Then my neck kinked as my dinner jacket bunched under me, flipped me sideways, and I lost sight of him as I fought to get my bearings back, stop my head from spinning.

My slide ended at last, dumping me on the utmost rear area of the ship, and I staggered, trying to get my legs to work, my eyes to focus. I continued to stumble along, trying to right myself as I forged forward, putting one foot in front of the other, repeating the process. It was a bad strategy, trying to gather myself on the march, for I was still staggering when I blundered into Ricardo's knife.

He was tired, and the thrust went low, the blade slicing into the meat of my right thigh. I bellowed and clutched at him, pinning his arms and carrying him to the rail. He bucked under me, fastened his teeth in my right ear, worried it like a dog, sharp slashes of pain jolting my scalp at each jerk. I pressed my mouth down over a scream, dropped my right arm off him, hammered a punch to his solar plexus. It should have juiced his intestines, but he tightened his gut muscles and my fist trampolined off them, springing back so fast it cranked my right elbow half out of joint. I ignored that, hit him again, thumping up under his ribs, trying to smash his lungs against his heart. He grunted. Christ, I'd gotten that much!

But then he popped his fists hard at my ears, and my brain exploded inside my skull. I coughed and coughed. I couldn't keep him. Vertigo had broken loose something in my head, my blood was gushing strength from my thigh, my ear was ablaze, my eyes had gone bleary. Ricardo writhed and squirmed out of my grasp, I fell to my knees, felt my gut convulse, half-digested food gushing from my mouth. My eyesight focused. I wished it hadn't. With wet eyes, I saw Ricardo lifting the dagger, cocking it precisely, poising it for a juicy bite of my skull. Then, on the edge of my vision, as high and far as heaven, I caught a glimpse of a shape I knew.

Three decks up, so far away that she seemed to be framed against the uncaring yellow moon, I saw Grace dip into her robe, pluck something forth, point it. The action was familiar. In my mind's eye, I saw her in her office, sweeping the .32-caliber Colt Pocket Positive to the point, taking dead aim, forcing the trigger back in a nine-pound, double-action pull—a smooth, rolling stroke.

The Zen masters, who practice the art of archery to search affairs of the spirit, have a saying, "One shot, one life." Their meaning is this: that a shot launched with perfect understanding mirrors the life that sends it on its way, that it flies true.

A tiny spark leapt from Grace's hand. Across the open space, through the darkness, piercing the sea fog, sped the Colt's whisper-light bullet. Ricardo's right bicep tightened for the death stroke, my eyes rolled upward as I saw it coming, my mind went blank, everything stopped. Something cracked, far off—the belated report of the shot.

Ricardo straightened suddenly, as if hearkening to the voice of a ghost in the misty darkness. His stretching movement carried him up and around, pivoting like a ballet dancer, his arms convulsing, face slackening. His body struck the rail, jackknifed over it, and fell. As it did, his hard grip loosened. The dagger sprang free from his hand, tumbling end-over-end into the outer darkness, into oblivion, as his body plummeted toward the sea.

Chapter Twenty-Six

THE REMAINS OF MORNING COFFEE sat cooling on a sideboard as Grace questioned Uncle Carlos in the captain's cabin—a snug, neat place, though I doubt Uncle Carlos appreciated it. Nautical charts lay precisely on a roll top desk next to a brass sextant. On the wall, a languorous South Seas scene shared space with a clock set in a tiny ship's wheel.

As the most damaged survivor of the night before, I was given the softest chair, off in a corner, where I leaked quietly into the bandages on my thigh and right ear. Grace had tried to confine me to my quarters with plenty of hot brandy to ease my suffering, but I wasn't going to miss this show, even if I did feel like a dog-chewed boot. After all, Grace was here, and still on her feet, despite the bandage that clung to her neck and the one that made her blouse bulge over her right shoulder-blade. Completing the party were Captain Wheelwright, who sat across from Uncle Carlos, and Fourth Officer Archie Kirk, who stood by at parade rest.

Our eyes were on Grace, and she drew out the moment for the benefit of Uncle Carlos, who was looking very gray. There was chalky gray in his sparse hair, unhealthy gray in his skin, speckled gray in his beard, white-gray in the mustache trailing limply down his face. She still had not spoken when Uncle Carlos himself opened the proceedings. He wet his lips and said haltingly, eyes elsewhere, "He was all I had."

199

"Tell us, in your own way," said Grace, her voice raw from the injuries Ricardo's fingers had inflicted on her throat. "You may take your time."

Uncle Carlos looked at the floor. "He was very young when I met him." The withered head came up, the eyes empty, and the voice thickened. "A runaway. He came in from the country, into Bueños Aires, and I found him in an alley there. Rags on him, dirty, but with those lustrous eyes, those fine shoulders. The whores had used him—they'd wanted a boy they could handle any way they wanted, as their customers handled them—they'd done filthy things with him, and they'd gone too far, his mind was off. I healed him, or thought I had, raised him up as an equal partner. Age was telling its tale on me, I needed a young man—"

"To help with the young women, the wealthy ones?"

Uncle Carlos head dropped again. "Yes." He coughed, and the cough sounded rough and serious—it made him weep and redden—but he controlled it, continued. "They couldn't keep their eyes off him, had to touch him. I used to say, 'Ricardo, you could have any of them. You could marry one, choose one with plenty of land and baggage.' But he wouldn't leave me."

Grace's voice was soft. "You are being kind now, are you not? In fact, he would not marry because he hated women, had set himself apart from them. For him, even the pretense of being close was too much."

Uncle Carlos nodded. "Yes, yes, that is true."

Grace clasped her hands, and looked over them at the decaying old man. There was a throatiness in her tone now, a deep feeling. "And you sent him out to kill."

Uncle Carlos' face twisted, his hands made spreading, brushing motions, his breathing pumped audibly. "I never sent him out to kill. Oh no, I never sent him out."

"You're lying," I growled. "He killed Jack Mullraney, butchered him like an animal, came close to finishing Mrs. Humiston."

The Uncle's head was down. He shook it back and forth in

confusion, true or acted. "I don't know, I don't know." He sighed, a rasping sound. "I never sent him out. He went out, I didn't ask. Sometimes there were news stories, bodies. I didn't ask, didn't dare. To ask was to lose him."

Grace glanced at my angry face, then at Uncle Carlos. "This is artifice," she said. "You schemed to kill me on this ship, it was your idea, your plan."

Uncle Carlos looked around as if begging for understanding. "To keep him! You were closing in. It was the only way to keep him."

Grace stepped to the roll top desk and looked at the sextant, burnishing it with her eyes. When she spoke again, her voice was still quiet, but now it was also smooth.

"You are a white slaver, are you not?"

Uncle Carlos had gone off somewhere. His hands shook with palsy, blurring the warty freckles on his skin, which seemed too thin to hold in the claw-bones of his fingers.

"Yes."

"And over the last three years, you have taken away several young women from New York City, as part of a scheme to sell them into prostitution in Argentina?"

"Yes." His mind seemed to wander. "And to take their goods. Diamonds, gold, whatever they had." He said, with a ghost of irony, "Their dowries…"

Grace grew impatient.

"Maria Greene?"

"Yes."

"Victoria Ingley?"

"Yes."

"Nancy Leonard?"

"Yes."

"Barbara Dunston?"

"Yes."

"Amelia Karcher?"

A choking sound. "Yes, but. . .she died."

"Died how?"

He spread his hands, and they fluttered. "Everything was fine, it was going well. She came away willingly, she was totally enthralled with Ricardo, she was even willing to travel under a false name to avoid complications..." Uncle Carlos drew a ragged breath. "But the steward was after her, too, this man Anderson. One night, late, up on the deck, he approached her roughly, tried to overwhelm her. He had no chance. Ricardo surprised them, there was a scuffle, and Ricardo stabbed him to the heart."

Grace tilted her head. "To save Amelia?"

Uncle Carlos looked at his hands. "Well, yes. For his own purposes, yes. But the scuffle had been a rough one, and Miss Karcher had been caught in the middle of it. Anderson had tried to use her as shield, and Ricardo's knife took part of her right cheek, clipped it away. Then she'd fallen on the deck, broken a leg. And that was all for her."

"Why did that make a difference?"

The old man turned a hand, businesslike. "She was damaged. As Ricardo said, 'No-one wants a whore gimping around with half her face gone.'"

Grace's face was granite. "He said that to her?"

"Yes."

"Just before he stabbed the life out of her and you both lifted her, carried her to the side and threw her overboard?"

Uncle Carlos blinked, as if surprised that this needed to be spelled out. "Yes. Yes, exactly. I had to go along, or he'd have put me over the side with her and Anderson."

Grace inhaled, let the air out. "And did you serve Ruth Cruger the same way?"

"Ruth Cruger? The girl in the newspapers?" Uncle Carlos surveyed the faces around him. He coughed, and his eyes were innocent. "The one who disappeared? Oh, no." He searched his pockets, captured a handkerchief, made a pass at his forehead. "What a stir that caused! I'm glad she wasn't ours. No, we had nothing to do with that."

We were up on deck, the wind in our hair. I swung heavily on the crutch tucked into my right armpit.

"You can't expect that kind of bastard to tell the truth," I said.

Grace put a finger to her lips. "You think not?"

"No. Look at the way he said Amelia Karcher 'died.' He wouldn't even say he was in on the killing until you bulled it out of him."

"Still, he did confess it."

"Finally." The rubber-covered tip of my crutch slipped slightly on the teakwood, and I winced. Grace, concerned, caught my arm.

I gritted my teeth. "I'm just glad this damn case is over. A little lying-up will serve me, a few stewards running here and there at my beck and call."

Grace smiled. "Why, Kron, you are exhibiting an out-of-character taste for the good life. I always thought you relished the rough side."

"Maybe, but I'm getting a taste for the smooth side, rambling about from ocean to ocean all snugged up in fine clothes, doubling up on meals and doing no work beyond winking at beautiful ladies."

I made a bit of a stumble-step, to make sure she kept a tight grip on me as we dipped down a passage toward the interior of the ship. "Yes," she said. "I can see how you would feel that."

She stopped suddenly, and I looked about, noting the number on the door. Grace said, "I'm sure you would like to see Luisa alone."

I sensed a trap here, for Grace was always up to something—that was what kept her interesting. Actually, after the doctor had dressed my wounds the night before, I'd slipped away, stumped down here for a bit to look in on Luisa—just in the line of being professional, keeping track of our troops—had tapped at the door, been turned away by a nurse with an abrupt manner. I'd got a glance at Luisa, though, pale on the bed, knocked out with a bit of Luminal to make her sleep. I had to admit she slept well, a gentleness to her mouth, a clean look to her forehead, like a kid who had been playing too hard, and who was getting a good rest. So, I'd done my duty, and that was done. What was this business of Grace wanting me to visit her now? I scowled, not wanting to get drawn in. "Oh?" I said. "Why would I want to see Luisa?"

Grace smiled. "I'm sure Luisa would like to see you. She seemed quite concerned about your wounds."

I looked at the deck, shrugged. "Oh, well. That's all right, then."

Luisa was propped up in her canopied bed, her left arm swathed in bandages, her hair fixed up beyond what you would expect from an invalid, quite a fetching twirl to the little spit-curls along her temples. She always had a nice luster to her hair, which glowed with silkiness you don't often see. She knew it, too, I was sure. And others knew it, I noted. On the sideboard rested a half-pound box of chocolates and a carton of Piedmont cigarettes. That got my eyebrows up, but she tossed a finger toward the gifts as if I couldn't see them for myself. "That Archie Kirk has been nice, hasn't he? Men in uniform have such good manners."

I made some sort of rumble down deep in my throat. Here was I, all diced up like a breakfast steak, making a special trip down to see her, and all she could talk about was men in uniform. Well, she'd see enough of them soon, though I wasn't sure the war would bring out their best manners. "You don't look so bad," I said. Her chin drooped a bit at that—I suppose my words had come out wrong. "What I mean is," I said, "You look like you're getting along, like you're not going to go south on us."

The droopiness moved along from her chin to her cheeks, and I thought I saw her shoulders sag, which didn't give her the top aspect for a young lady, though I must say she had enough looks so that she had some to spare. "So that's all you care about," she said, "Whether I'm going to die or not."

I tried for a smile, but my thigh was hurting, and my lips were strained against the pain. "That's a start isn't it?" I said. "Hard to operate if you're looking up at flower-roots."

Her eyes sparked. "And that's the only reason you care if I die, because it would mean I couldn't carry out missions, that I couldn't sneak around and do your bidding."

My collar began to get hot. "It's not my bidding," I said. "We both work for Mrs. Humiston."

She made a little angry sniff. "You more than me, I expect."

I stumped my crutch on the deck. "Yes, well, what about that?" I searched for a further reply, for it seemed I was being attacked unjustly when there were sins to be totted up on the other side. "Here you are kicking about your work—that's pretty odd, the way you've played it," I said. "You were eavesdropping on me and those two assassins while we were planning to do in Grace."

"Yes, and what if I was?"

"What if? You never passed along what they said after I left, that's what." I took a breath. "I know you didn't, because I just asked Grace. And Grace—though she tried to make you look good—had to admit it."

Her good arm began to beat on the bedspread as the color came up in her cheeks. "Grace, Grace! It's all 'Grace, Grace' with you, isn't it? Your Mrs. Humiston, your employer!"

Well, this put me off. Here I was accusing her of bad faith, of complicity with the enemy, and she was going on about Grace. But she wasn't through.

"Mrs. Humiston knows why I didn't tell," Luisa blurted, flinging the words at me like hot marbles. "I confessed to her last night, so she knows why. Because Stoker McCullagh got me in his grip, that's why! That's why I played a double game. Because he came to me after I joined up with you and said he'd got evidence on me for my confidence work, and would trump up more and send me along for a good long stretch that would keep me inside until I was very old. And, in spite of that, I saved Mrs. Humiston and she saved you and I got hurt and here you come down to me and say, 'Grace, Grace!'"

Well. Well. I stumped my crutch, looked away, cleared my throat a few times. She was crying furiously now, her one good hand up to her face, wet and glistening with the tears. Women. Some men understand them, I guess. Doctors, maybe. Not me. I was just as confused as I'd ever been.

I stood there being confused and watching her cry. And, I must say, as confused as I was, all I could think of was that time I'd gone to her apartment and gotten all mussed around with her because she was weeping then, and how she looked so pretty in spite of the weeping and how I hadn't meant to get mussed around, all I had meant to do was recruit her.

For a job. For a simple job.

CHAPTER TWENTY-SEVEN

I DIDN'T HAVE LONG TO think about what had got the wind up Luisa, though I gave it some strong concentration. At times, I thought — But, no, I was at least ten years older than she was, broken teeth, chewed ear, she certainly wouldn't be wanting my attentions. After our encounter, at any rate, she allotted a long visit to Fourth Officer Kirk, which showed what she was truly thinking. I repaired to Grace to discuss work, though I couldn't see exactly what work there was left to do. All I could see in front of us was a leisurely finish to our trip to Argentina, a pleasant layover, and a relaxing return voyage. You might say my thinking was wrong.

Before night fell that day, Grace and I and Luisa—because Grace wouldn't leave her—had pointed our noses directly away from Argentina and were heading back to New York on board the *Calpurnia's* sister ship, *Oceania*, which had passed the *Calpurnia* on the reverse run. To say that this took some doing—convincing the captains of both ships to rendezvous and heave to while a boat ferried the three of us from one to the other—would be an understatement. I learned later that several wireless messages (some indignant) shot back and forth between each of the ships and the Bright Star Line's New York headquarters before the deed was approved. Grace's force of personality helped, of course. It didn't hurt, too, that the Bright Star Line needed to make amends for botching the murder investigation of Amelia Karcher. And, of course, Grace's late father had been a friend of the owner of the shipping line. Grace had used every argument and had prevailed.

Confronted by the news from Grace that we were making an abrupt return trip, that we had another mission, I was dumbfounded. But none of my questions did anything to crack Grace's air of mystery and composure. There was something up. That was all she'd say, she'd had it planned, and now she was going to carry it out. If I didn't want to go along, well, I could stay aboard with Luisa and see her safely home. In a way, I got the feeling that Grace wouldn't have minded that. But I also got the feeling that part of her wanted me to go, and of course I was going to go, because mystery out of Grace Humiston meant danger, and I'd protect her from any danger if I could. True, I'd been blundering in that regard, and she'd had to bail me out, but I'd blunder on, by God, if there was any chance that I could lift an arm between her and a knife stroke or a bullet.

Four days after switching ships, we docked in New York. Luisa hadn't spoken to me the whole time. In fact, she'd found still another male friend on the *Oceania*, an American version of Archie Kirk, and walked with him on deck as soon as she was well enough. She was such an operator. Oh, well, who cared? I'd known that from the beginning, and worrying about that sort of thing was foolish. As for Grace and I, both of us had recovered sufficiently from our wounds so that the only remaining visual evidence of them was a bit of stiffness in Grace's right shoulder and my heavy limp.

Limping was no problem, not like that damned crutch—as soon as we made the dock, I threw it away. No-one met us, a turn of events that surprised me. Grace had extracted a promise from Capt. Wheelwright not to release to the newspapers any of the details of Ricardo's death until the *Calpurnia* docked in Buenos Aires, and to keep secret the change in our travel plans. Still, I had fully expected her to wire ahead to her husband, to have Howard Humiston waiting anxiously at the debarkation point. At the very least, I'd expected her to notify that damned nuisance, James Whistle, so he could fuss around her, seizing her baggage, clutching at her sleeve, that sort of thing. But as Grace and I slipped down the gangplank and disappeared through the arriving throngs into the streets of New York, not a soul approached us. Luisa had stayed behind, waiting for her officer to escort her off the ship.

Excellent. I liked this. I'll admit that in the four days previous I'd continued to entertain thoughts about Luisa, but I'd sighed and put them down, and now I turned back into familiar pathways—Grace, at least, was nearer to me in age—and perhaps there was some hope there. However, I was positively stupefied when, instead of directing the taxi to drop me off at the Boar's Head and continuing on home herself, Grace told the cabbie to take us both to the Hotel Wallick at Broadway and 43rd Street. I was equally amazed when she introduced herself to the desk clerk as Katherine Porterfield of Philadelphia, Pa., identified me as her cousin, Edward Banff, of Scranton, and asked for connecting three-dollar rooms. A few minutes later, I found myself sitting on a four-poster bed in a quiet room distinguished by elegant, subdued cornices, and wondering very strenuously what Grace was doing next door.

I did not have long to wait, for, abruptly, there came a knock on the locked connecting door, and Grace was speaking from the other side. "I am sorry to disturb you while you are still weary from your journey, but you must do something for me immediately."

My back straightened. I looked in the mirror, and was sorry to see that I needed a haircut. I harrumphed a bit. "Do I have time to take a bath first?"

"No, I am sorry to say you don't," Grace replied. "My need is urgent."

"Well, then," I said, wetting my lips. "I'll be in directly."

"In?" said Grace. "In? No, you must go out. Quickly. And buy me a monkey wrench. It must be the most expensive monkey wrench you can find. Indeed, I want you to buy the most expensive monkey wrench in New York City."

Two hours later, I was back, bearing an oily brown paper package bound with butcher cord. I followed Grace's directions, placing the package on her bed and stripping off the paper. The instrument reposed there, shiny and rather sinister, slim at its handle, its silhouette spreading as one's eyes progressed down toward its jaws. Grace, who was dressed for the street (not what I would have expected, given our impending situation), asked intently, "How much did it cost?"

"Two dollars and twenty-five cents," said I.

"Excellent!" said Grace, putting on her hat. She looked at the wall clock, which showed 5:22 p.m. "Come on! We just have time for dinner before the night's work begins."

I smiled, oddly attracted by this play-acting. Even a simple man can learn a trick or two, it doesn't pay to be too rigid. "I wouldn't call it work," I said slyly.

Grace looked at me rather strangely. "Your enthusiasm is commendable," she said. "Do you have your gun?"

The streets were daubed with shadow, and the yellowing, fading light was dusty as Grace directed the cabbie through streets unfamiliar to me. I knew we were in Harlem, but Grace's rapid-fire instructions to, "Turn here," "Double back," "Now, around this corner, wait for a few minutes, then start off again," kept me confused.

One sad fact was clear to me, however: Grace and I really were off for a night's work, and apparently a chancy one, for she was trying to ensure that we were not being followed. At last, just with the falling of the dark, we left the cab, hurried through an alley noxious with rotting potato peelings, decayed vegetables and discarded bones, slipped through the door of a drab rooming-house, moved quickly down a hallway, out a door, and across another alley. A badly fitted wooden door stood before us. Grace bent close to me, laid a finger to her lips, put her hand on the knob, twisted, pulled and slipped through into a dim hallway, with me so close behind that I could feel the breath swelling and relaxing her upper body.

The door whispered shut behind us, and the darkness was redolent of motor oil and grease. To our left, I could barely make out the shape of stairs leading upward—heavy feet were clumping around up there on the next floor, and I could sniff the musky odor of cooking beef. My eyes began to adjust to the dimness. Out of the half-light, a closet door emerged to our right and Grace, keeping her eyes on the stairway, slipped to that door, eased it open and gestured urgently at me to enter. I did, and she came after. The door creaked, and the outside world was gone.

The closet was large, black as the inside of a Doberman, and uncomfortable. We sat uneasily on the floor, enveloped in the smells of soap, chemicals and oil. The hard, narrow ridge of a mop-handle cut into my back, and my legs, caught against a wash-bucket, cramped quickly. Before five minutes had passed, the knife wound in my thigh began to stretch and ache, and the revolver in my hip pocket grew into a monstrous sharp lump gouging my right buttock. It was so dark I couldn't even see Grace's outline, though I could smell her perfume and hear the soft, measured pulsing of her breath.

Hours passed, or so it seemed to me. My whole body was tight and suffering: so cramped I feared I wouldn't be able to move at all when the time came. And still the time did not come. Disembodied, floating in darkness, I began to feel vertigo. Strange ideas occurred to me: I'd once read that miners trapped in cave-ins envisioned the most fantastic scenes—sword fights in medieval castles, visitations from monsters, trips across the frozen mountains of the moon. I was confidently awaiting a truly ferocious fantasy of this kind when, suddenly, I heard a muffled bumping and shuffling from beyond the wall. Grace put a hand on my knee.

We remained in that attitude for many long minutes more, as the concussions in the wooden walls and floors, and then somewhere below us, continued for a while, then receded. I was just beginning to think that Grace was going to keep me here forever (perhaps in retaliation for my indelicate overtures at the hotel?) when her hand stiffened on my knee, then was lifted. The closet door opened on the dim hall, which, by contrast to the blackness of the closet, seemed light as day. Grace, holding the door open, beckoned me to follow. Creaking painfully, I did.

The sounds from the upstairs apartment had ceased. Grace turned quickly to her right and I followed. Here, the smell of motor oil was strong, and the form of a long counter, the vague shapes of certain objects, finally oriented me: This was Cocchi's shop. We had entered from the rear, and now were approaching the trapdoor in the floor that gave on the basement stairs. The trapdoor had been thrown back. From below, I could hear occasional hushed voices, and the crunching of a spade in gravelly earth. Grace clutched my arm once and released it, a signal to exercise caution, then—wraith-like—she slipped through the opening onto the steps below.

I followed, pulling up sharply behind her as she halted halfway down the steps. Our movements had not been noticed by three men partially shielded from our sight by a cracked wooden storage cabinet drawn out from the wall. On the cabinet, to aid the weak light of the ceiling bulb, a lantern glared. From beyond the cabinet, there issued a stale, loamy smell—the odor of freshly turned earth. The spade thumped again, and, suddenly, an accented voice said, "Ohh, her hand is here."

Feet scratched and scuttled on the earth as a small silhouette lurched toward us, then stopped and hunched over just beyond the pool of lantern light. I heard the stuttering gush of a man retching, and a foul, acid smell reached out to me just as I heard Stoker McCullagh's voice say disgustedly, "You gutted her, and now you can't keep your dinner down?"

This was answered only by a horrified tumble of Italian, punctuated by the name of God and the Virgin Mary. The tall policeman's head, visible over the cabinet, turned now to the third man. "Take the spade, or we'll never get her out of here before sunrise."

The metal blade crunched again in the earth, more urgently now.

Abruptly, Grace reached back and tapped my leg, and we drifted the rest of the way down the stairs as I fumbled out my revolver. She stopped on the dirt floor and her commanding voice cut sharply through the dead air. "Alfredo Cocchi, I arrest you for murder! Captain McCullagh, I arrest you as an accessory to murder!"

Cocchi, still wretched from his sickness, jumped, shivered, and shuffled sideways to see who was speaking. Then he drew back, fetching up against the broken cabinet. I stepped briskly to intercept him. As I did so, I brought myself within the orbit of the cabinet just as McCullagh pushed it from behind. The heavy case, with its cargo of supplies, cracked and shook as it fell, taking down Cocchi's body and my own, kicking the revolver from my hand, exploding a dry wheeze of dust.

As the air cleared, I wriggled against the crushing weight on my chest. It wouldn't budge. Cocchi's thin crying reached my ears. He was further underneath, body broken, arms and head sticking out. I was pinned, hurt, but not crippled, for Cocchi's body had helped break the fall. But I was helpless, and mad with frustration as I struggled, looking upward to see the play go on without me.

McCullagh stepped forward holding a cannon-size revolver, the swaying ceiling bulb pumping his shadow against the wall, making it dark and long, then small, then dark and long. With him came the third man, still with the spade in his hand. Christ! I'd known it, I had just known it! It was James Whistle, and he was smirking at Grace.

McCullagh laughed easily. "It's a damn good thing I ordered up a meat wagon for this little lady in the ground, for it looks like we will have a whole parcel of bodies for transport."

Near me, Cocchi moaned, cried, and thrashed about like a lobster crushed by a bucket, his little arms and hands scrabbling on the earth. "Oh Mary, Mother of Jesus!" he wept. His twitching rocked the cabinet painfully on my body, but I couldn't keep my eyes off the doings above me.

Grace stared at Whistle, drew a long breath, and said, "I expected better of you, James."

Whistle's face curdled with anger. "You expected everything, paid nothing. It was as if you knew."

Grace, I was sure, was up to something. Her left hand, holding her purse, drifted slightly lower, her right hand slightly higher, as she said, "And what is it that I should have known?"

Whistle grimaced, refused to answer, but McCullagh laughed and spread his hands. "Why, that little James here isn't a Harvard lawyer at all, Mrs. Humiston. Just a shirt-tail Mick from Southie who used to work as a bus boy in the Harvard dining halls to pick up the lingo."

Grace's right hand jerked, but McCullagh's gun-barrel moved more quickly. "Freeze that purse, or I'll spill you all over the ground."

Grace's hand stopped.

"Throw the purse over here."

She complied. Whistle dropped the shovel, lifted the purse and extracted the .32-caliber Colt Pocket Positive. He was just raising the pistol in McCullagh's direction when the cop leaped at him, pistol-whipped his left temple. Whistle sagged to the ground, shivered once and slept.

McCullagh chuckled edgily. "What a pity this is, my little confederate turning against me." The cop sighed. "He produced plenty of grand information about your goings-on. You'd have thought that would have convinced me, wouldn't you?" He coughed. "It did, for a while. It even led me to figure I'd better dig up this girl while you were gone and put her some place you'd never find her. But I came to suspect you'd lodged him in my hip pocket. And it's clear you did. Who else could have told you we'd be here, and you just fresh from an ocean voyage?"

Grace looked compassionately at Whistle, then at me. She had only one thought, I could see: to save us. It would take some fast footwork. To McCullagh, she said, "Do you intend to dip your hands further in blood just to guard your filthy little racket?"

The policeman drew his lower lip down gravely. "Well, as to that, I have slipped in so far that I don't see how I can slip out again. Once I decided to turn a blind eye on Cocchi when I learned he'd killed the Cruger girl. . ." He shook his head. "That pretty much decided me, set me on a course. And I must stay that course, even if it means the disappearance of all present company."

Grace spoke urgently. "It is only petty graft. Almost absurd— bribes from motorists to get out of expensive traffic tickets. How much does it even bring you?"

McCullagh grinned. "The monkey wrenches are cheap and the bribes cost plenty. It's not bad. And it looks clean: just a little extra business in a motorcycle shop." He paused. "How did you tumble to it? Whistle didn't tell you, for I didn't tell him. Was it that stupid cop who stopped you on the way to the ship?"

So Stoker was in a mood to jabber. Good. I knew that Grace would be glad of the talk. If only she could continue to talk, she could continue to plot.

"The policeman's overreaching helped," Grace said. "He dropped Cocchi's card in our car. But the key came from Jack Mullraney. The night Cocchi stabbed him to death at the Stag Cafe, Jack left a clue that pointed right to Cocchi, though it took me some time to work it out. Why Cocchi fell in with Jack at the Stag, I'm not sure, but I suspect Cocchi—knowing Jack's bad reputation—was trying to get Jack to betray me. Jack played along to get information. They both got drunk, and Cocchi revealed the monkey wrench scheme. Then Jack messaged me."

McCullagh's eyebrows twitched. "Messaged you how?"

Grace took a long breath. "Jack managed to carve a monkey in the bar, probably showed it to Cocchi as a joke." Her voice went soft. "By that time, Jack must have suspected he might not get out of the situation alive. After he was stabbed, he completed the message by thumbing a hole in the word 'ranch' in a headline in a bit of newspaper he'd stuffed in his shoes." She paused, bit her lip. "I knew that was important, for there was a bit of dried blood on the headline, which meant he'd spent his last breaths doing that job for me." She paused again and sighed, and that sigh was a long bit of mourning for Jack Mullraney. "At first, I thought the monkey carved into the bar related to De Souza. De Souza kept a monkey, engraved the symbol in his front window. But that was too obvious. Jack could never have carved that clue right in front of Ricardo, had Ricardo been the killer."

She put a finger to her lips, playing the moment for effect, to draw it out. "So what could the message actually be? I tried the two words in combination—'ranch monkey,' 'monkey ranch.' Neither made any sense. Then I recalled a transaction I'd tumbled upon in this shop one night when I dropped in unexpectedly to interview Cocchi. A man came in, a well-off man, and paid $15 for a monkey wrench."

Grace smiled with self-deprecation. "The price seemed a bit high to me, but I wasn't sure. At first, I thought the coming war might have put a premium on steel and tools. By the time I interpreted Jack's clue, we were hot after De Souza and Alvarez, and I had no time to verify my speculation. As soon as things settled down, though, I sent Kron shopping for the most expensive monkey wrench in New York. And he confirmed my suspicions, for he came back with a wrench that cost only two dollars and twenty-five cents."

From the ground, Cocchi moaned. He wheezed and clutched at his neck-bandanna, trying to free his airway, pulling the cloth free to reveal an infected wound in his neck. There it was, the work done by the point of Grace's umbrella. The grease, which had hidden it previously, had spread germs, caused it to turn.

McCullagh stepped forward and kicked him hard in the leg. "Little shit! He couldn't do you properly himself, so he tried an old Mafia trick —hiring your bodyguard to kill you. Told Mullraney he would cut him in on the monkey-wrench bribes. Then he said something dirty about you, and Mullraney went up like Vesuvius. Cocchi saw what he'd brought on himself, and had to kill the man he was trying to hire."

On Cocchi's spittle-flecked lips, words formed, and his eyes sought the only person he thought might comfort him. "Am I going to die, lovely lady?"

"Do you feel death?" asked Grace.

He wept. "Oh, I do."

"Then you must repent."

"Oh, I do repent."

McCullagh moved his gun barrel impatiently and stepped in close to Cocchi, but his bones were steeped in Irish Catholicism as thoroughly as in Irish whiskey. He watched, listened, but held his ground.

"Are you a Catholic, Alfredo?" asked Grace.

"Yes, yes," the little man blubbered.

"And have you committed the mortal sin of violating Ruth Cruger and murdering her to hide your sin?" Sin murder, *Peccato omicidio?*"

"Yes!"

"And of killing Jack Mullraney?"

"Yes!"

The fever of confession carried Cocchi along now, purging all the deception and blood. He gasped out the admissions eagerly, hoping for salvation.

"And of attacking me, intending to take my life?"

"Yes!"

Grace raised a hand to her chest and her eyes searched upward. "And do you know that God in Heaven sees all, forgives all?"

"Oh, please pray for me, lovely lady."

"Prayer is not enough in your faith, is it, Alfredo?"

The little man's eyes searched for hers, fumbled with the concept. McCullagh's eyebrows drew up sharply, suspiciously, but he was used to sensing danger in the swift movement of a man's hand in his pocket, the sweep of a blade or a club, the ratcheting sound of a gun's hammer being cocked. He did not fear a quick tongue, nor a discussion of religion. To his sorrow.

Grace, her bright eyes looking into Cocchi's said: "To be saved, one needs both faith and good works. Is that not so, Alfredo?"

McCullagh caught not the sense of it, but the emotional flow. He cursed and started to step past Cocchi, in close to Grace, to make the shot certain. At that moment, Alfredo Cocchi understood. One of his muscular, grease-stained little hands came up suddenly and caught Stoker McCullagh's trouser leg like a thorn.

The policeman stumbled, tried to recover, but Cocchi held on like death itself, rocking his body to hold the tall man's leg in his clutch. And I took advantage of the slight up-and-down movement of the cabinet, struggling free just as McCullagh sprawled, his trigger finger tightening at the last moment to explode a shot directly into Cocchi's chest.

Grace swept forward and briskly smashed her right elbow into the side of McCullagh's head. He reeled and dropped the gun, and then I was all over him, launching a roundhouse right that collided with his left ear and a left hook that whistled over his head. McCullagh rolled away, gun lost, shaking his head. He came to his feet, scrambled for the stairway. I struggled to follow, hobbled by the knife wound in my thigh, found myself able to thrash after him only at three-quarters' speed. McCullagh turned at the bottom of the stairs, bounced a backhand right off my dome, leaped upwards.

This was a desperate situation, for he must have confederates posted not far away. I couldn't let him go. I caught his right leg; McCullagh pulled it free in two jerks. Up the stairs he went, and up I went, too, furious with frustration. Behind me, I could hear Grace scrambling for McCullagh's revolver, but in these close quarters it wouldn't matter—she'd never be able to get a clear shot. I tripped and my knees thumped painfully into the stairs. Stoker led the race now by three solid feet, and it was a lead I'd never overcome. He was gone.

Except that— At the top of the stairs, a huge, awkward shape loomed. Cocchi's wife. She made no move, merely stood, braced on her cane, blocking the cop's way. It gave me a chance, and I put a hand on a step and pulled. McCullagh saw my move, and his right hand suddenly fell to his padded right hip pocket and flicked upward clutching a short billy club, hard and iron-heavy. He cut at my forehead. He missed. I dodged, and slipped off-balance, tripped again, lay awkwardly on the steps at McCullagh's feet.

The cop balanced up for one more strike into my forehead, a blow that would crush my skull and lay my brain open. He swung, and I sensed the blow was well launched. Just then Cocchi's wife chose to take a hand, stepping in and whipping her cane downward. I'll never know if she, too, was aiming for my head, or whether she was taking revenge for her husband, realizing that McCullagh had blown a hole in him. In any case, her plunging cane snapped down on McCullagh's right wrist, cracking the bone. I seized the broken wrist and twisted, and McCullagh gasped with agony. He kicked out with his right foot and caught me in the belly. I fell, the wind knocked out of me, and McCullagh leaped to the top of the stairs, knocked Mrs. Cocchi sprawling, and made a wild rush for the shop's front door.

Up to this point, I'd been having a very bad day—weary from the journey on shipboard, stiff and aching from my long wait in the broom closet, scratched, skinned and bruised from the falling cabinet and from the pummeling I'd taken from McCullagh. Add to this the breath-robbing pain I was suffering from the knife wound in my thigh, which had cracked open and was weeping blood through my pants. Taken all in all, I was one very sore, angry human.

All this came together, suddenly, in one explosion. I staggered to my feet and pushed Mrs. Cocchi aside; I roared and shook like a torched munitions factory; I blazed forward, struck the fleeing McCullagh in the back and helped him exit, not through the door, but right through the front window. Glass tinkled, smashed and cartwheeled away as we struck the sidewalk and bounced.

Stoker McCullagh—a hard, bitter, battered skeleton—still managed to get to his feet and lash out with both feet and his one good hand. But I drew back a punch that reached all the way to Newark and sent it forward into his face with the force of Manifest Destiny. McCullagh's head bounced like the loose head of one of those little porcelain Dutch Boys that nod in the breeze on many a knick-knack shelf. Then I grabbed his uniform blouse and readied another blow even as he sagged. The punch was reaching back somewhere in the region of Atlantic City, ready to ride forward on greased rails, when Grace put a hand on my shoulder.

"Kron!" she said. "Enough."

Chapter Twenty-Eight

THE SMALL FORCE OF OFFICERS Stoker McCullagh had assembled to back him up were grouped under a streetlight a half-block away, emitting cigarette gusts, back-slapping and laughing, and generally having their way with the world. The crash of Cocchi's window brought them running, but they soon skidded to a stop when Grace cocked her revolver in their faces. At just that moment, the ambulance McCullagh had ordered up to spirit away the girl's body whirled around the corner, grinding its gears as it screeched to a stop. Grace thrust her revolver in at the driver's window to encourage him, I bundled McCullagh through the meat-wagon's back doors, and we were off, down the street and around the corner.

We didn't go far, for we still had Whistle—and, for that matter, Cocchi and his wife—to worry about back at the scene. We swung down at the nearest saloon, swept through the startled patrons, and Grace demanded a telephone. Within seconds, she sent a call out for the only real counterbalance to a thoroughly corrupt city police force, and it quickly coalesced at the saloon and joined us in a triumphal trooping march back to Cocchi's motorcycle shop.

Reporters were our marching companions—the amoral dregs of the literary world, with drawn, alcohol-sick faces, twitching noses and gleaming teeth. There was Campaneris, the night man of the *Tribune*, with his unwashed union suit showing through a poorly buttoned shirt and a red silk handkerchief leaping from his coat pocket; Texley, the general assignment reporter from the *Times*, all celluloid and cleanly blocked bowler hat; and the *World's* police beat handler, Sweeney, with an Adam's apple big as a baseball, a young Irishman said to be the finest stylist of them all. They all brought their drinking companions, which made quite a crowd.

All around the roiling mob stalked the fast-talking news photographers, setting up their heavy cameras as if they were machine guns, from time to time cutting loose with salvos of flash powder. In the confusion, Grace slipped away to check on the survivors in the motorcycle shop, while I kept an eye on the scene outside, watching the reporters jostling and capering, jabbing questions at the bleeding McCullagh, their eagle eyes and frantic pencils holding all the corrupt cops at bay pending the arrival of the District Attorney's police—the flying squad of the latest reform movement.

Twenty minutes later, here they came, tumbling out of a Model T, big mustachioed men who affected tweed sport jackets and swore political allegiance to the little man now parting them like Moses dividing the Red Sea—District Attorney Jacob Flint. His mouth hard as the coin-slot in a porcelain piggy bank, Flint inspected McCullagh's crushed nose, battered teeth and broken wrist with professional interest, asked me a few questions, then had the wounded cop led away under guard.

The newsmen clamored for admittance to the basement, but Flint denied them, wanting to control the publicity for his own ends. Self-minded he might have been, but he was efficient. Within half an hour, medical personnel he summoned tended to Mrs. Cocchi's bruises, removed Cocchi's body, tended to the scalp-wound of James Whistle, and stood by as two young policemen and I completed the exhumation of the young woman whose disappearance had begun the death hunt. In the final stages, I laid down my shovel and Grace and I stood by, she clutching my hand as Ruth Cruger emerged from the earth.

The girl was wearing the same clothes she'd worn on her errand in December, when all she'd wanted were her sharpened ice-skates—her excuse to pop in next door on Ricardo. Her shroud was the long blue velour coat she had donned to protect her from the elements, her kid gloves were still on her hands, her blue velvet sailor hat still clung to her hair. Her killer had wrapped her white waistcoat around her head and tied a thick hemp rope about her ankles in a slip-noose, either to bind her while alive or to lower her into the pit after she had been killed. Another rope was tied about her waist. Her head had been crushed by a heavy tool, and a stab wound had laid open her abdomen.

Flint—speaking, perhaps, for the benefit of two reporters who had somehow slipped past the cordon into the basement—muttered, "Someone will suffer for this."

Grace looked at him with disdain. "Someone already has," she said.

The headlines in *The New York Times* were the most restrained in the city, and they were lurid enough: FIND RUTH CRUGER BURIED IN CELLAR OF COCCHI'S SHOP (subheads: "Skull Crushed and Body Dressed, Even to Gloves and Coat, as She Stepped from Street," "Found By Woman's Effort"); 'RIPPER'S' MARK FOUND ON BODY OF RUTH CRUGER (subhead: "Autopsy Shows Death Due to Crushing of Skull and Fiendish Use of Long Knife"); LAYS POLICE GRAFT TO HEADQUARTERS (subhead: "Commissioner Wallstein Finds Lack of Supervision of Motor Cycle Men's Work.")

Grace refused to read the initial news reports. She closeted herself with the Cruger family, comforting them as best she could, and bustled about ensuring that Whistle and I got the proper medical treatment. Only when convinced that publicity would expose the sexual predators she'd been battling did she give an interview, which appeared in the *Times* under the headline: MRS. HUMISTON, THE WOMAN WHO SHAMED POLICE IN THE RUTH CRUGER MURDER CASE.

For the readers, she laid out the situation clearly. "I started out with the conviction that Ruth Cruger was a good girl," she said, "and I knew that one of her training and character never would figure in an elopement or anything of that kind. Working on this conviction of mine, I knew that the police theory of 'waywardness' was all bosh and that Mr. Cruger's repeatedly expressed belief that his daughter was being forcibly detained was correct—or at least partially so.

"I say partially correct, for, while the father clung to the hope that Ruth was still alive, I never for a minute thought so."

She went on to explain—more or less—how we had come up with the solution to the Cruger mystery, giving Luisa, Whistle and me perhaps more than our due in that regard. And she expanded upon her desire for legislation and a Bureau of Moral Health to do away with the kinds of activities that Uncle Carlos and Ricardo had worked to their advantage.

"Why, had I the power, I would cause to be inserted in the laws of every state an act that would make the tempting of a young girl a serious offense punishable by an adequate penalty," Grace told the reporter. "I would call such practices 'criminal persuasion' and I think that if the white slaver knew he violated the law at the very beginning of his 'trade' there would be fewer girls in the underworld."

Despite such departures, the interviewer seemed most interested in Grace's investigative techniques, pressing her repeatedly about how her methods might compare to those of a certain legendary English detective.

"I never read Sherlock Holmes," Grace replied firmly. "In fact, I am not a believer in deduction. Common sense and persistence will always solve a mystery."

Chapter Twenty-Nine

IT WAS A FULL WEEK before things began to settle down. Little as I like to admit it, my wounds and the strain of my final—and finally satisfying—encounter with Stoker McCullagh had finally caught up with me, and I'd spent a few days in the hospital, really resting up more than anything else. Grace, of course, came to visit regularly, though she refused to talk shop until I was better, and even Whistle showed up, the prim little bastard, carrying a box of my favorite cigars. He'd a great white bandage splashed across his head where Stoker had taken him down.

"That's an expanse of cloth to waste on a bump," I told him. "You'll never need a pillow again, just regular changes of your dressing."

His blue eyes were innocent. "I didn't want any wounded parts of me to fall off, as they tend to do with you." His eyebrows went up. "Tell me, did they give your ear a proper burial at sea?"

The little bastard. I took a long puff on my cigar, wheezing out the smoke to cover my grin. "Tell me," I said, "Are you really a lawyer or not? And are you really a shanty Irishman or not?"

He spread his hands. "Shanty Irishman, that I am. I ran the streets of Boston as a kid, and I can roast a stolen potato over a garbage-can bonfire as well as anybody on earth."

"And the lawyer part?"

"No, though Mrs. Humiston calls me an 'embryo lawyer,' which perhaps is apt. I worked the dining halls at Harvard, stole books, read them at night in the boiler rooms. I picked up the talk, a knowledge of law, then went to Mrs. Humiston, saying I was a graduate." He turned a hand. "She was unconventional, and I thought she could bridge me into a legal career."

I sucked smoke, emitted a derisive bark. "And she saw through you."

He sighed a cultured sigh, tucked a finger alongside his nose. "In about 30 seconds," he admitted. "She broke me down, got the true story out of me. But she didn't turn me away. Instead, she picked me up, said she'd train me in her special trade."

"Ah," said I sourly, "she tends to pick people up."

He tipped a look at my long face. "If you mean you, that she's used you, that's not the truth at all."

I raised my eyes to the ceiling, let the cigar smoke drift. "Then why did she keep me in the dark about you and Luisa?"

He massaged his jaw. "You are too honest, it's that simple. In disguise, you do well. But, normally, your emotions are too much in your face. Your face would have betrayed me and Luisa, if you had known. Not knowing, you convinced McCullagh that I was crooked."

I grunted. "How did I do that?"

"By bashing me down at the scene of Jack's murder. It showed you were suspicious of me. That was our great break in the case. Mrs. Humiston trolled me as bait for McCullagh, and you reeled him in. If you hadn't done that, I never would have been able to send her an urgent, coded message on the *Calpurnia* to return quickly to New York."

I mulled this. "Is that so?" I shook my head, letting out a long draft of air, getting used to the idea of being worked myself while we were working everyone else. Being worked by Grace. Grace—those eyes, and that straight jaw, and those honest cheekbones, and always playing the game with a little something extra in her pocket. Grace. Sweet Jesus. I shook my head again, edging out a rueful look, nipping my lower lip in my teeth. She always had it up on everybody, even on me, and who could match her? Who could do the things she did? My belly grew warm, though it's supposed to be your heart that does so. Grace.

I threw back my head, opened my mouth, and let out a laugh. Not just a laugh, really. It was a bellowing explosion that shook my hospital bed, rippled through my body all the way from the toes, flung cigar ashes out in great spirals. It should have brought my nurse on the run, but the face that poked through the doorway was not that of the nurse —severe, straightforward and plain. No, this face was sweet, with the easy bloom of youth, the lips trembling fetchingly with uncertainty and concern. Luisa.

I found Grace in her office going over a green-canvas-covered account book. She looked up casually, a light morning breeze from the window lifting and ruffling her dark hair. "Kron!" she exclaimed, jotting an entry, then tossing her pen aside. "I didn't know you were to be released."

I flipped my hat into the corner, scoring easily on one of the hooks of the hat tree. "I released myself. Too much lying down gets dispiriting." I rummaged in my pocket, aimlessly clinking my change. "Or maybe my curiosity about our recent adventure just got to be too much for me. There were some items even Whistle couldn't clear up."

She smiled widely. "He's quite an efficient young man, isn't he? He'll make a lawyer some day, if we can reform his evil ways."

I put my head over to one side. "He'll never get them reformed around here. Evil's your meat and drink."

"Oh, now," she said. "You give me too much credit."

"I doubt it," I said, dropping into a chair. "For instance, how did you line up on the corrupt cops to begin with?"

She waved a hand. "Oh, that was no great feat. Remember, Cocchi said he'd been beaten by police probing Ruth Cruger's disappearance. My experience is that the police excel in that area, and are remarkably thorough, but Cocchi showed no marks of a beating on his face or hands, or at least none I could see when I drew close to him. No bruises, no lumps, no lacerations. Cocchi was a simple man, a poor liar. So how did he come up with that story? Probably because the police had threatened to beat him, but desisted when he told the truth. There was only one reason they would have done that: if they were linked to him in some dirty business."

I put a finger to my right temple. "Some dirty business with money in it. The gold cross on his wall showed an unusual source of income."

"Exactly! And, later, his getting money to develop his toy Ferris wheel showed the same thing. He was afraid we'd find out about his hidden wealth, so he came up with a cover story."

"So did Stoker. Or maybe the cover story fell into his lap—the white slave racket." I mulled this. "Prior to the murder, had he been turning a blind eye to De Souza?"

"I doubt it. McCullagh would not have let white slavers work without exacting tribute. And he wouldn't have thrown them to us if they were bribing him. I'm sure he learned of them only after Ruth Cruger dropped from sight." Grace nodded, sharply. "Cocchi must have told him. Cocchi's lust, which led to his attack on Ruth, had been sharpened by watching them work. He was very familiar with them. Cocchi sometimes went so far as to wear crushed-almond cologne similar to Ricardo's—I smelled it when I was attacked in the street." She paused, reflecting. "Cocchi, no doubt, saw Ruth visiting the jewelry shop when De Souza wasn't there. Ricardo kept that from his Uncle, who knows why? He had met Ruth ice skating, but perhaps he felt she wasn't rich enough to be a proper mark. Cocchi thought she *was* one of their marks, however, and gave the slavers to McCullagh. Then McCullagh gave them to us as obvious scapegoats."

The gears were clicking neatly into place. They always did with Grace. "When did you first suspect that?"

"When I saw the list of missing women Jack bought on the sly. It showed fine penmanship, indicating a clerk had done it, someone under Stoker's command, not a half-literate cop snatching scraps of information." She paused, bowing her head as she reviewed her analysis. "Stoker had brushed off the investigation of each of the original disappearances. The families reported them as possible elopements, which needed to be hushed up, so he knew he would not come under political pressure to solve them."

"But, Amelia Karcher—"

"Yes, yes. That situation might have changed when Amelia Karcher was killed, but Stoker knew nothing of that. She was traveling under a false name and the Bueños Aires police, who had been paid off, didn't report the killing." Grace looked up. "When Cocchi killed Ruth, her disappearance fit neatly into the pattern. Stoker guided us on a course that took us after the slavers, thinking he had successfully diverted attention from Cocchi."

"But he failed, thanks to you," I said. "And because of you, Stoker will be spending the rest of his life in a cell."

She shook off the compliment, rose, took a turn toward the window. She had a way about her, she had a way with me, and I had other questions for her. I was reminded that this last adventure had caused hell's own rift between her and her husband. "And you," I said, "where will you be spending the rest of your life?"

Her smile was now all for me and there wasn't a more tender one on the face of the earth. She came around the desk to me, extending her hands, and I came to my feet, catching her fingers. "Kron," she said, "you are the dearest companion I have ever known, the finest and steadiest."

Somehow, I seemed to know the speech. There are certain things you must be wary of in a woman, and one of them is excessive praise. It means that there is an open door in your near future, one leading out of her romantic life. I squeezed her hands and found myself able to issue a cautious smile. "You have come to terms with Howard, patched things up."

The gleam in her eyes changed, and now it was one of keen respect. "You are the cleverest man I have ever known."

"That's all very well, then," I said, letting out a long breath. "For I have reached an understanding with Luisa."

She was back at her desk now, reaching for the account book. Next to it lay the .32-caliber Colt Pocket Positive. "I expected you might. She's a young woman with excellent qualities. I saw that instantly, and knew she would do the right thing."

"Oh," said I, "and how did you know that?"

She smiled. "Usual methods."

Usual methods. Hmmm. She was always holding something back. This after she'd said such brave things about me. And here I was, just accepting it all. "So you're not going to tell me?"

"Oh, Kron."

I was irritated, but I didn't want to leave it like this, we'd had such a splendid moment. My eyes strayed back to the pistol. I sighed. "Keep your secrets then, I suppose I must learn to live with them." I paused. "At least I am living. Thanks to you."

"For what?"

"For that shot on the ship, the one that knocked Ricardo out of the game. It saved my life."

"You're welcome."

I took two steps, put a hand on the doorknob, turned back. "Excuse me, but I wasn't sure you could shoot."

She'd re-opened the account book by this time, but now she snapped it shut. "Well, that's a fine thing to say. It sounds as if you are deliberately trying to hurt my feelings."

"I'm not!"

She persisted. "You are, and I know why. It still grinds on you that I didn't consult you about Luisa and Whistle."

I dropped my hand from the knob. "All I meant was—"

"All you meant was that you could not believe a woman could come to your rescue." Sadness crept into her eyes. "This, after all we have been through."

I stepped toward her, spreading my hands. "All I meant was, I had never seen you do anything but dry-fire that pistol at that damned death mask on the mantel. Before the night you scored with that long shot on Ricardo, for all I knew you had never fired a single round of live ammunition."

"Oh, well. . ." Her upset look was fading.

"So I apologize."

Grace fluttered a hand. "Oh, don't apologize," she said, picking up the book and spreading its pages. She meant to dismiss me, but something told me not to go. So it was that I caught her out at last. She cast her eyes down, her lips quirking as she pretended to read, and—trying to toss it off carelessly—admitted: "In point of fact, I never had."

ABOUT THE AUTHOR

Charles Kelly, formerly a reporter for *The Arizona Republic,* was co-winner of the Arizona Journalist of the Year Award in 1992. During his career, he investigated the 1976 contract murder of *Republic* reporter Don Bolles, located several missing heirs, and helped a wrongly convicted American tugboat captain get out of a Mexican prison. He is the author of the novel *Pay Here,* issued in 2007 by Point Blank Press, the story "The Eighth Deadly Sin," published in the collection *Phoenix Noir,* issued in 2009 by Akashic Books, and the self-help book *Finnegan's Way: The Secret Power of Doing Things Badly.* His biography of an amnesiac hard-boiled novelist, *Gunshots in Another Room: The Forgotten Life of Dan J. Marlowe,* has been called a "masterpiece" by Ed Gorman, the legendary mystery author and editor. Kelly lives in Scottsdale, Arizona.

<<<◇>>>

Made in the USA
Lexington, KY
06 November 2018